The Mourning
of Angels

-EDMI

The Mourning
of Angels

For Lydia
with every good wish,
Patricia Taylor Edmisten
May, 2002

Patricia S. Taylor Edmisten

To order additional copies of this book, contact:
Xlibris Corporation
1-888-7-XLIBRIS
www.Xlibris.com
Orders@Xlibris.com

Contents

A mi familia

Also by Patricia S. Taylor Edmisten

Nonfiction

Nicaragua Divided
La Prensa and the Chamorro Legacy

Translation, prologue, and afterword
The Autobiography of Maria Elena Moyano
The Life and Death of a Peruvian Activist

Author's Note

THE characters in this book are composites of people I've known or imagined. Although history, experience, and memories have contributed to the narrative, it is a work of fiction. All translations from Spanish to English are my own.

Prologue

MY beloved Lydia, my darling son Gabriel,

I want to return to you, but I do not know what will happen to me, and I am afraid. Those who commit these crimes do not question what they do. They obey, living in fear of change or of being punished if they do not conform. They turn those who hold different beliefs into monsters who must be subdued.

As monsters, we may be tortured or executed, and the assassins will feel patriotic because they have done their duty. But right now, my loves, I need to believe that your spirits will not be vanquished by their ignorance or by the evil they do.

If I am to die, I want you to know that you are the good that I have searched for in life. I have lived briefly, but, dearest Lydia and Gabriel, in that short life, I found and loved you, and, with you, I embraced a new vision for Peru.

Please tell my mother that there has been no mother sweeter, no mother more courageous, than she.

I kiss you, my family, my loves, now and through eternity.
Rafael

I

Leaving Home

Yesterday I went out naked
to challenge Destiny,
with pride as my shield
and the helmet of Mambrino.

Alberto Guillén, *Deucalión*, 1920

"PERU! Lydia, that's so far away," my mother moans into the phone from the motel room in Hollywood, Florida, where she and my father are escaping Milwaukee's spring snows. "But sweetheart, you know we'll support you, if that's what you want."

Although I'm grateful for my parents' support, I, too, have doubts. Who joins the Peace Corps? Like heaven or hell, no one has come back to tell about it, but it has to be better than correcting lisps and articulation disorders at the twenty rural schools I visit in southern Rock County, Wisconsin. I'm almost twenty-three, and I don't want to spend the rest of my life teaching the correct tongue and lip placements for the "snake" sound.

I live with Betty and Roger Radich. She's a librarian, and he's one of my colleagues and a golf professional who travels on weekends. Betty hates being alone when Roger travels, so they invited me to rent an airy bedroom in their Victorian house. Now, when Roger golfs, Betty and I go on long bike rides, sometimes stopping to pick wild asparagus for supper. In the evenings, she and I sit in the small library and listen to Joan Baez and Pete Seeger.

Betty and Roger know about my confusion, and now, when only days remain before I have to decide whether to accept the Peace Corps call or not, Roger speaks to me in my office. "Lydia, I wish I could have had this opportunity. You're not married. You have no children. You're absolutely free. How can there be a contest between what you're doing now and the Peace Corps?"

*

On June 14, 1962, I fly from Milwaukee to New York City and then take a Mohawk connection from Idlewild Airport to Ithaca, the home of Cornell University. I've been on a plane only once before, when I escorted my younger brother Johnny back home from Florida, after he had an emergency appendectomy.

The campus, with its grand old buildings, makes me think I'm not embarking on some fly-by-night scheme, but I feel out of place. "*Hola*, are you sharing this room with anybody?" asks the tidy woman in the yellow shirtwaist and matching headband. She has sandy hair, blue-gray eyes, a finely shaped nose, and cheeks that look like she's just skated on an icy pond.

"*Hola*, yourself," I greet her. "Come in. I've taken the bed by the window, but you can have the other one. My name is Lydia Schaefer."

"Susan Blain," she says, walking toward me, extending her hand. "I'm from Rochester, Minnesota, you?"

"Milwaukee, and please no jokes about the beer."

When she smiles, I notice her perfect teeth. "*Por supuesto qué no.* We're both Midwesterners; we have to stick together," she says, swinging her white vinyl cosmetic bag onto the lumpy bed. "Where's the bathroom? I haven't brushed my teeth since I left Rochester at dawn. My father's a dentist; he'd kill me if he knew I had waited this long."

"Down the hall on the right. It's old, just like everything else here, but the plumbing seems to work. I'm going to clean up and have my picture taken for the directory. Want me to wait for you?"

"*Por favor,*" says Susan, flying out the door with her toothbrush and toothpaste.

I hope I can keep up with her Spanish. Thank you Divine Redeemer High School for the two years of Latin and the two years of Spanish; thank you Marquette University for the two of Spanish. When I'm in a restaurant in Peru, I want to say more than *Yo qui-er-o-a-gua* in baby talk.

After putting on white pedal pushers, white flats, and an orange, calypso-style blouse, tied so just a sliver of my stomach shows, I smooth my pageboy and wait for Susan who emerges from the shower, pinker than before. "Let's see what the Peace Corps men look like," she says, strutting out the door.

While Susan greets the volunteers milling in Willard Strait Hall, waiting to have their pictures taken, I read in the orientation package that there are one hundred nine of us, that we'll be in class ten hours a day, six days a week, and that we'll spend two hundred hours in Spanish language study. We'll learn the basics of butchering and slaughtering and take classes in poultry care, first aid, food preservation, Peruvian history, American studies, and communism. Physical training will include a course in equitation, should we be assigned to the high sierra, where the only transportation is by horse, mule, or foot.

*

Fernando Arollo, my Spanish teacher, is a petite, narrow-faced, Mexican graduate student. Although his main job is teaching Spanish, he spends a lot of time criticizing the Catholic Church. "The Church is like a comfortable mattress for the people," he says. "It puts them to sleep, so they don't have to take responsibility for their own actions."

I feel the quivering in my stomach that tells me I want to respond but am unsure of what to say. Noting my distress, he says, "Miss, do you have a problem with what I just said?"

"Where I grew up, the Church stressed individual responsibility," I blurt, feeling my face flush, wishing I had kept my mouth shut, but the Jesuits had taught me to question.

"Ah, Miss Schaefer, right? A good Catholic girl, no? You think the Church can do no wrong because you've never been exposed to anything outside of your perfect, little hometown. You know nothing about the world, and now you think you're going to save it." He spits out the last few words.

Thinking I'm too rigid to work in Peru, Fernando refers me for psychological testing, but the psychologist decides I'm sufficiently flexible to deal with a new culture and recommends I transfer to a different Spanish class and keep a low profile.

*

A rumor circulates that a Peace Corps assessment officer is posing as a trainee in our group, spying on us, trying to weed out those who could become problems once in Peru. Then, with with only three weeks of training left, eight men from Peace Corps Washington come to evaluate our progress and pour over our files and test scores. Three young male trainees and one older woman slip away. They have been "deselected." The next cut will take place in Puerto Rico.

*

On July 18, the armed forces of Peru, dissatisfied with results of the June elections, take control of the government. The United States refuses to recognize the military leaders. President Kennedy calls the coup "damaging to the spirit of the Alliance for Progress" and recalls our ambassador.

Undaunted by international events, our trainers teach us to deal with life in the Andes, so I pay attention when the Cornell veterinarian anaesthetizes a standing cow, makes the Cesarian incision that forms a large rectangular window in her side, and removes the calf. Oblivious to the open window, the mother licks away the glistening, viscous coating encasing her offspring.

Joey Amado, a thirty-five-year-old trainee, having studied photography in the Army, will document our training program for Cornell. He will become my first Negro friend. Among the photos Joey takes are one of Susan immunizing a chicken and one of me skinning a sheep, nudging my balled-up fist between the hide and the carcass.

On Joey's birthday, Susan and I surprise him with a party at a road house overlooking Lake Cayuga. I wear a spiffy white dress with spaghetti straps and put on heels. Claire Henry, a trim, twenty-one-year-old medical technician from Miami, who wears cat's eye glasses, teaches us the stroll. Joey's eyes moisten when we bring out the cake and sing.

The night before our departure for New York City and then Puerto Rico, Joey, Susan, and I walk to the Palms, a dinky bar in downtown Ithaca. "Here's to the three of us, to our friendship, and to Peru," says Joey, lifting his martini, taking a quick sip to avoid losing any of the crystal liquid.

"We made it," I say, "despite my rigidity."

"*No seas tonta*," Susan says, telling me not to be foolish. "I would have reacted the same way in Fernando's class, even though I'm Presbyterian. The three of us will survive whatever they send our way, won't we, Joey?"

"I couldn't have made it without you gals," says Joey.

"What are you talking about, Joey? You're the most popular guy in Peru III." I say.

"Yeah," Joey says, "only because everyone wanted their picture taken."

"Not true, Joey," says Susan.

"You underestimate yourself, Joey," I add.

"Susan—Lydia—you mean well, but you've got a lot to learn; not everyone's like you. After running around with you, I don't think you have a mean or prejudiced bone."

Flipping her hair back from her face, Susan asks, "What do you think, Lydia, should we tell him the truth?"

Joey orders another round. Before finishing my third martini, I slump over in the booth, passed out on alcohol for the first time in my life. Joey will later refer to me as the most "graceful" drunk he has ever known.

*

We receive a $25.00 clothing allowance for Puerto Rico, and I buy men's work boots, two work shirts, and a pair of jeans. In anticipation of the harsh, dry, Andean winds, each woman trainee receives a complimentary bottle of Tussey lotion.

At commencement, John Patterson, U.S. Ambassador to Peru, tells us the political situation in the country has eased. The military junta has agreed to hold free elections and promises to respect the results. It has restored freedom of the press and has released President Prado from jail. We sing "The Star Spangled Banner" and the Peruvian national anthem. The campus priest offers the benediction. I remember Fernando Arollo's remark about religion being a mattress for the people.

After a goodbye picnic the next day, a chartered bus takes us to the Great Northern Hotel in New York City. Susan, Joey, and I see *West Side Story*, and the next day we fly to San Juan on Trans Caribbean Airways. Heady stuff for two girls from the Midwest and a guy from the streets of Los Angeles.

II

Puerto Rico

Where to?
It doesn't matter! Life hides
nascent worlds
yet to be discovered.

Alberto Guillén, *Deucalión*, 1920

BUSES carry us along the coast from San Juan to
Arecibo and follow washboard roads to the interior.
Hot winds whip up whirlpools of grime that smart
our sticky legs and blow up our sweaty, cotton dresses.
The men remove their suit coats, pinch wet, short-
sleeve shirts away from their bodies, and loosen their
ties. Finally, we stop at a small wayside stand to drink
from *cocos bien fríos,* very cold coconuts.

Back on the bus, I'm breathing with my eyes,
sucking in images of naked brown children playing

near shacks that are surrounded by banana, breadfruit, and guava trees. At last the buses deposit us at Camp Radley, one of two camps where the Peace Corps tests the mettle of soft North Americans.

We'll sleep on cots in large tents with elevated wooden floors. There are fifteen women in my tent. We have footlockers for our personal belongings. "Always shake out your boots before putting them on in the morning," warns an instructor. "You don't want to get stung by a tarantula or scorpion." The first few nights I lie awake, listening to rain dripping from leaves, to the forest animals that cackle and howl, and to the *coquís*, the tree frogs, their calls unlike the traffic noise I went to sleep with on West North Avenue in Milwaukee.

At dawn, a burly staff member yells for us to get out of our sacks and on with our push-ups. In the mud, our soft bodies behave like slimy jungle slugs. I am out of shape for the mile run and can barely chug into camp for the cold shower before breakfast.

Rock climbing follows Spanish every morning. Then there's trek, where we learn to identify edible plants and tree snails. Next it's survival swimming, drown-proofing, dinner, more classes on Peruvian history and culture, followed by lights out at 10:30.

Duties rotate among the volunteers. We might set up the long tables in the dining room before meals, clean up after meals, or scrub the latrines. I'm learning to live with unidentifiable crawling things, unshaven legs, damp sheets, and the smell of mildew.

At our third rock climbing class, Susan and I pray for an early start to the afternoon deluge so we won't have to climb El Diablo. Donning helmets and gloves, we encourage each other, enduring the cajoling of the instructors above who pull in the belay ropes, as we search for foot and hand holds. At the top, more confident and suffering from only a few gouges, we lean out into space and rappel to the bottom, controlling our descent with the double rope passed under one thigh and over the opposite shoulder. The next day, Mrs. Washburn, a sixty-two-year-old trainee, noticing our anxiety, smiles and says, "Nothing to it, girls," before she bounces her way down the face of a massive dam, a few miles from Arecibo.

Because Camp Radley doesn't have a pool, we pile into open trucks for the short ride to Camp Crozier, where we learn to drown-proof. For ten minutes, hands tied behind our backs, we curl up into balls and float with our faces in the water, lifting them out to breathe. Then, after swimming four lengths with our hands still tied, we must execute front and back somersaults, before recovering an object from the bottom of the pool.

Our instructors teach us to hyperventilate, how to take rapid breaths for a minute before we try to swim two lengths underwater. Near the end of my second length, just when I think I'm going to die, I hear Susan shouting from the deck and see her hands splashing at the end of the pool, signals that I'm nearing the finish.

A day later, wearing garage mechanic overalls, we swim a mile through the rough Caribbean surf off the coast of Arecibo. At the end of the swim, we remove the bulky clothing without removing our two-piece bathing suits, but fail at blowing up the sleeves and arms of the overalls to make life preservers.

"Susan," I whisper across my cot to hers that evening, my limbs still like water-logged stumps,

"What could these stupid activities have to do with our work in Peru?"

"What things?" she mumbles.

"Drown-proofing, rock climbing, swimming with overalls."

"*Ay, Lydia, te preocupas demasiado.* You worry too much, but if we're kidnaped and thrown into a lake with our hands tied, drown-proofing might come in handy," she says, rolling from her back to her side.

"Seriously, Susan, don't you like to know why you're doing something?"

"If I thought about everything foolish I've ever done, I'd never try anything, but it has occurred to me that you may never have to skin another sheep, and I may never have to cut off another chicken's head. I don't think they give a damn about our success in survival swimming or rock climbing, Lydia. They're putting us in these situations to see how we'll react, how we'll handle our fears. Now go to sleep. You think too much."

*

To prepare us for the upcoming three-day trek to the town of Utuado, Jerry Cohen, a tanned staff member with impressive shoulders, who seems never to have suffered from insecurity, leads our small group of women, made ungainly with heavy knapsacks and poor fitting hiking boots, into the rain forest. After several hours, I fear he might be leading us in circles, so I surreptitiously snap off the ends of some of the branches we pass. But then he drops us off, one by one, at various sites in the forest. He knows whom he has left at each location, and we'd better be at those spots, alone, in the morning, or we won't pass trek, or worse, we might get lost. Having learned what plants are edible, we should have no trouble surviving. For those too squeamish for tree snails, we carry dehydrated soup and canned peaches.

Using a call that mimics the whistle signal from *West Side Story*, Susan and I locate each other. We cover the ground under a rocky overhang with banana leaves, build a smoky fire with wet twigs from the forest floor, and huddle near it with tin cups of reconstituted chicken noodle soup.

"Don't you wonder what brought us to this place, Susan? You and I didn't even know each other two months ago, and here we are, sitting together on a dark rainy night in a Puerto Rican forest, watching out for tarantulas."

"You mean, why did we join the Peace Corps?"

"Yes. Why did you join, Susan?"

"At the risk of sounding corny, I like JFK, and he seemed to be speaking to me when he asked us to give something back to society. What about you?"

"Part of it was idealism, but I also wanted to travel, especially to Latin America."

"Why Latin America?" Susan leans back on her elbows.

"In high school I had a Spanish teacher who spent her summers in Latin America. In the fall, she would fill our heads with her adventures. My mother must have influenced me, too," I say, tossing more twigs on the fire. "She always loved Latin music and dance. In 1936, when she was twenty-one, she and her cousin traveled by bus from Milwaukee to Miami, arriving with swollen feet and legs. Then they took a boat to Cuba. My mother's first love was a Cuban man."

"Sounds as if you have a neat family," says Susan, checking the ground behind her for spiders.

"Yeah, but it's taken me this long to realize it. When I was sixteen, my mom talked my dad into driving the family from Milwaukee to Acapulco. The trip was grueling; it took a week to get to Mexico City. The roads were awful. I'm still amazed when I think of it. Most of the kids in my neighborhood never even left the state during vacations. I got altitude sickness in Mexico City, sunburn poisoning in Acapulco, and the whole family suffered from intestinal problems. After we got home, my dad said that Okinawa in 1945 and Mexico in 1956 were enough, and that he'd never leave the United States again, but my mother loved Mexico."

"I couldn't wait to get away from Rochester, Minnesota," Susan says, scraping the tiny noodles from the bottom of her tin cup. "I love my parents, but I grew up in a regimented household. My father wanted every tooth in our mouths to be perfect and every action to meet his approval. Although I know my mother loves me, she has trouble showing affection and gives in to my father on everything."

"And here we are, not even sure we're going to Peru, or if we do get there, what region, or what we'll be doing once we get there."

"You have trouble letting go of details, Lydia."

"Give me a break, Susan, these are more than details. I will admit, though, that my high school friends used to call me Mother Den."

"Mother Den? Why?"

"They thought I was like a den mother, always wanting everything organized."

"Good night, Mother Den. I'm glad we're friends," Susan says, curling up on her pile of banana leaves, covering herself with her poncho.

"I'm glad we're friends, too, Susan."

*

The Puerto Rican Health Department has asked the Peace Corps to assist them in a project that will get us talking to families in the interior who lack running water. We'll use our Spanish to learn how many people live in each house, whether or not there's a latrine on the property, and, if so, how far away it is from the family's source of water. Once we've inspired their trust, we're to ask permission to do an experiment in the latrines, explaining that the Health Department is concerned about parasites.

Most of the people reluctantly cooperate and let us go "honey dipping." We stick a six-foot-pole down into the latrine to get a sample and break off the swab end of the pole into a glass jar that holds a preservative. At the end of the day, we carry knapsacks full of "honey" to the camp.

*

The staff groups us according to physical condition and provides our sex-segregated groups with topographical maps before sending us on a four-day trek across the island. Standing in the back of an open truck, trying to maintain our balance, six other women and I travel to Lares, thirty miles southeast of camp. Using the contour lines that indicate mountains and valleys, we must find our way back to Camp Radley.

It's hot, but at mid-day there's a heavy, cooling rain. This makes further travel impossible, so we take cover in an abandoned shed. By late afternoon, the sun grills our necks, and a woman invites us to drink freshly squeezed orange juice inside her shack. Giggling, her children peek at us from the doorway.

At nightfall, in the small village of Angeles, we meet two teenage girls who invite all seven of us to their home. There's a small living room, a tiny bedroom, and a closet-sized kitchen. We slop mud through the doorway, but their mother begs us not to worry, to make ourselves at home. She makes coffee and says three of us are welcome to spend the night with her and her two daughters; she will ask a neighbor to take the remaining four women.

Susan, Claire, who is the medical technician from Miami, and I share our rations with the mother and daughters. After supper, Susan asks permission to play an old guitar standing in a corner and leads us in "Michael, Row your Boat Ashore." The mother and daughters applaud and sing "Cielito Lindo."

At bed time, Claire positions herself between Susan and me, her head between our feet. The mother tucks the mosquito net under the thin mattress on the double bed and bids us goodnight. She slips into the second bed with her two daughters.

We start out early the next morning, fording three streams before lunch and greeting peasant families who stop everything to watch us pass. We startle a woman who sweeps up her laundry basket and runs inside her house. When she sees we're women and not an army platoon, given our khaki pants, she comes out smiling, and we apologize for frightening her. She explains she has never seen girls wearing pants like ours.

By late afternoon, we catch up with a group of women trainees who, because they were less conditioned than we, started their hike eight miles closer to camp. We resist the urge to brag. A farmer invites us all to spend the night in the second floor of his granary and gives us permission to use the family's bathroom. His wife brings us candles and a spray to keep the bugs away.

The staff was right about the third day being the roughest--it's all straight up. The swirls that represent mountains on the topographical map look alike. The slow group decides upon their route, but my group stands around, arguing about which direction to take. When a farmer approaches and offers to help, saying he knows the land well and will take us to our destination, we wonder if this would be cheating. We agree that by accepting his help, we are being resourceful and fall in after him, traveling so quickly that, when we check the map again, we realize we're only about two hours from camp, and here it is only 3:30 p.m. on the third afternoon. We have a day's leeway. To show off, we decide to build a fire, cook, and eat at the camp's entrance. We enter at 12:01 a.m. on day four, take showers, sleep in our own beds, and watch the rest of the women straggle in throughout the day.

*

"Washington will decide my fate tonight," Joey Amado says. "God, I want to go to Peru with you."

"You'll go, Joey," Susan says, "It's just a matter of formalities."

"No, you guys don't understand. There were things in my background they're just now discovering—bad credit, a bit of a record—but nothing serious, I swear."

"I don't think they'll keep you out for that," I say, hoping I'm right. The three of us hold hands, pray, and wait on a bench outside the administrative building.

*

When the month-long physical training program in Puerto Rico is over, Joey, still unsure of his status, and not wanting to return to Los Angeles, returns with me to Milwaukee for home leave. My parents, who have never known people of another race, are welcoming, but I see my mother studying us from an upstairs window while we wait across the street for the Sherman bus to take us downtown to a movie.

Joey's case is still on hold when I receive instructions to be at the Miami International Airport on September 21 for a 7:00 p.m. departure on a Panagra charter. On the way to Billy Mitchell Field, I try to imagine what it will be like not seeing my family for nearly two years. Before boarding the North Central flight for Chicago, I embrace my parents, brother, and grandfather, holding each long and fast. Then I turn to Joey who will go to Washington, D.C. to plead his case. "So long, Joey," I say, kissing his cheek. "I know we'll meet in Peru. You *will* be there; I can't imagine it otherwise."

"I hear you have a knack for getting your prayers answered, Lydia girl; I'll be counting on those prayers."

"You got em' Joey." I climb the stairs to the plane, turn, and wave goodbye to my family and Joey. From my seat, I stare back at them, wishing the two years were over, and that I were returning to my family, my home, and my own bed.

III

Arequipa

From fire, water, earthquake free me Jesus
Christ , . . . from authorities, magistrates , . . .
priests, from all the gentlemen, thieves , . . .
free me Jesus Christ. From those who raise
false testimony, from haters, men or women,
from drunks, from those who do not fear
God and justice.

Felipe Guamán Poma de Ayala, *Nueva
corónica y buen gobierno, 1615, in Loren
McIntyre, The Incredible Incas and their
Timeless Land, 1975*

ALTHOUGH spring has officially arrived in the
southern hemisphere, it is still cold, and the *garúa*,
the gray mist that shrouds Lima from April to
December, makes for a somber welcome. Eighty-two

of us arrive, twenty-seven fewer than our original
count. A few volunteers lumber off the plane, hung-
over from the free alcohol on the DC 6. A bus takes
us to the Hotel Alcazar, where Susan and I sleep till
noon.

After lunch, we explore Lima. Although we just
missed the changing of the guard outside the
government palace on the Plaza de Armas, we view
the statue of the conquistador Francisco Pizarro. We
see the scraggly fig tree that, according to legend,
he planted when he founded the "City of Kings" in
1535. Pizarro's remains rest in his own chapel in the
Cathedral on the same plaza. After viewing the
catacombs in the colonial church of San Francisco
and the intricately carved wooden balconies of the
Palacio Torre Tagle, we stop for coffee at a restaurant
on the Plaza San Martín. Ragamuffin boys shine
men's shoes next to the statue of Peru's liberator,
astride a regal horse.

A man is sketching at a table near the window.
He is probably in his forties and handsome for his
age, silver at the temples. Turning to us, he smiles,
picks up his pencils and sketch pad, and asks if he
might join us. "*Por supuesto*," says Susan.

He is Tomás Rivas Peña, and he has read about
our arrival in the newspapers. "*Encantado, señoritas*,"
he says, bowing his head slightly, before pulling up a
chair. He asks the waiter to bring us another *cortado*,
a Peruvian espresso, and is pleased that we have asked
to see his drawings. There's one of a small boy, dressed
in rags, selling newspapers, and another of a poor old
man, playing a guitar on a street corner. The artist insists
we each take a sketch as a *recuerdo* of our meeting.

After telling him about our homes, Tomás invites
us to his studio to see his work and suggests that,

later, we may wish to stop by the Ministry of Land and Agriculture to see one of his murals. Susan and I exchange glances, but Tomás notices and assures us his motives are innocent. We agree to accompany him and walk the few blocks to his apartment and studio.

Paintings litter the small room, in disheveled stacks, on easels, in boxes. He invites us to choose a painting from a stack on a table, but we hesitate, not wanting to feel obligated.

"*Por favor, Lydia y Susana,* I may never see you again, never be able to thank you properly for the work you will do here for the next two years. Let me thank you for my country. These paintings are not much, the work of a native son of Peru."

I choose a painting of a cello player, dressed in a tuxedo, his bow drawn. The face is long and narrow, his legs and arms delicate, but the cellist's hands are large and muscular. Tomás also gives each of us a small sketch, models he worked from for the mural at the Ministry of Land and Agriculture. Mine is of a young boy, mouth gaping in horror, hair standing on end, as though he were fleeing a predator.

We thank Tomás, taking his address, and walk to the Ministry, where we stare at the panoramic mural of Indian families running in terror from the conquistadors. In the middle, fleeing the Spanish, is the little boy who originated with the sketch Tomás had given me. All the Indian men have large, strong hands, like the hands of the cellist.

Susan returns to the hotel for a nap, and I visit the sanctuary dedicated to Saint Rose of Lima, the first saint of the Americas. There is a small, peaceful garden next to the adobe hut that was built by Saint Rose in the early 1600s as a place of prayer and repose. As I leave the sanctuary, I drop a donation into a metal box and pick up a card with a picture of St. Rose. On the back is a paragraph about her. At age five she is said to have taken a vow of virginity; she received the habit of St. Dominic at age fifteen; for sixteen years she lived a life of mortification and penance, and she died in 1617 at age thirty-one. I feel worldly by comparison, and I wonder how, at age five, St. Rose knew what constituted virginity.

At 7:00 p.m., buses take us to a reception at the opulent residence of the American ambassador. We meet politicians and journalists and drink *pisco sours*, a frothy concoction of clear grape brandy, lime juice, egg white, and angostura bitters.

*

During the ensuing days, volunteers hang around the Peace Corps office, waiting for news of their assignments. So far I've been assigned to Arequipa, Puno, Vicos, and now I'm back to Arequipa, because the Peace Corps coordinator there says he needs a volunteer to work with hearing impaired children.

We get more immunizations. My arm turns red, puffy, and itchy, an allergic reaction to the horse serum used to treat rabies, and the doctor advises me not to keep a dog while in Peru, not to pet one, not to ever let one lick me.

Finally, I see my name and Claire's on a list of twenty-five volunteers bound for Arequipa, Peru's second largest city. It's in the southern Andes, at an altitude of 8,000 feet. Some volunteers, previously scheduled for Arequipa, are now going to Chimbote, a booming fishing town north of Lima. It's said to have a dreadful smell because of the fish meal plant.

Susan will go north to Trujillo, to work as a translator aboard the Ship HOPE. I'll miss her. A few volunteers, fluent in Spanish before training, and newly equipped with basic Quechua, the language spoken by most of the Indians in Peru, will go to an experimental agricultural station run by Cornell University in the northern Andes.

*

The bus driver heads south along the Pan American Highway. Small villages interrupt miles of rocky, Pacific shore on the west and sweeping sand dunes on the east. We spend the night at a tourist hotel on the coast that has been constructed by the government to accommodate weary travelers for whom no other lodging is available.

We arrive in Arequipa at nightfall of the second day. Skirting downtown, we head up a dark, gravel road toward Ciudad de mi Esperanza, City of my Hope, one of the *barriadas* where the poor live, where we will live. Those of us not sick with dysentery help the others off the bus.

Volunteers from Peru I and II greet us. They arrived only three weeks earlier, their training having been extended because of the Peruvian political mess. They lead us to the school that will be our temporary quarters. One classroom will house the twelve women, the other, the thirteen men. The "experienced" volunteers explain how we're to pump and carry water from outside the school to flush the toilets inside, and that nothing but human waste may enter the toilets.

After we've chosen our cots and stowed our luggage, the bus driver takes us to the public showers downtown, where for three *soles*, twelve cents, we bathe bodies, that, given the altitude, feel like ship ballast.

Newly clean, a state I'll learn never to take for granted, we walk to the Dalmacia Restaurant, down narrow sidewalks crowded with shoppers, wearing heavy sweaters against the prickly, evening chill. No one stops and says, "Welcome to Arequipa, we're glad you're here." The passersby stare at our troop of oversized North Americans; they don't smile.

*

I awake before the other women and step outside the school to survey my new neighborhood. Although some full-blooded Indians live in Ciudad de mi Esperanza, most of the residents are mestizos, of mixed Spanish and Indian blood. They have come down from the high sierra to find work. Because they appear to drop out of nowhere, erecting ramshackle houses overnight, they are known as *paracaidistas*, parachutists.

Gray and white dominate the landscape. No road is paved. There are no trees. Nothing green. No spring flowers interfere with the dreariness. Looking up, however, there is visual relief. Misti, a 19,150-foot volcano, said to be dormant by experts, but alive to those who know her tremors, rises proudly over The City of my Hope. Snow lavishly bleeds down her sides, like the white mantle of a madonna. It was in the green valley below us that Inca Mayta Capac, on his journey southward from Cuzco, found the beauty and climate so agreeable that he proclaimed to his followers, "*Arequipay*," meaning, "let us stay."

*

Irving Worthington, the Peace Corps coordinator for
Arequipa, gives us one day to rest and one day of
orientation before we begin our work. For some it's
easy. Two of the home economists will join a nutrition
program already underway in the *barriadas*. Men
with construction or plumbing experience will join
a government-sponsored housing project. The rest
of us must carve out our own niches. If I want to use
my training, I'll have to develop the job myself, but
this might be a good time to try something new.

On day three, Claire and I climb a garbage-strewn
embankment behind the school to Runa Chica, one
of the newest and poorest *barriadas*. Despite its
barrenness, Runa Chica has a splendid view of Misti
and of the peaks Cha-Chani and Pichu-Pichu.

Curious about our presence, the mothers swarm
around us, begging for assistance. "*No hay agua.*"
There's no water. "*No hay ayuda médica.*" There's
no medical help, no blankets, not enough food.

Half-naked children approach us with distended
bellies, hair infested with lice, skin raw and cracked
from the cold dry air, and nostrils encrusted with
mucous. I pick up a tiny girl with ratty hair, a snotty
nose, and filthy nails and hate myself for worrying
about contagion. She smiles at me and reaches for
my sunglasses.

Families here rarely eat fruits or green vegetables,
forced to survive on potatoes, beans, and rice. Up to
ten persons may live in a shack made of tin or scraps
of abandoned building materials. A woman invites
me into her house to see her child, who, she says,
has scarlet fever. The mother looks expectantly at

me, thinking that at last she's found someone to help her child.

After a long day in Runa Chica, I return to my cot in the schoolhouse with stomach cramps from the "Russian salad" I ate in town last night. It must have been the mayonnaise mixed into the cooked potatoes, carrots, peas, and beets, but I can't complain, given what I've just seen. The biggest obstacles to my well-being are the absence of a daily shower and latrine duty. This evening I'll wash the toilets, empty the trash cans in each stall, and burn the toilet paper. Tomorrow I'll bring aspirin for the sick child.

*

In the market I pay $11.00 for a neatly crafted hand-made guitar, reminding myself that, although I'm spending this money on a luxury item, the man who made it has a family to feed. Using a teach-yourself book I brought from the States, I learn "Beautiful, Beautiful Brown Eyes" and "Tom Dooley."

*

Claire and I speak to Irving Worthington, the boyish-looking Peace Corps coordinator, about our idea to start a nursery school in Runa Chica. We explain that the small children there are at risk when their parents go to work, and that, frequently, three-year-olds are left in the care of seven-year-olds. The school could also be used in the evenings as a place to teach preventive health measures to adults.

"It's a perfect project for the Peace Corps," Irving says. "We can put volunteers to work, help the people, and use the project to get publicity for our work in Arequipa."

Families in Runa Chica respond favorably to our idea and are eager to help in the school's construction. On a Saturday afternoon, volunteers and residents use tin siding to erect the John F. Kennedy School. One of the volunteers places a *Time* magazine photo of the president at the front of the classroom.

In the festivities that follow, the Peruvians urge us to share their *chicha*, an alcoholic beverage made from fermented corn. I should decline, but my throat is parched, and I want to celebrate with our hosts.

During the night, I awaken with wrenching abdominal pains and chills. Three women give up their army blankets, and I'm still shivering. Claire sits with me, holding my head when I vomit, washing my face, covering me. The Peace Corps trainer was right. Homesickness is worse when you're sick.

At dawn, I fall into a deep sleep and don't awaken till mid-afternoon when I drink a little hot chicken broth. Natalie Perigo, a stout, former Marine, in her early thirties, stays with me, trying to cheer me with talk of her family and hometown, but I fall asleep again and dream I'm on a Greyhound bus. I go to the bathroom at a rest stop, and when I come out the bus is gone. I inquire of the owner of the restaurant how I can get to my destination. He tells me there's a small airport nearby, and that there will be a plane in seven hours. Then a big bus pulls in, but it is headed in the direction opposite the airport. I wonder if I should board the bus anyway, but it leaves before I decide. The bus doesn't have a roof, and everyone looks free and breezy, and they wave goodbye to me.

*

Feeling better the next day, I'm teased about finally succumbing to "Atahualpa's Revenge," named after the Inca king betrayed by the Spaniard Pizarro.

At recess on the second day of my recovery, after a lesson on colors, in this colorless land, all the little boys run from the play area to the edge of the steep hill that separates Runa Chica from Ciudad. I try to stop them, but they are on urgent business: All ten line up, baby penises in hand, and pee over the edge. The school is too close to the hillside used as a community latrine and too close to mounds of stinking, fresh, human feces.

IV

Cuba

I have an avowed and resolute ambition: to
assist in the creation of Peruvian socialism.

José Carlos Mariátegui, *Siete ensayos
interpretivas sobre la realidad Peruana,*
1928

ON October 22, Claire and I are eating *bíftec a la
Milanesa* at the Capri Restaurant in downtown
Arequipa when Richard Marler, a New Jersey
plumber, and Peter Casten, an electrician from New
Hampshire, rush in, scanning the faces of the diners.
Seeing us, Richard orders, "Claire—Lydia! You've got
to come with us right away! Just leave your food!"

"What's going on?" asks Claire. "We've just begun
to eat."

"Forget the food! This is an emergency! We don't know what's going on," says Peter, "but Irving will let us know back at the school. It has something to do with Cuba." We quickly apologize to the waiters and leave our food and money on the table.

At the school, Irving Worthington tells us there's trouble with the Soviet Union and Cuba, and we should pack one bag containing necessities, in case we're told to evacuate. We must stay locked inside our quarters until told otherwise.

Are we on the verge of World War III? I want to speak to my parents. If there's a war, I want to be with them. I have brought along the small, short-wave radio my dad gave me as a going-away present, but I can't pick up any international news, nor the expected 8:00 p.m. broadcast by President Kennedy.

Irving returns later that night and says it's all right for us to go to work tomorrow, but we must not walk alone. We must avoid the downtown and return to the school by 5:00 p.m. He tells us to buy whatever food is available in nearby stores and to cook our meals at the school.

We open tins of Argentinean corned beef and packages of stale crackers, drink warm soda, and stay close to the radio. At 2:30 a.m. we awake to the sound of car tires digging into the gravel school yard. In the morning we find the words *Viva Cuba* painted on the door.

On October 23, we work in our *barriadas*, arriving back at the school by curfew. Irving alerts us to the "heavy communist element" in Arequipa and to anti-American demonstrations in the Plaza de Armas. He tells us to move our own cots and baggage to the houses of the already-settled volunteers because the school is an obvious target. He reassures us that the

Peace Corps will move us to the Hotel Turista, should the situation worsen. I wonder why we would be any safer in the tourist hotel.

Claire and I move into a two-room house with two women from Peru I. In the evening, there is a demonstration in the Plaza de Armas, and the Peruvian cavalry breaks it up with tear gas.

On October 24, we go to bed early, having consumed two bottles of cheap red Peruvian wine. At midnight, we again awaken to barking dogs and tires crunching gravel. Peeking out the covered window, as though victims of an air raid, we try to see the driver, but it's too dark. He blows the horn and departs. He repeats this pattern two more times. Is it a signal? Whoever it is knows that volunteers live here because a Peace Corps jeep is parked outside. Shortly after his last visit, we hear loud booms from downtown and see flares from that direction, then nothing.

I pick up London on my radio. The United States and the Soviet Union are close to war. I picture a gutted Milwaukee, my parents wandering through the ruins, or dead. In a letter I later receive from my mother, I learn that Soviet warheads had, indeed, been pointed at Milwaukee.

*

On the sixth day of semi-confinement, we receive an order telling us to prepare for evacuation. An article in the local communist newspaper *Frente* has apparently urged its readers to "kill every American man, woman, and child in Arequipa." Now we can't go to our jobs because the head of the Peruvian Secret Police has ordered us to stay in our rooms until we evacuate. Guards have been posted outside all the Peace Corps dwellings in Ciudad.

*

Claire and I have permission to attend Sunday Mass on October 28. The priest celebrates Mass in Spanish instead of Latin, a change made by the Second Vatican Council, convened by Pope John XXIII to address the spiritual renewal of the Church.

After Mass, we stretch out our absence to inspect the two rooms we hope to rent when the Cuban ordeal ends. We scoot inside the out-of-place wrought-iron gate to avoid being run over by a herd of llamas hurrying down the dusty, unpaved street. The family lives in two rooms in the back of the pink cement-block house, the only painted house in the neighborhood. They invite us to see the neatly swept backyard and the cistern where water is collected during the rainy season. Although it's not very private, there is also a clean latrine. A free-roaming turkey that the owners have been fattening for their daughter's fifteenth birthday party eyes us suspiciously.

We hope Irving will approve these rooms, but we fear he won't because the house is too pretty compared to the others around here. It rents for two hundred fifteen *soles* a month, or $8.00 U.S., reasonable, considering it boasts an electric light in the living room/bedroom.

Returning to Ciudad, we join the party the guys are throwing to commemorate what appears to be the end of the crisis. I bring my new Trini López album, and Claire and I dance the cha-cha to "Corazón de Melón" and drink *pisco* mixed with a warm orange soda called Fanta. Other volunteers mix their *pisco* with

Inca Kola, a yellow soft drink that tastes like bubble gum. Some of the volunteers are pairing off. Although the Peace Corps men like me, I get more attention from the Peruvians who can't seem to watch me walk by without making comments under their breath.

My ear for Spanish is still developing, but my eyes understand a leer. It must be my height. They're not used to tall women, and at five feet-ten inches, they must wonder if I work the same way other women do. Also, with my olive skin and dark eyes, they can't figure out where I'm from. Since arriving in Peru, I've been asked if I'm from Armenia, Argentina, and Spain.

By October 30, the night we call Beggars' Night in Milwaukee, the danger from the Soviet Union has passed. Kruschev will withdraw the missiles in Cuba that threaten the United States. We are proud of President Kennedy.

Drinking instant hot Nescafé at breakfast, Claire and I compare our childhood Halloween experiences. I remember the cold nights, the heavy sweater under my costume, the crunchy leaves, the pennies, popcorn, and apples all stuck together at the bottom of a paper bag. Claire said "Trick or Treat" when she went from house-to-house in Miami, but in Milwaukee, the group of rag-tag kids I went with shouted "Halloween Handouts!" On Beggars' Night, our small band would have to sing for the customers in Lerner's drug store before the pharmacist would give each of us a chunk of thick milk chocolate, broken off with an ice pick from a large tray in the bottom of his glass candy counter. It was the same chocolate he melted down and ladled over two scoops of vanilla ice cream to make delicious hot fudge sundaes.

*

After Irving approves our rooms, we buy rose-colored cotton fabric to make curtains and bedspreads to decorate our pink bedroom. For our kitchen we make a wobbly counter out of wooden crates and cover it with blue oil cloth that matches the walls. The landlord loans us a small kitchen table, two chairs, and a mirror. The Peace Corps will supply us with basic kitchen equipment.

*

Since my arrival, my parents have been slipping a dollar bill or two in their letters to me. I guard them between two of the cement blocks in our make-shift sofa. Added to the money I brought from home, I have enough to buy a battery-operated, portable record player and still pay my share of the first two month's rent.

Although our living conditions have improved, the water situation remains a challenge. Once a week, a truck driver deposits water into a centrally located tank. Adults and children run to the tank with empty containers, pushing and jockeying for position in front of the single tap. All other activity ceases when the water truck arrives. We store our drinking water in large clay jars outside our door and use the rainwater from the cistern behind our house for washing our clothes and bodies. We've become adept at bathing with only two basins of water, one to scrub, the other to rinse. Rough spots, like barnacles on oysters, begin to grow on my skin.

Activities that would have taken little time back home consume inordinate amounts of time here. For example, just to get hot water for tea or coffee, the alcohol stove must be pumped the right number of times before the wick on its burner ignites when struck with a match, and the water must be boiled for at least twenty minutes.

When we have a little money, we prefer to eat at a downtown restaurant, where we can also use the bathroom and not deal with the turkey that patrols the latrine at home. Because the latrine has no door or roof, only a short privacy wall, we use a fly swatter to keep the turkey at bay. This fencing further provokes him, and our reach is too short to thwart his pecking beak. We try brandishing a broom instead, but it's easy to lose your balance while poised over the seatless toilet. If Claire and I are home at the same time, we stand guard for each other at the latrine entrance, jabbing the jutting turkey with the broom. When one of us has dysentery and is too weak to get to the latrine, the other is nurse, emptying the bedpan, broom in hand. It takes coordination.

*

On November 1, All Saints Day, we get the news that Joey Amado has been deselected. What stupid shortsightedness! I am sick for my friend. Will he write to Susan and me, or would that be too painful for him?

*

We've been meeting some Peruvians from the small middle class in Arequipa, and our social lives are improving with the help of the American-Peruvian Cultural Society whose members are hosting a potluck supper for the volunteers. Irving is nervous about our participation. To squelch a popular rumor

that we're spies working for the CIA, agents of
Yankee imperialism, he insists we avoid the
restaurants and keep to the *barriadas*, not mixing
with the other North Americans here, not showering
in their homes. We should keep our noses clean and
our bodies dirty.

*

After two months in Arequipa and six months in the
Peace Corps, I wonder what significance my teaching
in Runa Chica has. Maybe all I'm doing is baby sitting.
The chance of these children ever attending public
school is remote.

*

I continue to attend Mass at Our Lady of Good
Counsel, the church run by the Maryknolls. There I
meet Father Daniel O'Shea, a tall, curly-haired priest
who has the women in the parish in the palms of his
Irish hands. Father Dan invites me to teach a small
class of retarded and physically handicapped
children. The class, held in the church hall, is staffed
by women from the parish, but they are in need of a
specialist to head it up, to teach and guide the
mothers. Here is where I could make a contribution,
and, by training future teachers, a lasting one. I'd
also be able to use the knowledge from my special
education minor.

"I don't know, Lydia," Irving says to my proposal.
"It may not be such a good idea."

"Why not, Irving? I thought for sure you'd be
happy with the idea."

"I like Our Lady of Good Counsel. Don't forget I'm Catholic, too."

"So what's the problem? You were eager to have me work with handicapped children when you visited Cornell during our training."

"Yes, well, then I thought a public school could use you, not a wealthy church school."

"But the school in this case isn't wealthy, and it will take children from all over—not just the children of the rich—and there's a modern classroom, with bathrooms."

"But the Peace Corps' image is important, Lydia. We can't have our volunteers giving the impression that they've come here to live and work in high style. I'll have to check with Lima before I give you an answer."

"Irving, please. I'm not asking for a room in the Tourist Hotel; I'm asking you to let me do my job. Father O'Shea and the mothers invited me. That's got to count for something. I thought we weren't supposed to shove projects at the Peruvians or tell them what they need."

"Lydia, I don't appreciate your jibe—you know my wife and I are only living at the Hotel Turista until we find a suitable house—and I'm telling you for the last time, I need to speak with Lima."

"Go ahead and speak with Lima, Irving. I'll be waiting to hear what Hal Rugger says."

"Your attitude won't help things, Lydia," Irving warns.

*

A week later, I get a message that Irving wants to see me about the school. "I have good news for you, Lydia.

Lima says it's okay for you to work with the handicapped children, but you'll have to do it in a *barriada*, and any upper class families with handicapped children will have to bring them there."

"That won't work," I say. "Some of the children can't walk; they're in wheel chairs. We have no decent place in the *barriadas*. I can't imagine Father Dan or the volunteer mothers agreeing to this."

"Sorry, that's the final word," he says, picking up some papers.

"Answer me one thing, Irving," I say, before going to the church to tell Father Dan. "Do you agree with Hal Rugger?"

"It's not for me to agree or disagree," he says without looking at me.

*

After I explain the situation to Father Dan, he speaks with some of the mothers, and one of them, Mrs. Tucket, a woman from Massachusetts, married to a Peruvian of British descent, suggests there be a door-to-door canvas in the *barriadas* bordering the church to get a count of the number of handicapped children. Enough mothers might be found to transport these poor children to the church school until a bus could be rented or purchased. The statistics might influence local politicians to provide funding to transport the children. Instead of taking the school to a *barriada*, we will be bringing the *barriada* to Our Lady of Good Counsel.

Rugger and Worthington can't say no to this. True, it is only the wealthy women who have cars, but if they're willing to go to the homes of the poor, they might develop relationships with them, creating a real Alliance for Progress. The children of the rich and poor would learn and play together. I take the new development back to Irving.

"This certainly seems to be a compromise on their part," he says. "Fortunately, Hal Rugger flies in from Lima tomorrow, and we can put it to him."

By the time I get to the obligatory meeting the Peace Corps director for Peru has called, the school is already filled with volunteers. Hal Rugger stands at the front of the room, shaking hands. I stand against the back wall.

Rugger, with furrowed brow and hair the color of evaporated milk, takes ten minutes to tell us the good things he's heard about our performance before delivering his warning: "Now I know you'd like a hot shower at night, and you'd like a stiff drink and a decent dinner, but that's not why you came to Peru. You came here to live the way your counterparts live. Toward that end, I want you to avoid unnecessary associations with the rich, and that means no showers and no dinners at their homes, however tempting the invitations.

"Keep in mind," he continues, after inhaling deeply on his cigarette, "that you're a novelty for rich Peruvians; there's a certain prestige in showing you off to their friends. Sure, maybe they'll feel sorry for you, but don't jeopardize our work here for a swim in the country club pool, an elegant meal, or a shower."

"Hey, Hal," Richard Marler, the plumber from New Jersey, says. "Who are our counterparts here anyway? Don't the volunteers who teach in Lima have comfortable apartments? I'm not asking to get into a plusher place myself, but to point out the inconsistencies in this policy."

"Some of the volunteers in Lima do live well, but all of you are in Community Development—the backbone of the Corps—the core of the Corps." Hal laughs at his own word play.

"Look, Hal," I say, standing straight, my stomach clenching. "No one is asking for major concessions. Sure, I'd like to have a hot shower now and then, but more importantly, I'd like you to explain how the gap between the rich and poor can be bridged if we can't go near the rich, and if they, on their own, never go near the poor." I take a deep breath and notice that all eyes are watching me.

"You're right about the rich being curious about us," I continue. "They wonder what we're doing here, living and working in the slums and leaving the most prosperous country in the world to do it. Why not involve the rich in solving some of Peru's social problems? We've got to start thinking long-term here, not just what looks good for the moment."

I look down at the floor, awaiting his reply, but the volunteers are applauding and smiling their approval at me. Those closest to me are reaching out to shake my hand, saying, "Nice going, Lydia."

Hal and Irving exchange looks before the Peace Corps director answers. "It's true that all of you may not be suited for the Peace Corps. We're a fledgling organization, and we tried to do a careful screening of potential volunteers at Cornell and Puerto Rico, but as you know, several of your members have already left. They didn't have what it takes, and it may be that, even though you've been in the Peace Corps six months, some of you have become malcontents. You know who you are. Just remember evaluation is an ongoing process. It's an honor to serve, and if you can't hack it, perhaps it's time to return to your

namby-pamby universities back home." He looks at
me and says, "Miss Schaefer, please see me after the
meeting."

I wait for the room to clear before approaching
him. "Sorry if I offended you, Hal. I'm just impatient.
There's so much to do here, and I don't know how
we can fix things by ourselves."

"Lydia, I won't beat around the bush," Hal says,
before taking another drag. "When you challenged
Irving about the school, I took a look at your record.
You did the same kind of upstaging in your Spanish
class at Cornell. You should think twice before
drawing attention to yourself again. I know how to
handle troublemakers, especially pretty, well-
educated troublemakers."

"Draw attention to myself? I'm just trying to be
useful. I don't want to go home in eighteen months,
feeling my stay here has been a waste of time. You
know that's been a problem for some of the
volunteers—that's why they've been leaving. They
come with high hopes and a desire to work, but they
get overwhelmed by the poverty and feel helpless
and unequipped. You encourage us to find our own
way, and when we do, you pull in the leash."

"The way you're headed, Lydia, you'll be lucky if
you make it another eighteen months. I trust there
will be no further debate on this issue," he says,
turning to shake the hand of a volunteer who's been
waiting to see him.

"Forgive me for being dense," I say, not letting
him go just yet, "but are you saying that I can't work
with the women from the church?"

"You got it, baby. You're finally catching on."

I drag myself home, wanting to sleep, but Claire
won't permit it. "We're going to celebrate the stand

you took today, Lydia," she says, offering me a *Perú Libre, pisco* and a small amount of her much-coveted Coca Cola.

That night, thinking over Hal Rugger's words about drawing attention to myself, I remember being an eleven-year-old girl scout. One Sunday afternoon, our troop visited the television studio of WTMJ in Milwaukee. The master of ceremonies invited the shortest cub scouts and the tallest girl scouts to the stage. Despite my embarrassment, my mother, the troop leader, persuaded me to walk up to the stage. The master of ceremonies paired the tall girls with the short boys and explained there would be a jitterbug contest. I knew what the jitterbug looked like, so I led the cub scout, and, at one point, for the effect it would create, picked him up under his arms and twirled him around. The audience applauded wildly, and we won.

I remember back even further, when I was five or six, and the only child on our block not invited to a birthday party of a girl I didn't like anyway. My pride and feelings hurt, I rummaged through a large box of comic books in my brother's closet and selected a few of the least rumpled ones because I had no money for a gift. I placed the comics in a paper bag, walked to the birthday girl's home, and rang the bell. Her mother opened the door, felt sorry for me, and asked me If I'd like to join the children trying to drop clothespins into a milk bottle.

*

Soon it will be Thanksgiving. My rebel status has earned me a place on the Thanksgiving dinner committee. I'll be working with people from the

American embassy, people who have hot showers and, because they have commissary privileges, have canned soups, peanut butter, and dill pickles on their shelves.

*

On the Monday before Thanksgiving, a cab arrives at our door of our little painted house. The children in the street flock around it to stare as Lima artist Tomás Rivas Peña emerges. Shortly after arriving in Ciudad, I had written to formally thank him for the drawings, never expecting to see him again. He had found the Peace Corps office in Arequipa, and the Peruvian secretary, impressed at meeting the famous artist, gave him our address. He had been invited to give a lecture at the University of San Augustín and thought he would take advantage of his presence in Arequipa to visit his new Peace Corps friends.

I explain that Susan had been sent to Trujillo, and, after introducing him to Claire, I invite him to stay for dinner, grateful that we had bought meat at the German butcher shop in town. While the rice is cooking, Tomás goes to the bodega to buy some wine, and Claire borrows a third chair from the landlord.

Setting aside the rice from the single burner on the alcohol stove, I use the space to make *lomo saltado,* sautéing chunks of red meat with onions, garlic, thinly sliced potatoes, and red pepper. While I spoon the mixture over the rice, Claire tells Tomás what a heroine I've become for having stood up to the Peace Corps director. "*Delicioso,*" says Tomás, trying the food, yet still attentive to Claire.

After dinner, Claire offers Tomás a local cigarette, known as "Inka Stinkahs" by volunteers who crave

American brands. "Lydia," Tomás says, "Claire has told me what you tried to do in the meeting with your boss. It was a brave thing. Did you accomplish what you wanted?"

"No, I didn't. In fact, I may have made things worse."

"Ah, Lydia, my sweet young friend, you remind me of myself when I was much younger," he says, his dark lashes closing a second over eyes that seem to have no pupils.

"I consider that a compliment," I say, folding my arms. "In what way do I remind you of yourself?"

Pushing her chair back from the table, Claire excuses herself. "Sorry to interrupt, but I promised to help our landlord's son with an English lesson. It was great meeting you, Tomás, and I hope you'll visit us again the next time you're in Arequipa."

"The honor was all mine, Señorita Clara," he answers, getting up from his chair to give her a kiss on the cheek.

"See you guys," she says, walking out the door.

"*Me gusta,*" Tomás says. "She is so fresh and eager, but now, where were we? Yes, how do you remind me of my youth? Well, by confronting authority— questioning—the way you did with your Señor Rugger."

"But aren't you still confronting people, Tomás? What about your mural in the Ministry?"

"Yes, it is true that I continue to confront; critics have said the mural forces one to look into the face of evil, into the avaricious face of the oppressor and see the terror of the young boy who flees, but it is up to each person to read into the mural what he will."

"But you're a famous artist," I say, pouring the last of the wine. "You can disagree without worrying about the opinions of others."

"There were those who opposed my idea for the mural, Lydia. They did not want to offend the people of Spanish descent in Peru, and they did not want to elevate the Indians or add to their discontent."

"Then how did you get the design approved?"

"By talking quietly to a few key persons about my ideas, without trying to persuade them, by giving the ideas time to take hold, by waiting."

"I think there's a lesson in this for me."

"Not unless it seems right for you." Tomás stands up and pushes his chair under the table. "It is getting late, and I had better get back to my hotel. Is it possible to get a cab from here?"

"No, taxis don't usually come here, and there's no phone, but the bus should still be running. I'll walk to the bus stop with you."

The streets are deserted, except for a few stray dogs that begin to follow us. As we pass the dark houses, more dogs join the stragglers, until a pack forms. The dogs begin to snarl and growl, nipping at our heels. I remember my allergy to the rabies vaccine. Tomás bends and picks up a handful of stones and forcefully throws them at the dogs. I do the same. The dogs skulk away, and we safely reach the bus stop, a weak circle of light under a mist-veiled street lamp.

I'd like to keep Tomás near, consult him whenever I lose my bearings in this bizarre culture of Peace Corps policy and Peruvian reality. As if sensing my need, Tomás grabs my shoulders and turns me toward him, pressing his fingers into my arms and locking his eyes on mine. "Lydia, I want you to be my woman. I want to make love to you. Come back with me to the hotel."

I look up the street for any distraction, grateful to see the headlights of the bus through the mist. His arms drop to his side, and I struggle to say something that won't hurt. "Tomás, I can't. I'm sorry. I like you very much, but I'm not ready for that kind of relationship."

"It's all right, Lydia, don't worry," he says, brushing the damp black hair from his forehead. "I'm the one who should apologize." He boards the bus, shoulders bent, looking much older than when we first met in Lima. Perhaps a woman has never before refused him.

In bed I have second thoughts. What would it be like to be this superb artist's lover, to enter headlong into my first affair, to have his sensitive fingers and hands on my body, to have the wisdom and guidance of a gentle, intelligent man?

I pick up my rosary from the fruit crate beside my bed. It's Monday night. The first Joyful Mystery: The Annunciation.

V

Ica and the Flood

But life always triumphs. Man is the same as
the river, deep and with his misfortunes,
but always willful.

Ciro Alegría, *La serpiente de oro,* 1935

SUMMER and Christmas bring rain, overcast days,
and damp, chilly evenings. Walking into the
seventeenth-century Baroque church of La
Compañia on Christmas morning is like entering a
child's vision of heaven. Every inch of the nave and
altar dome is gilded or ornately painted with biblical
scenes. The Jesuits who built this church hoped that
the sumptuous painting of the resurrected Christ
would remind sinners that it is the Easter event upon
which Christian belief rests. If Christ had remained
in the tomb, He would have been a good man, a

prophet, but not God's Son, not divine, and Christians would have no hope of life beyond the grave. Walking back to the bus stop after Mass, I pass store windows decorated with aluminum Christmas trees.

Claire and I invite our landlord and his family for hot chocolate, and they bring *empanadas* stuffed with meat and olives. Later, Claire gives me a white lace mantilla to wear to Mass, and I give her "Feria de Octubre," a popular recording of music she loves from the October bull fighting festival in Lima.

Christmas melancholy descends like syrup. What is the value of my work in Runa Chica? We've given the mothers a safe place to leave their children, but in two years, when the volunteers leave, what will have changed? There will be more children in each family and fewer resources to go around.

Even though it's summer, it's cold. In Wisconsin, where the seasons are more sharply defined, you dress warmly, wear boots, go ice skating, and you wait it out. Here, with the constant damp chill, you draw your lethargic body up tightly, protecting your heart from the hard, muddy poverty until fall, when the white sun relaxes your skin, muscles, and bones and quickens your sluggish blood.

*

There has been a flood in Ica, a city four hours southeast of Lima. I will be part of a relief team. Is this Irving's way of getting rid of me?

On a late March afternoon, Celeste Renfro, a chubby, red-headed nurse from Nebraska, and I leave for Ica in a *colectivo* we share with three other passengers. At 4:00 a.m., fourteen hours later, we arrive in Ica and camp out in the lobby of the Hotel Colón, on the Plaza de Armas. The carpets squish underfoot. The receptionist offers us a musty smelling, red velvet sofa, away from the door, where we sleep for three hours.

We clean up in the ladies' room and have rolls and *café con leche* in the dining room before lugging our suitcases to the Caritas office on Calle Cajamarca, taking wide steps over the gutters that still run with dark sewage, the dregs of the five feet of water that covered these streets a week ago.

Padre Joaquín Benavides, who resembles Fidel Castro, is the director of Caritas, the local Catholic relief agency. He welcomes us with a Castilian accent and a strong handshake. From his drab office, he directs the distribution of U.S. powdered milk, flour, and cooking oil. He explains that an operator wouldn't open the dikes when the Ica river crested because he feared the water would destroy the cotton crop belonging to the richest man in Ica. Instead, the water swept away the fragile adobe and straw houses of the poor, killing many, injuring more, and leaving nearly everyone in the *barriada* Oculto homeless.

The Padre introduces us to Señora Gutiérrez, a widow who has offered to host the women volunteers until we can arrange for our own housing. She takes us across the noisy street to her flat and shows us the room we'll share with six other women. Celeste and I roll out our bedding, reserving spots near the window. After showering, we ask Señora Gutiérrez for directions to the *barriada.*

Oculto is a cesspool of mud, garbage, teeming flies, and rats, and it stinks. "*Bienvenidas a Operación Limpieza,*" says Trent Kendal with his Boston accent, welcoming us to Operation Clean-up. He strides toward us, hand extended, the dried muck on his jeans almost betraying his privileged background. Trent invites me to join the other volunteers shoveling mud and debris; Celeste scouts out the injured.

The Peace Corps men and women work together, hands blistered, feet sodden in mud-filled shoes. The Peruvians stand around and watch. Who are these fair-skinned people who do this filthy work? Soon, however, their amazement gives way to shame, and a few women join us; then the men help. At sunset, older women arrive with huge pots of rice and Lima beans that we devour. At nightfall, we slump back to our rooms, wait our turn for a cold shower, clean the mud from our toenails, and put cream on our ragged hands.

The next day there are blankets, rice, corn meal, and Quaker (pronounced "Quahkerr) oats to distribute. By late afternoon, I can't move my neck without pain and return to the room to rest. Señora Gutiérrez sees me holding my neck to one side and questions me. "*¿Ay hija, qué tienes?*"

"I hurt my neck, Señora. I don't know what's the matter," I say, holding back tears.

"Lie down, Lydia. Let me look at you," she says. "Listen, I think a jealous woman may have given you the *mal de ojo*. It is important to find out if you were given the evil eye, so the spell can be broken."

She instructs me to be quiet while she makes small versions of the Sign of the Cross over my entire body. When she finishes, she sighs with relief. "*Gracias a Dios*, you do not have the evil eye."

"What were you looking for, Señora?"

"If you had started to cry, daughter, I would have

known some jealous woman had given you the evil eye."

"But why would anyone be jealous of me?"

"We never know these things, but it is possible you have something the other woman wants—a lover, perhaps—and you have youth and beauty."

"Thank you, Señora, but I haven't felt beautiful for a long time."

"Now you rest, and I'll bring you some aspirin," she says, closing the fly-specked curtains. I miss my mother and wish I were home, in my own bed, with clean sheets, a chocolate malt, and new magazines.

*

In two days, I feel better and join Celeste who is using donated materials from the volunteers' first aid kits to turn a Caritas storage shed on the river bank into a make-shift health clinic. I take up a collection among the volunteers to buy additional bandages, antiseptics, and antibiotics at a downtown pharmacy, where no prescriptions are needed. Word of the clinic gets out, and we are soon swamped with patients. At first I'm dependent on Celeste's expert instructions, but gradually I become desensitized to treating the festering wounds. I never get used to the sick babies, however.

Most of them are malnourished, but parasites feed well in their swollen bellies. Flies light on their eyes, crusted shut with discharge; neither the infants nor their mothers have the energy to flick them away. Many of the mothers have tuberculosis, and I give them shots of streptomycin.

*

Marcia O'Neil, a new volunteer from Rhode Island, arrives in Ica. She will work with a credit cooperative that will make small loans to people needing capital to re-start their businesses after the flood. Despite her pudginess, with her red-brown hair, creamy skin, and freckles, Marcia looks like she belongs on an Irish travel poster. Because she will be working in town with small business owners, instead of in the *barriadas*, she is allowed to have housing similar to that of her Peruvian counterparts. I learn that she is looking for a roommate to share her house. It has a bathroom with a cold water shower and a flush toilet. She is pleased that I'm Catholic, and we agree to share rent and expenses.

The living room, bedroom, and bath in our new house are aligned in a straight row, a Peruvian shotgun house. Feathers from the chickens living on the roof float through a bar-covered opening over the passageway leading to the kitchen. We take turns sweeping up the feathers and wonder if we're susceptible to chicken-borne diseases, and what are the health risks from the DDT we dust on our military-style cots to kill fleas. Then there's the cat, that, days after we moved in, fell through the iron grate and bolted through the house, leaving a trail of sickening stool.

As in Arequipa, we don't have a refrigerator, so we go to the market nearly every day to buy eggs, fruit, and vegetables. I'm learning to dicker with the market women for the best prices, trying not to insult them by arbitrarily offering a price much lower than what they first ask.

*

As fall approaches, and the weather on the hot coastal strip cools, I begin to gain weight. Intermittent bouts of dysentery, however, keep me from worrying about temporary gains. After recovery, I splurge with a dish of *manjar blanco*, a condensed milk concoction we buy at the local bakery. Marcia and I eat huge gobs of it right from the waxed paper in which it is wrapped.

The two-burner kerosene stove is an improvement over the single burner alcohol stove I used in Arequipa. We've made meat loaf in the top of a double boiler, but you have to keep adding water to the bottom pan, so it won't scorch. It's surprisingly good with lots of ketchup. Having a stone sink and cold running water in the kitchen is also a luxury.

You can't put out your trash in garbage cans because scavengers will dump it on the sidewalk, sort through it, and steal the cans. Instead, we bundle our trash in newspapers and tie it with string before placing it on the street for the garbage men who come at dawn. Some people, nevertheless, find it irresistible, and we find the contents, including the soiled, pink paper you can't put in the toilet, strewn over the sidewalk when we leave for work in the morning.

*

Having settled into a routine, I enjoy evening walks to the Plaza de Armas, the central square that is surrounded by centuries-old Ficus trees. After dinner, with the flood water gone, families amble to the plaza, where the elderly sit on benches around the fountain, watching the flirting rituals between the cocky, adolescent boys and the coy, self-conscious girls.

Is there someone in Peru for me? Marcia is already in a steady relationship with José Estrada, who works with her at the credit co-op.

On a Friday evening, Ingrid Swenson, a statuesque blonde from North Dakota, and I go to the movies. *Breakfast at Tiffany's* makes me feel more alone. Audrey Hepburn is elegant and petite, and we feel like unfeminine clods, with our too-tall bodies, worn clothing, scuffed shoes, and dry skin.

After the movie, as we're about to enter my house for a cup of instant coffee, a short, stocky man calls to us: "Señoritas, do you like this?" he asks, exposing himself. Instead of ignoring him, I chase after him, screaming that he is a jerk, an asshole. He flees in disbelief. What is happening to me? I would have beat the shit out of him had I caught him.

The following Sunday, I'm kneeling in the Cathedral before Mass starts when a young priest leaves the confessional, walks toward me, and says in imperious Spanish, "¡*Vete de aquí con ese vestido de playa!*" I think he's ordering me to leave church because of the "beach" dress I'm wearing! I look at the women on both sides of me. They are modestly attired. But he can't mean me because I'm wearing a powder blue dress with a high neckline and cap sleeves, and Claire's white mantilla covers my head, shoulders, and arms to my elbows. But he says the words again, this time louder and angrier, and he points at me.

Without a word, I step around the people in the pew and walk out of the crowded Cathedral, avoiding stares, feeling like a woman caught in adultery, waiting to be stoned. I rush toward home, talking to myself through tears and snot. An old priest, wearing a long dark tunic, tied with a white knotted cord, hurries toward me. I stop him, explaining what has happened and ask how another man of God can treat someone like that. He apologizes for the behavior of the young priest and invites me to return to church, but I refuse. His concern softens my anger, and I remind myself it is the people who comprise the Church, and I should not let one troubled priest with unexamined scruples keep me away.

I buy a bottle of red *Copa de Oro,* put Ella Fitzgerald on the record player, and plunk myself down in the green canvas lawn chair in our living room. Taking a swallow of wine from the bottle, I think about the young priest at the Cathedral. Had I tempted him? Why else would he throw me out of church? I'd like to tell him how much he hurt me and ask him if he was behaving in a Christ-like way; I would remind him that he's a man, not a god, and what right did he have to judge me in the first place? Although I'm not a perfect Catholic, I've tried to live a decent life.

I recall Sister Mary Ladislaus who looked and sounded like her name. The final "s" was not pronounced, so we called her Sister Cole Slaw. In seventh grade I had attended a spin the bottle party with school friends. One of the girls squealed, and, in front of the class, Sister called me "a cheap penny girl." I wish Sister Ladislaus were in this room now. I'd have a few words for her, even if she had, upon the occasion of her final vows, chosen the name of a Hungarian king who had been canonized.

But then, to prove my decency, I had asked Sister Mary Angeles if I could be one of the girls who cleaned the sacristy of St. Anne's Church. The Gothic structure, built in the 1920s, was a mysterious place.

The altars lining the side aisles, with their shiny mosaic images of saints, appeared to be portals to paradise.

Sister Mary Angeles granted my wish and instructed me in my solemn duties. Reverently, I dusted the statues of Mary, Joseph, and the saints and replaced the spent beeswax candles that believers had lighted in prayerful offerings to the Mother of Perpetual Help. Behind the altar, I waxed the dark brown, lustrous cabinets that held the priests' vestments.

I wondered if priests had penises. I knew what my baby brother's had looked like, but I had not seen another one until my oldest cousin Ralph came down to the basement where my girl cousins and I had been playing. A hard, red member was sticking out of his pants. He called, "Hey, Lydia, have you ever seen a boner?" I wondered if priests could have a penis and still turn the bread and wine into the Body and Blood of Christ.

After seeing Ralph's penis, I didn't want to hear my mother tell me that men put their penises into women's vaginas to make babies. To me it didn't matter if a man and woman were married and loved each other. How could love make that behavior any less disgusting? I shared my mother's lesson with my best friend Brenda Stadler, but she didn't believe it.

Ella Fitzgerald is singing "All through the Night," and I remember how Brenda and I used to practice the popular ballroom steps, learning them from her older sisters who went dancing at the Roof Ballroom on Friday nights and at the Eagles Ballroom on Saturday nights. They layered crinolines under full felt skirts and wore tight sweaters with narrow scarves tied around their necks. They cinched their waists with wide belts, accentuating their hips, looking daring and naughty, but at the end of the evening they said goodbye to their dance partners and went out for cheeseburgers and cokes at the Kopper Kettle.

When Brenda and I turned eighteen, we became dancing fools. Most of our partners were sailors who took the train to Milwaukee from Great Lakes, sporting short hair and summer whites. Those from the east coast were especially good at the jitterbug and Latin steps. I didn't have to lead any more, like I did at Divine Redeemer, when we danced during lunch breaks to Tony Bennett's "Rags to Riches" and the Four Ace's "Love is a Many-Splendored Thing."

At the Eagles Ballroom on a New Year's Eve, I was dancing with a sailor who was at least four inches shorter than I. He held me too tightly and pressed his groin against me. When I felt something hard, I thought of my cousin Ralph and pushed back, sticking out my rump. When the orchestra played "Auld Lang Syne," the sailor opened his mouth and gave me a French kiss. It felt like he were trying to swallow me head first, as though, in spite of my height, I were a mouse, and he, a python. I left him standing in the middle of the ballroom and fled to the bathroom to rinse out my mouth. I think I'm still afraid of the male anatomy and of what men do with it.

When I first arrived in Peru, I winced every time I saw a man urinate in public. I still don't like the sight, but I'm getting used to it. Even though the men pee against a wall, with their backs toward me, I still have to negotiate, on my way to work, the yellow-green rivulets they make in the sandy soil. Each fresh, public pee adds to the acrid smell that has accumulated in the hot sand from public pees over thousands of years; I smell the urine of the Spanish, Incas, and pre-Incas.

I was grateful when the Peace Corps men, after the initial flood clean-up, dedicated themselves to the building of latrines. Using the latrines would have diminished human excrement in the river bed as well as disease-carrying flies, but the people used them as storehouses instead.

*

Hung-over in the morning, I take a freezing shower, eat an avocado and a piece of old bread, and walk to the clinic. Celeste is visiting the poorly equipped hospital in downtown Ica today, trying to arrange for medical interns to work at our clinic. When I unlock the clinic door, I disturb battalions of flies sleeping on the ceiling, and they retaliate, dive-bombing for my face. Brushing them away, I reach for the fumigator, directing it at the ceiling, pumping rapidly, my eyes slits, as pesticide-soaked bodies fall on my head and shoulders. The black corpses fall like a biblical plague, littering the floor and the sheets covering the medicines and syringes. While the fumes dissipate, I walk to the house of Alicia Peralta, the teen-aged Peruvian girl who has been helping us in the clinic.

Alicia's sisters are prostitutes who bring their men to the two-room shack they share with their youngest sister. Only twelve, Alicia is not ready to enter the business, and she probably won't. She eyes men with suspicion and has a tough, boyish look about her. When we first opened the clinic, Alicia warily approached us, asking questions about our language and clothing, but soon she expressed a desire to work with us. We accepted her offer, needing someone who could speak Quechua.

Alicia grins when she sees me at the door. How does she manage such cheerfulness? I put my arm around her shoulders, and we walk along the stinking, dry river bed back to the newly whitewashed and now fumigated clinic. The fresh paint and the red cross over the door distinguish it from the brown reed shacks that look more like animal pens than human dwellings.

We brush the dead flies from the chairs and tables and sweep the dirt floor. Alicia is business-like as she welcomes the first patient, writing the woman's name in the record book and charging her one *sol*, or four cents, to ensure the patient has an investment in her own health, but Alicia doesn't charge for the baby the woman holds.

The Quechua-speaking woman complains of a vaginal infection, a frequent problem when men are not careful about their hygiene, a task complicated by the scarcity of clean water. The frail baby boy has diarrhea, and his limp arms and legs look like thin rolls of dough. The mother has no more milk, and her flattened breasts droop over an emaciated frame, encased by skin that has lost its elasticity and softness.

Careful to read the warnings on the package, I give an antibiotic to the woman from a stash of samples we've received from a U.S. pharmaceutical company. I know I'd be arrested for doing the same thing back home, but who else is going to work here? I tell the mother to boil the water she will give the baby now and to boil the water for the formula she will give him when his diarrhea has stopped, cautioning her, because there's no refrigeration, not to store any excess. She can't read, so I ask her to repeat the ratio of formula to boiled water. Many mothers tend to over-dilute it so the milk lasts longer.

One after another, the women arrive with sickly babies at their breasts. Some suckle toothy three-year-olds, who stand stubbornly before over-worked teats, tugging on them, reluctant to give up the only softness in their lives. I've heard that some Indian mothers, wanting to wean their toddlers, paint frightening faces on their breasts.

"*Gracias, doctora,*" says a prematurely aged woman, gathering her dirty skirts and baby to her weathered body. I am uncomfortable with the patients' use of an honorific I don't merit and inform them of the mistake, learning later that Peruvian Indians often use *doctor* to address any professional.

*

On a quiet Sunday afternoon, my movie buddy Ingrid Swenson and I go to a matinée. Missing popcorn, we buy candy from a street vendor and take seats toward the front, where fewer people shout yeas and boos at the movie characters, and where there's a fainter smell of urine than in the back.

We note the arrival of two tall, handsome criollos, the designation for people born in Peru who claim a pure Spanish blood line. They see us, look at each other, and take seats right behind us. Ingrid and I exchange light elbow jabs.

Apart from the Peace Corps men, who are more like brothers than boyfriends, they're aren't many tall men in Ica. Come on, make the first move. During the previews, there's a tap on my shoulder, and I'm looking into the mischievous eyes of Paulo Carilo, who introduces us to his friend, Fernando Ortiz.

After the movie, disregarding Peruvian cultural mores, we accept their invitation to go for a drink at the Hotel Mossone at the Huacachina oasis. Separated from the blight of the *barriadas* by only eight miles, the oasis, nestled midst high sand dunes, has a spinach-green lagoon, surrounded by towering date palms. We sit in rocking chairs on the hotel's veranda and sip *pisco sours*, make small talk, and watch pot-bellied men rub slimy lagoon algae on their bald heads.

Paulo and Fernando invite us to dinner, and, for a short time, we are proud North American beauties, pursued by two dashing criollos. Dark Fernando, attentive to blonde Ingrid, is debonair with classic Spanish features. Paulo, of Italian descent, has clear blue eyes, light brown curly hair, and smiles easily. There are white linens on the table, the Pacific fish is fresh, and the waiter pours *Nectár de Ica* wine.

After dinner, Paulo and I dance in the lounge to a sultry selection on the juke box. Holding me firmly, he nuzzles his mouth near my ear and sings, "She swore to love me and never forget those tropical nights near the sea."

*

At thirty-three, Paulo is the oldest man that has ever interested me. He's district manager for a farm equipment company and visits clients throughout southern Peru. The following week I join him every evening after work at the Chinese restaurant known as the Chifa. We sit in a dark booth, hold hands, and drink cold beer before sharing an intimate meal.

The night before he returns to Lima, we have the house to ourselves. We dance to Antonio Prieto's,

"Más allá," a big hit. Our bodies aligned, a demanding ache settles in my groin. He eases me down to the straw mat covering the cement floor.

"No, Paulo, please don't touch me there."

"Don't refuse me, Lydia. It's natural for me to want to touch you, to want to make you happy."

"You won't make me happy if you do that, Paulo. Please stop."

Holding my hand upon the erect penis straining against his trousers, he says, "Then you touch me, Lydia. You will know how much I want you." Instead, I want to scream, yikes, what is this? I quickly withdraw my hand.

Sitting up, Paulo asks, "Lydia, what's the matter with you?"

I sit up too. "It's just that all my life I've been told sex outside of marriage is wrong. If we make love, I may feel good for a moment, but then I'll feel rotten and I'll need to go to confession. I know how ridiculous this must sound to you."

"Confess that you are a healthy woman, with healthy desires, to a priest who probably has his own woman on the side?"

"I don't think that happens where I come from, Paulo. Also, I've never been with a man."

Shaking his head, he says, "You're a beautiful twenty-three-year-old, a North American, and I'm to believe you have never slept with a man?"

"Believe what you like. It's the truth."

"Ay cariñito, let me show you how beautiful physical love between a man and a woman can be," he says, nuzzling my neck.

"And what if I get pregnant?"

"Don't worry, Lydia. I know when to withdraw."

"But why do we have to do more than this?"

"You may not need to do more than this, Lydia, but I do," he says, getting up, brushing straw from his clothes. "I'll call you when I'm back in Ica."

Before falling asleep, I remember a horrible incident I had with my mother. I don't recall how old I was, perhaps nine or ten. We had been grocery shopping at the A & P, and, as we were leaving the parking lot, I read out loud the word "fuck" from a movie house door. I had no idea what the word meant, but my mother assumed I did and backhanded me. I cried over the pain and unfairness of the blow.

Other memories come to mind: Our family had taken a summer cottage with another family, good friends of my parents. Their little girl and I played doctor, examining body parts we should not have examined. She told her mother, who told my mother. Because I was older, and should have been setting a good example, my mother locked me in the outhouse for a long time.

I also remember that when my mother would serve my father dinner, he would frequently reach under her dress and pat her. I would cringe, thinking he was doing something dirty. It occurs to me that I'm afraid of more than sin and pregnancy; I'm afraid for a man to touch me in a place I've always associated with shame.

*

A few weeks later, Paulo returns and takes me to dinner at the Hotel Turista in Nazca, a few hours drive from Ica. We sit beside the modern swimming pool and drink *pisco sours*, listening to boleros and the erotic cooing of the white doves who make their home in the hotel's lush tropical garden. After

shrimp cocktail and a delicately prepared filet of
Pacific Corvina, Paulo leads me to one of the hotel
rooms. What did Eve feel when she approached the
forbidden fruit? If I bite, will my life also be filled
with pain and suffering?

Surprised that my hymen is still intact, Paulo
abandons his plan and walks to the bathroom. In a
narrow rectangle of light, I glimpse his penis standing
at nearly a ninety-degree angle to his body. It reminds
me of the one I saw on a farm horse while visiting my
great Aunt Pauline on her Wisconsin farm.

VI

Celinda

All my bones are alien.
Perhaps I stole them!
Perhaps I made my own
what was assigned to another,
and I think if I had not been born,
a poor man would be drinking this coffee.
I am a bad thief . . . Where shall I go?

César Vallejo, from "El pan nuestro," *Los heraldos negros*, 1918

RELIEVED to be at the clinic this morning, after my near fall from grace last night, I listen to the patients with renewed dedication, until I hear a fuss at the door. A slightly built girl pushes in front of the ailing women and elderly men who stand in line. The girl-child, who can't be more than eight or nine, throws back the dirty cloth that covers the burned body of a screaming baby. "*Señorita, ayúdanos, por favor,*" says the girl, pleading for help.

Celeste has not yet returned from Lima. The only hospital is three miles away, and no cabs enter Oculto. The girl explains that while crawling on the dirt floor of their home, her baby sister had knocked over a kettle of water boiling on an alcohol stove. I ransack the cabinet, looking for burn ointment. Having found some, I scrub my hands and gently apply the medicine to the raw flesh that shows under cracking skin. I tell Alicia to close the medical post and order her and the baby's sister to follow me to the hospital.

The streets in the two *barriadas* we must cross are jammed with people and vegetable carts. Weaving in and out of the noisy crowd, I carry the now-silent baby, ignoring the curious stares of the vendors and their customers.

The woman at the admitting desk explains that the doctors can't treat the baby without the parents' consent. With her eyes cast downward, Blanca, the baby's sister, answers that their mother is dead, and that she doesn't know the whereabouts of their father. The clerk says there's a way around this problem if I consent to become the baby's *madrina*.

I hold my godchild above the font in the hospital chapel, praying that Celinda Valdivia will not end up a sacrificial offering, while the priest, through the sacrament of Baptism, welcomes her to the Christian family. He then anoints her eyes, ears, nostrils, lips, hands, and feet in the sacrament of Extreme Unction. Should her body not recover, her soul will find eternal rest.

After we leave the hospital, I treat Blanca and

Alicia to a Fanta and a sandwich. "Will you be all right, Blanca?" I ask.

"Yes, Señorita, thank you for helping me," she says, savoring the orange soda.

"Do you think you'll be able to find your father? Does he have a job?"

"No, Señorita. He does not work, but I might find him with his friends who also drink."

"Do you want me to come with you?"

"No, Señorita, thank you. I think I should go alone."

"What about Alicia? Maybe she should go with you."

"Yes, Señorita, that would be fine. I do not think my father would object."

"Alicia, I know you will take good care of Blanca." I touch my young helper's shoulder.

"Do not worry, Señorita Lydia, I will take care of her." Alicia puts her arm around Blanca's thin shoulders.

"You know where I work, Blanca. Alicia, you know where I live. Let me know as soon as you find him."

"*Sí, señorita*," Blanca says, smiling wanly.

"*Adios, Blanca*," I say. "*Ciao, Alicia*."

"*Adios, señorita*," they say simultaneously. Blanca turns to walk away with Alicia but suddenly turns, runs to me, and grasps me around the hips, holding me tightly.

✳

It is the hour of siesta, and I return to my bedroom to rest before returning to the clinic. Had I further harmed the baby by my unskilled treatment? Should I have applied the ointment? I was afraid to apply

bandages directly to her raw, cracking skin because
they might stick, but I was even more afraid to leave
the burns undressed, fearing infection from the dust.
Oh, God, this is not what I had in mind when I joined
the Peace Corps.

I have no right to do this work, and the Peace
Corps has no right to put me in this situation. It's
one thing to share hygiene information, give vitamins,
even immunize, but to treat third-degree burns is
something I'm not equipped to do. I should be doing
what Irving Worthington *said* I'd be doing in Peru—
working as a speech therapist. Even though I disliked
my job in Wisconsin, the work was predictable; there
were no emergencies. But how can I practice my
profession in a second language I'm still learning in
a country where the majority of people don't even
get a basic education? I have been terribly naïve. I
return to the clinic without eating lunch, barely
responding to the people who greet me.

Back from Lima, Celeste is attending patients.
She knows what has happened with the baby, but
she doesn't challenge my decisions. I help her treat
a boy with a puncture wound, flushing the wound
with sterile water, bandaging it, and giving the child
a tetanus shot.

After writing my parents that evening, I decide
to ask for a few days leave. I bet Susan is ready for a
break too. Maybe she can join me in Lima. Celeste
can check on the baby, but what about Blanca? What
will happen to her? And to all the other Blancas in
Peru? But then, in the long run, how can my going
to Lima matter one way or the other?

*

Two weeks later I pay the sixty *soles* and board the *colectivo* for Lima, eager to see Susan. The sand dunes on the outskirts of Ica touch a cloudless, autumn sky. A sphinx would look at home.

The Pan-American Highway turns north and follows the Pacific coast. Opening my window, I breathe deeply of the air, pungent of seaweed and the guano covering the rocky shore. Except where mountain streams irrigate the land on their way to the Pacific, a desert stretches the length of Peru's 1,400-mile coast. The Humboldt Current, a cold, northward-flowing underwater stream keeps the moist Pacific air away from the coast, causing the aridity. Because of the plankton it carries, the current also keeps the sea life plentiful. The fish bring the seabirds that roost on the off-shore islands, depositing thick layers of the nutrient-rich fertilizer.

At the Hotel Alcazar, I luxuriate in my first hot tub-bath in months and take a nap between freshly ironed sheets. I awake to a loud knock on the door. Susan, pretending to be the maid, asks if she can clean the room.

"Susan!" I pull her into the room, hugging her. "Am I glad to see you!"

"*Igualmente*," she says, throwing her bag on the floor. "You look worn out, Lydia. I want to hear everything, but let's wait till after we eat *Beeg Boy cheeseburrrgerrrs* and hot fudge sundaes at Todos."

Over coffee and ice cream, I tell about Celinda. Susan squeezes my hand. Her eyes are moist. "I'm sorry, Lydia—for Celinda, for Blanca, for you—I wish I could take your pain away."

"Talking to you has helped."

"You did what you could. It's in God's hands now."

"I'm beginning to wonder what being 'in God's hands' means," I say, playing with my napkin. "Humans permit the poverty of the *barriadas*, the disease, and filth, and when there's a death, they say it's God's will. Maybe God lets innocent people suffer to remind the rich that the poor are *their* responsibility."

"Lydia, you can't believe that," Susan says, putting down her cup. "God doesn't want children to suffer."

"No, but we permitted the conditions that nearly killed Celinda. Should we then ask God to intervene when we've screwed up so badly?"

"We permitted?" Susan sops up the coffee under her cup with a napkin.

"Sure, would we have behaved differently had we been raised here with the same privileges as wealthy Peruvians? And you know that most North Americans think all the poor need to do to better themselves is to work harder. They'll proudly tell you that without any thought of the benefits they inherited simply by being born white in the United States."

"There are a lot of compassionate people back home, Lydia," Susan says, cocking her head to one side, her speech more precise. "After all, who gave you and me our values? I work on a hospital ship where doctors and nurses from the United States fight to improve the lives of the poor you're talking about. We've had many children with cleft lips and palates. Without plastic surgery, they would always have infections, and they wouldn't be able to eat like the rest of us. Recently, the doctors operated on a mother whose upper teeth had pushed through a lip with a double cleft."

"Easy, Susan," I say, patting her hand. "That's a lovely exception, but given the enormity of the problem, it's too little."

"Yes, for some it is too little. It was too little for the girl whose uncle brought her down from the sierra. She was losing her vision, and the doctors patiently explained that there was nothing they could do for her. Before they left the ship the uncle asked his final desperate question: 'Won't you at least give us some drops?'"

"He needed hope, Susan. Maybe the doctors should have given him the drops." I look at the restaurant bill. Enough to feed a poor family for a month.

"Aren't you sometimes overwhelmed, Susan? Is it just me?"

"No, it's not just you, Lydia. When I feel like that I pray and try to remember a few words of wisdom."

"Will you share them with your friend?"

"I don't know who said it, but I remember hearing that when we help one person, we help the whole world."

"We could really use you at our clinic, Susan."

"Who knows? The Ship HOPE will soon leave for Ecuador. Maybe I can get a transfer to Ica, but right now, I have an idea," she says, reaching for the check.

"When I see that look, Susan, I know I'd better be on my guard. What do you have in mind?"

"Trust and follow me," she says, before applying fresh lipstick.

We take a *colectivo* back downtown and walk down Avenida Nicolás de Pierola until we come to a large red door. "*Adelante, por favor, señorita,*" Susan says, ushering me inside.

"You've got to be kidding, Susan. This is Elizabeth Arden's. We can't afford this place."

"For God's sake, don't be so serious."

"But what do I say to them? What will I ask for?"

"They'll look you over and tell you what you need."

"But I *need* everything!"

"Come on, Lydia, just a little job."

A heavily made-up woman with lots of jewelry asks me what services I'd like. I can do without the facial, never having had one, and I don't want some stranger giving me a massage, but my hair needs cutting.

The woman in the chair next to mine wears a bathing cap. I ask what she's having done, and the beautician explains she's having her hair streaked. I ask if it works on brunettes, and she says, oh, yes, gold highlights would look *magnífico* in my hair. Once in a lifetime. And what do I care, so far from home.

My head looks like a mushroom dome, and the hot rubber cap pinches. Were I bald, this is what I'd look like. I should have worn more make-up. The beautician picks up a long hook and pokes it through the cap, gaffing a narrow hank of dark brown hair, pulling it through the hole. She repeats this action until my head is throbbing, and I look like Medusa, with serpentine strands of hair sticking out all over the cap. After applying the peroxide solution to the snake hair, the lady sees my anxious look, pats me on the shoulder, and tells me to be patient while she's gone. I'll look sexy with blonde streaks, she says. After setting, drying, and back-combing my damaged hair, all that shows is the blonde—a yellow caul over the head of this olive-skinned, brown-eyed girl.

"*Me gusta*," says Susan, eyeing me carefully, sporting a smart new cut herself.

"My parents should see me now," I say.

"No, not your parents, some gorgeous hunk."

"I can't deal with the one that's in my life right now."

"You can tell me all about him at our next stop. We've been in the Peace Corps eight months, and we're going to celebrate."

Sipping dry martinis in the lounge of the Hotel Bolívar on the Plaza San Martín, I confide in Susan about Paulo, and she tells me about the married doctors on the Ship HOPE. On our walk to the Chalet Suise, a man smiles at me and says, "hello, blondie." After our cheese fondue, Susan and I dance the rest of the evening, teaching German tourists at the Swiss restaurant the Peruvian *vals* and *marinera*.

On Sunday, after accompanying me to the Cathedral, Susan asks, "Why can't Mass be simple, like a Presbyterian service?"

"It is elegantly simple," I say. "Everything leads up to the Eucharist, then there's the Eucharist, and then we give thanks for the Eucharist. Don't let the standing, kneeling, and sitting throw you."

On Monday we say goodbye and promise to write. Susan says she will look into a transfer to Ica. I dread the ride back there. Ordinarily, I enjoy the banter with the children who flock to the car windows when the *colectivo* slows in each town along the Pan-American Highway, but today they are intrusive. In San Vicente de Cañete, however, I buy *habas*, toasted Fava beans, from a tiny girl whose arms barely reach the car's windows. The older children, descendants of Negro slave cane cutters, sell balls of raw brown sugar, wrapped in dried cane leaves.

The bathroom in the roadside restaurant is a hole in a urine-soaked floor over which you stand. I roll up the legs of my slacks, so they won't be wicks for the urine. On the door is the word *damas*. No lady should have to use such a place.

Back on the bus, waking from a nap, I discover there has been a sand slide on the Pan-American Highway, and cars and busses are lined up in both directions. We'll be delayed several hours, until bulldozers arrive to push the sand into the sea.

We get underway at sunset, and, as the driver turns inland, I strain to get a last glimpse of the Pacific and think of my godchild Celinda. Has her father been found? Tomorrow I'll visit her at the hospital and try to check on Blanca. I hate the thought of returning to the flies and stench of the *barriada* and the thought of not seeing my family for another sixteen months. Maybe I should return to the States before the end of my term.

Our driver and the driver of a second *colectivo*, both trying to make up for lost time, take turns passing each other. We're in a drag race in the Atacama desert. Our driver tries to pass, but the second driver accelerates; we're speeding, neck-and-neck. A huge Ormeño bus is coming at us, and I shout at the driver, "For God's sake, move, I'm not ready to die!" With only seconds to spare, we cross in front of the second car. I tell the driver he'd better let me out before doing that again. The other passengers laugh.

*

Back in Ica, I walk to the hospital to see Celinda. A nurse remembers me and says she's sorry, but my godchild has died, and the father was never found. The next day I take $50.00 from my hiding place, go to the bank to exchange the dollars for *soles*, and return to the hospital to pay the bill. Maybe my care had contributed to Celinda Valdivia's death, a baby already handicapped by the accident of having been born in a Peruvian slum. No one knows where Blanca, the baby's sister, lives.

*

To take my mind off Celinda and Blanca, Paulo invites all eight volunteers to his farm in Hacarí, an hour's drive from Ica. Inside the weathered farmhouse, we sit near the stone fireplace, drinking straight *pisco* from tiny glasses. For supper, we eat *sopa a la criolla*, a chicken soup with vegetables, accompanied by white goat cheese, grapes, bread, and red wine. With Paulo nearby, I'm sure I can complete my two years.

That night Paulo takes us to a cockfight at a rickety, circular barn. He opens a cage and withdraws an impressive fighting cock, a *Flor de haba*, named after a flowering white bean plant. Its long tail feathers, the color of dried red peppers, stand up proudly behind his regal head. Paulo strokes his bird and tells us it has been bred for fighting and winning. The first fighting cocks came to Peru on Spanish galleons, he says, and he speaks soothingly to the bird, before returning it to its cage.

Taking me aside, Paulo explains why a cock fights: "*Lydia, querida,* it is said that within the small brains of these birds resides a corner that longs for its mate. The cock it will fight possesses this same instinctual drive. They behave toward one another as though possessed of a jealous passion—the way I would behave if you were to leave me for another." I shiver.

The other volunteers approach. Paulo lights a cigarette, rests his foot on one of the spectator benches, and describes the culture of cockfighting. The cocks are cared for by a *preparador* until they are eighteen months old. The trainers make sure the birds get proper nutrition, exercise, and rest; they keep them alert and ready for the day of their first fight.

On the day of the fight, the *amarrador* carefully fastens a steel blade just above the cock's left foot. In this way, he lengthens the cock's own natural spur. A good *amarrador* knows the perfect point at which to fasten the blade, and he must be sure the length of the blade is just right, choosing one from a set of blades that range from seven to nine centimeters in length.

Paulo introduces us to a *careador*, or second. He has had years of experience and is known for his deftness at separating the cocks when they are locked in combat or have been fatally wounded.

I accompany Paulo around the ring, noticing that the women volunteers are the only females here. Guiding me toward a wiry man, Paulo says, "Lydia, I want you to meet Señor Velázquez, the judge."

The elderly man, dressed in an embroidered white shirt, a *guayabera*, looks at me as if I were the only woman in the world. "*Encantada señorita*, you and all of your North American friends are welcome here. We are honored that you have come."

Paulo explains that the judge is the most important person here; he has complete authority over the proceedings. He inspects the placement of

the blades, and, when the fight is over, rings a bell
and announces the winner to the audience. His calls
are like those made by a Supreme Court—they can't
be appealed. The judge also has the responsibility
for maintaining order; he forbids disturbances caused
by sore losers or by those who drink too much *pisco*.

"A good judge," says Señor Velázquez, "renders
the perfect call when a cock has hit home. You have
to know how to apply regulations that are so
complicated they resemble a legal code. I have been
doing this for fifty years, Señorita. My ancestor, Don
Emilio Velázquez, a judge for twenty years in Sandía,
Spain, used to tell me, 'He who is not familiar with
cocks, and does not know how to lose a bet, will never
respect the judge's call,' so I do a lot of teaching,
too."

"Don't some cocks fight with their beaks?" I ask.

"Yes," the judge says. "Cocks are classified as
piqueros if they are trained to fight with their beaks,
or *navajeros* if they use a blade. You will see cocks
fight with their beaks in the north of the country
and also near Arequipa, but here we prefer
blades."

"The fight," Paulo says, "is more violent and
spectacular with blades, but it is swifter and less cruel
than when the birds fight with their beaks. The blade
must be sharp enough to kill, without giving the
appearance of offending the victim. One more thing,
Lydia: If one cock retreats, the other wins outright."

A man, dressed in a crumpled white suit,
circulates among the crowd, taking bets. Then two
men, their lips pursed tightly around cigarettes, step
into the ring, carrying cocks under their arms. They
adjust the blades on the birds' legs, touch the birds'

heads together, to provoke an aggressive response, and place the cocks on the circular dirt floor.

The dirt sprays in all directions. The cocks waste no time finding a vulnerable spot—the neck or the chest. I avert my eyes while Paulo shouts for his bird to win. No wonder there are no Peruvian women here. Looking up, I see blood spilling from the neck of the *Flor de haba*, its white feathers now the color of Burgundy wine. It buries its beak in the sticky, blood-thickened sand.

A bell rings, and the judge emerges, announcing that the *Moro*—the Moor—the cock with blue-black feathers, has won. There is much applause and an equal amount of disgruntlement. Paulo retrieves the wounded cock, hoping it can be nursed to health and returned to the ring, but its wounds are mortal, and it will end up in the cooking pot, an ignominious end for a royal creature.

*

Back at the farm, we sit by the fire with steaming cups of hot chocolate and cinnamon. Paulo plays the guitar and sings "Bésame Mucho." He looks at me longingly when he ends the song, "*Que tengo miedo perderte, perderte después.*"

I translate the words in my heart. "I'm afraid of losing you, of losing you." If my will were truly free, I'd sleep with Paulo on this chilly evening and not think of mortal sin in the morning.

In grade school, I confessed my sins to young Father Berkholter, of the angelic face. Depending upon the nature of my sins, I might feel faint before entering the confessional. It wasn't the expected penance that frightened me, but the humiliation at having to admit to a priest, who probably never had to go to the bathroom, that I had "entertained unclean thoughts."

Paulo waits till the volunteers drift off to their rooms and beckons me to follow him, probably the last invitation he'll extend to me if I don't accept. He takes me to the heavy, ornately carved bed in his room and removes my sweat shirt, bending to kiss my A-sized breasts. I take off my boots and jeans and silently say, "Forgive me, Father." Paulo makes me feel there is no impure place on my body.

VII

Betrayal

Come, kiss me!
What does it matter if something dark
is gnawing with its teeth
at my soul?

Magda Portal, *Una esperanza y el mar*,
1927

PAULO has returned to Lima. Winter has arrived. I wear flannel pajamas and use three army blankets at night. Getting out of bed in the morning requires the discipline of a monk; our rooms are like the meat refrigerators used by Milwaukee butchers. No cold showers now. Marcia and I take sponge baths with heated water. By noon I can remove a thick sweater, and my hands are warm.

I press my hands against the burning foreheads of infants and children, and, following Celeste's instructions, pinch together enough flesh on their tiny, wrinkled bottoms to give injections of antibiotics. At night I write long letters to my parents but still don't tell them about Paulo.

*

With the political situation heating up over the upcoming presidential election, there are demonstrations in the Plaza de Armas. University students engage us in political debates over beers at the Mogambo restaurant, but even when their voices get loud and strident, they never level personal insults at us. They may view us as pawns of U.S. foreign policy, but they never say so, and they respect us for working in the slums—something none of them—well-dressed and of European stock—has ever done.

There are three leading presidential candidates: Victor Raúl Haya de la Torre, General Manuel Odría, a former president, and Fernando Belaúde Terry. In the elections that were held while we were in training, these same candidates accused each other of voting fraud, and each claimed victory. Tensions mounted throughout Peru. The military leaders, not wanting Haya de la Torre to win because of his liberal land reform and economic policies, called Belaúnde Terry the victor.

While we were at Cornell, the United States, fearing a coup d'etat, threatened to cut off economic assistance if the military intervened. But the generals seized control anyway, jailed President Prado before the end of his term, suspended Congress and the Constitution, and proclaimed General Pérez Godoy junta chief. In response, the United States cut off all aid, except certain humanitarian programs. If the situation had not been resolved to the satisfaction of the United States, we Peace Corps volunteers might have been sent to Sierra Leone.

But the political parties reached accords with the military junta, and the upcoming election was scheduled. President Prado was released from prison when his term expired, and the United States resumed diplomatic ties, sending us as a proof of its goodwill. I wonder why there can't be an election like we have in the United States, where the people trust the military to stay in its place, and the military trusts the people to govern.

Banners for political candidates wave from buildings and trees. Some campaigners have etched their candidate's political slogans on the sand dunes surrounding Ica. Others, with their megaphones blaring, fan out over the city, urging citizens to vote for their candidates, accusing members of the opposition of the only sin that matters: being soft on communism. You earn that characterization if you advocate any social program that might benefit the poor.

*

Belaúnde Terry wins the election, and, as predicted, Haya de la Torre claims fraud. So the new president's plans for social reform can be realized, he calls for the resumption of U.S. Alliance for Progress funds, but the United States is wary, afraid that some of its petroleum interests will be nationalized. Meanwhile, the Indians who visit the clinic talk about Diego Torrente, a rebel leader with whom they sympathize.

Criollos and many mixed-race mestizos, however, accept the government's line—that Torrente is a subversive, a Communist, trying to upset the cultural patterns of the Indians and the country's traditions.

Torrente, a former student at the University of Cuzco, wants to end the feudal custom obliging Indians to work lands without pay. In the high Andes, they've been forced to contribute ten to fourteen days of labor each month in exchange for small parcels of land to cultivate for their own families, or for the right to graze the few livestock they might own. Bilingual in Spanish and Quechua, Torrente has organized a federation of farm workers and says force is justified to end the unethical traditions stemming from the Spanish theft of land from the Indians.

I know what's wrong with communism—the State as sole employer, prohibitions against religious worship, restrictions on travel, speech, assembly, press censorship, the collectivization of labor, the erosion of personal incentive—but why are people attracted to such a stultifying system in the first place?

But capitalism, at least the kind practiced in Peru, doesn't help the poorest. A tiny percentage of the people have great wealth, and they have no contact with the fifty percent of the population who are poor and Indian, except for those they employ as servants. Moreover, the rich criollo class has little respect for those Indians who try to better themselves and disparagingly refer to them as *cholos*. Even some mestizos, trying to conceal their own Indian blood, say the problems on the coast will disappear when the Indians return to the Andes.

＊

After two weeks of not hearing from Paulo, I run into Jerry Parker, a volunteer from Arizona, assigned to an irrigation project. He has just seen Paulo. "In Ica?" I ask, my heart pounding.

"Yes, I saw him talking to Señor Flores, the guy who owns all that land along the river. They were standing next to a brand new tractor, the kind Paulo sells. By the way, Paulo had a kid with him."

That means Paulo will come by tonight or get in touch with me tomorrow. The little boy must have been Señor Flores' grandson.

But Paulo doesn't contact me. After waiting three days, I go to his office near the Plaza de Armas, hoping we can have lunch at the Hotel Colón. I've not been back to his office since the first time, when the secretary gave me a dirty look. Because he travels so much, he's rarely there anyway. I've asked him why he keeps a house in Lima when most of his sales territory is in the province of Ica, but he responded vaguely, something about needing to be in touch with the central office in Lima.

I smile at the fair, curly-headed child playing with a toy tractor in Paulo's office.

"*¿Lydia, que haces aquí?*" says Paulo, appearing from a back room.

"I came to see you, Paulo. I heard you were in town."

Paulo introduces me to Señor Flores. The tall, aristocratic man bows slightly, his eyes proposing a future liaison.

"And who is this handsome young man?" I ask, ruffling the boy's curls.

"*Es mi hijo,*" says Paulo, putting his hand on the boy's shoulder.

"—Your son is beautiful, Paulo," I say, smiling at the boy again. "—But I'm interrupting, and I should return to the clinic. It was a pleasure meeting you, Señor Flores." I reach for the door knob. "Ciao."

"Wait, Lydia," Paulo calls.

Ignoring him, forcing back tears, I walk toward the church of Our Lord of Luren. The ancient wooden doors stand open. Sun streams through the stained glass, and a dusty haze floats above the altar, forming an aura around the crucified Christ. The church smells of burning candles, withered roses, and incense from morning Mass. I genuflect and enter a pew in the back. Could Paulo be a widower? No, there would have been nothing to hide. He's married.

Kneeling, I look up at the image of the suffering Christ. Droplets of crimson blood from the crown of thorns cover His face and chest. In His right side is the deep, raw wound of the lance. Looking at the anguished face, I ask for the strength to end my relationship with Paulo. I find a holy card in the pew, a supplication to the Lord of Luren:

¿Qué haré Señor mío de Luren, si no acudo a Ti?
What will I do, my Lord of Luren, if I don't flee to You?
¿Que haré Señor, si no iluminas mis pasos?
What will I do, Lord, if You don't illumine my steps?
¿Qué haré, si no reconfortas mi espíritu?
What will I do, if You don't comfort my spirit?

I sit back in the pew, put my face in my hands, and weep. The same priest who had tried to console me when I was thrown out of the Cathedral a few weeks ago approaches. "My daughter, why are you crying? Do you want to talk?"

"Please, Father, I want to go to confession."

In the blackness of the confessional, I whisper, "Bless me father, for I have sinned. It has been two months since my last confession. I have slept with a married man."

I speak of my love for Paulo without divulging his name, explaining I didn't know he was married, acknowledging that I knew it would have been wrong to sleep with him, even if he had been single.

"You have done the right thing by confessing, daughter," says the priest. "You must be strong to resist further temptation, but the Lord does not tempt us beyond our capacities. Can you do this thing?"

"I will try, Father."

"Good, now for your penance, I want you to say the rosary and ask for special help from the Blessed Mother."

I silently say the Act of Contrition. ". . . I firmly resolve with the help of Thy grace, to confess my sins, to do penance and to amend my life."

Making the Sign of the Cross, the priest says, "I absolve you from your sins, in the name of the Father, and of the Son, and of the Holy Spirit."

*

That evening Marcia opens the door to Paulo and his son. Before facing them, I check my face in the bathroom mirror. My eyes are sorrowful wells of shame and humiliation. I splash cold water on my face, put on lipstick, and greet them, forcing a smile for

Carlitos, whom Marcia invites to the kitchen for cookies.

"*Lydia, mi amor, perdóname. Te quiero, con todo mi corozón.*" I pull away from Paulo's embrace and avoid his pleading eyes.

"Paulo, I don't want to see you any more."

"Listen to me, Lydia, I love you! My wife and I—we are not lovers—you are my only love. She had to go to Piura to care for her mother, and the maid was sick. I had to bring Carlitos with me to Ica."

"You deceived me, Paulo, and you were selfish. You betrayed your wife and me."

"*Sí, sí,* you deserve better, *mi amor,* but I did not want to lose you, and I knew you would leave me if I told you the truth."

"You would have been right. Goodbye, Paulo."

"You are being too harsh, Lydia. Don't do this."

"Paulo, even if you love me, I can't be with a married man, and I don't want to love a man who lies to me.

＊

I go to bed early and dream I've come before a combination church and military tribunal. The priest who threw me out of the Cathedral because of my "immodest" dress wears a black robe and cowl. Behind him is a rack, the kind used during the Inquisition to force heretics to confess. Paulo is dressed in a perfectly pressed khaki uniform. Medals blaze on his chest. He taps his thigh with a riding crop, walking back and forth before me.

Dirty, head bowed, barefoot, wearing a tattered dress, I sit on a stool before the two men. My hair is matted and my fingernails broken, as if I'd been trying to dig my way out of a cell.

"With what crimes is this woman charged?" asks the priest.

"With the crime of seduction and with the crime of being a woman," says Paulo.

"Serious crimes, indeed," says the priest, walking toward me. "And what evidence do you offer to prove your charges?"

"My aroused organ. As you can plainly see, your excellency," Paulo says, stroking himself. "I am helpless just thinking about this woman. The corrupt nature and body she has inherited is further evidence of her crime."

"But, in what way did the accused direct her lewd nature against you, my son?"

"By saying 'no,' of course, your eminence. By refusing me, she stokes dark desires over which I have no control."

"Of course, my son," the priest consoles Paolo. "As a man you must try to control these impulses, but the good Lord, in His almighty wisdom, is aware that men's physical drives are no match for the wicked ways of women. What say you to these charges, young woman?"

"I am guilty, father, of only one crime—that of being a woman—the general lies about the rest."

"See your excellency! She is hopeless! By her falsehoods she digs a deeper pit in hell."

"You do not appear repentant, my daughter."

"How can I repent what God has made me?"

"And you, my brave *caballero*, what remedy do you seek?"

"I want her torn on the rack till she confesses her sins," says Paulo, his light blue eyes glinting.

"Yes, we shall see if the rack can change the mind of this willful creature," says the priest.

The priest and Paulo seize me, pulling me toward the rack. They shackle my arms and legs in spread-eagle fashion, the priest on one side, Paulo on the other.

"Do you confess, daughter," asks the priest, bringing his face so close to mine I can smell his sour breath, "to using your seductive powers to lead this noble gentleman astray? Do you confess to the crime of being born of Adam's rib and therefore inferior and subservient to his male progeny? Answer carefully. The fate of all women rests on your answer. Tell the truth, and all females will enjoy the protection of men and the Church. Lie, and you will be stretched between the Church and mankind until your willful ways depart, which, I assure you," the priest gloats, "will happen the instant before you die.

"Should you not confess," hisses the priest, "know you, also, the fate of the women you leave and the fate of the girl children they spawn: Females will bear the scorn of all men, because the Creator God made them with less intelligence, less courage, and less moral strength than He made the male of the species."

"But He made all of us in His image!" I shout into the priest's face. At that, the men take the cranks, turning them easily at first, checking my face for pain. There is a tingling sensation, like a good stretch in the morning, then the tension increases. My skin tears from the body it protects, and my bones loosen from their sockets.

"Do you repent?" asks the priest.

"We are neither Jew nor Gentile, neither male nor female," I whisper before waking from my nightmare, afraid of falling asleep again.

*

A week after I say goodbye to Paulo, a letter arrives from Susan. The Ship HOPE is on its way to Ecuador. Susan's transfer has been approved, and she will arrive in Ica in three days.

Marcia doesn't know Susan but generously suggests she move in with us. We rearrange our bedroom to accommodate a third cot and acquire another fruit crate for her bedside table.

The *colectivo* arrives at our front door at midnight. After we hug, I introduce Susan to Marcia, and the three of us carry an enormous quantity of luggage to the bedroom.

"My Lord, Susan, do you have an outfit for every day of the year?" I ask.

"Ay, Lydia, don't you know that clothes make the woman?"

"Not where we work, Susan."

"But you can never tell whom you might meet. I heard that a writer and photographer from *National Geographic* were just in Vicos, doing a feature on some of the volunteers from our group."

We sit around the table, drinking wine, hearing about Susan's exhausting trip from Trujillo. "There was this little guy sitting next to me, see, and every time we took a curve, he tried to give me a feel. I kept trying to inch away from him, but there was a man on my other side, too, and I didn't want to roll over on him. I finally slapped the lech's hand and said, ¡qué barbaridad!"

∗

At the clinic, Celeste teaches Susan how to give streptomycin injections to mothers and children with tuberculosis. Because Susan's Spanish is excellent, and she had a little training in Quechua at Cornell, she also takes charge of the educational program, with special emphasis on the disease cycle and food preparation. Drawing huge posters, she shows our patients how unwashed hands and flies contaminate food and lead to bacterial infections and parasitic infestations.

∗

Susan is five feet-nine-inches tall, Ingrid is six feet, and I am five feet-ten inches. Every day men ask us about our height. "¿*Cuántos metros tienen?*" they ask. How many meters do you have? Do you mean how long is the stick we're going to hit you with?

On our way downtown to get a Donofrio fudgsicle, sold from bicycle carts near the Plaza de Armas, a man shimmies up the lamppost. He looks down and calls us *monumentos*.

One of his friends moans, "¡*Ay, si tuviera una escalera para llegar a ese cielo!*" We stifle our laughter. He has told us he desires a ladder to reach the heaven of our bodies.

A third man, leaning against a building, narrows his eyes, scrutinizes our long bodies, and slides his tongues over wet lips. Then he slowly sucks in air between clenched teeth and rolls his eyes in simulated ecstasy.

We decide to call ourselves *Las Altas Fabulosas*, The Fabulous Tall Ones, and go to the Mogambo for coffee where we compare other *piropos,* the flattering or lecherous comments we've received since coming to Peru.

Eyes half closed, leering, Susan whispers, "¡*Ay mamacita bonita, qué lindas piernas tienes!*" Then, looking pensive, she adds, "Frankly, I was pleased to hear he thought I had pretty legs. I always thought mine were a bit too thin, but I could have done without the 'pretty little mama' bit."

"My God, I am dying from so much beauty," I groan, holding my hand to my heart.

"Señorita, don't look at those flowers, or they'll die of envy," Ingrid says, plaintively.

Susan stretches out her arms, looks up, shakes her head and says, "¡*Si tuviera hijos de esa hembra!* What do you think, girls, was it really the children he wanted to have with me or the sex?"

We walk home, arm-in-arm, confident in our womanhood, confident in our futures.

The White House
Washington
June 17, 1963

Dear Miss Schaefer:

You have recently completed your first year
of service in the Peace Corps.

At home and abroad the Peace Corps has
been recognized as a genuine and effec-
tive expression of the highest ideals and
the best traditions of our Nation. You and
your fellow Volunteers have made that judgment possible.

I am proud of your participation and I trust
that in your second year of service your con-
duct and performance will continue to re-
flect credit upon you and the Peace Corps.

Sincerely,

John F. Kennedy

VIII

Rafael

But men have a head and a heart, thought
Rosendo, and these make all the difference,
like the wheat that only lives because of its
roots.

Ciro Alegría, *El mundo es ancho y ajeno,*
1941

CELESTE'S efforts to get a medical intern to work
at the clinic have paid off, but I don't want to take
orders from some spoiled medical student from
Lima's upper classes. Rafael Serrano, however, is
neither spoiled nor rich. He is soft-spoken and
respectful and doesn't hurry the patients. His
manner communicates they are his equal.

"Doctor," an Indian woman, pleads. "I cannot find
the oils a *brujo* told me would take away this ugly

birthmark on my face. Can you help me? I have twenty years and still am not married."

"Señorita," says Rafael, taking her hand, "your birthmark distinguishes you from all other women. I can tell you have a beautiful soul, and someday the right man will discover you. The frog, snake, and lizard oils will not help. Do not return to the *brujo.* Please trust me in this."

"I trust you, doctor," the young woman says, her serene smile sufficient thanks for Rafael.

Rafael's hands convey the high regard he has for each patient, and his sensitive explorations, palpitations, and probing all have a disturbing sexual effect on me. His long, narrow face, defined cheekbones, blue-black hair, and Asiatic eyes remind me of the paintings of Modigliani whose works I studied in an art appreciation class in high school. And here I thought it would take a long time to get over Paulo.

*

The winter passes, a rosary of satisfying days working beside Rafael. I'm excited, nevertheless, about the invitation to attend an evening reception to honor President Belaúnde at his palace in Lima.

Marcia and I dig out our best clothes, scrounging for hosiery, hoping there are no runs, and that our garter belts still fit over tummies swollen by rice and beans. Only Susan is prepared.

*

In the presidential palace, crystal-refracted light makes the marble floors gleam, and our shoes look shabby. President Belaúnde speaks for thirty minutes, praising our work, expressing his desire to help the poor. I wonder if he has had any first-hand experience with the poor before I savor an exquisite little sandwich between sips of my *pisco sour.*

*

The Friday evening after my return to Ica, while Susan and Celeste stay on in Lima after the reception, Rafael and I close the clinic. He pays meticulous attention to the sterilization of syringes and needles.

"*Ciao, Lydia.*" He uses the popular Italian phrase for goodbye.

Ciao, Rafael, hasta lunes." I don't want to wait till Monday to see him.

*

While doing dishes with Susan after her return from Lima, I tell her about my growing feelings for Rafael. "You've got to be kidding," she says. "You were just mourning Paulo."

"Don't you think I've thought of that? I was crying in church over Paulo, and now I'm thinking maybe God is answering my prayers by bringing Rafael into my life."

"Ay, Lydia, don't you see you're infatuated? You're on the rebound."

"And if I am? Susan, you've got to admit this man isn't ordinary. Sure I find him incredibly attractive, but he also has character."

"And just what is it about his character that appeals to you?" Susan asks, swinging the dish towel over her shoulder.

THE MOURNING OF ANGELS

"He does what he thinks is right, without worrying about the opinions of others. He speaks from his heart. He has inner strength, yet there's a gentleness I've never seen in other men."

She nods her head, and the sarcasm shows on her face. "And you know this about him already?"

"It shows in the way he treats people."

"Even doctors can be cads, Lydia."

"You like him, too, Susan. Admit it. Maybe that's why you're discouraging me. Are we going to end up fighting over the same man?"

"Don't be *ridícula*," Susan says, bending down to store the dishes in the orange-crate cabinet, making more noise than necessary.

"Susan, I know it sounds silly, but this man is going to change my life."

"¡*Ay, mi Dios*! You're right, it sounds silly," she says, hanging up the dish towel, leaving me alone in the kitchen.

Now I'm glad I never wrote my parents about Paulo. With a cup of tea at my elbow, I tell them about Rafael, about how content I am to work with him, and how I dread his departure.

*

"I'll miss you, Lydia," Rafael says, after locking the medicine cabinet. We work well together."

"I'll miss you, too, Rafael. So will the patients. Working here won't be the same without you."

"Lydia, I know this is last-minute, but I would love to prepare dinner for you tonight."

"I'd like that, too, Rafael, thanks." Thank you, God.

At the market Rafael bargains with the women vendors who tease him while he selects potatoes, cheese, peppers, and figs. They want to know who will cook the food, and who wears the pants in the family. "I will cook; it is she who wears the pants," he jokes back.

We take the back streets, stopping at a worn wooden door. A small boy holding a soccer ball answers the bell. Rafael gently wrests the ball from him and kicks it toward an imaginary goal in the courtyard, eluding the laughing boy before allowing him to capture the ball and make the pretend goal.

Rafael's room is on the other side of a plant-filled courtyard. Old medical books line the walls; some deal with plants and their curative powers. Wall hangings with Incan motifs decorate the room. There's a small stove and sink. A narrow bed covered with an alpaca rug is snug against a wall. I sit on a straight-backed chair at a paint-chipped table while Rafael lights candles. Then he offers me a shot of dark rum with the "Flower of the Sugar Cane" label. My first cautious sip is rich and smooth.

"Can I help, Rafael?"

"Just talk to me, Lydia, and I shall wait on you. You deserve a little special attention."

"Tell me about your plans first. Your internship is nearly over. You must be excited about finishing."

"I am eager to get home," he says, washing the peppers, "not only to see my parents, but to begin my work. Many of the people there still consult *brujos* when they are sick, just like the woman with the birthmark."

"Since I've come to Peru, I'm constantly reminded of how different worlds exist simultaneously, how back home my family, although not rich by U.S. standards, has every convenience and good medical care—Do you want me to chop those peppers for you?"

"But you have not taken your advantages for granted," Rafael says, handing me a knife and a cutting board.

"No, but I can leave Peru after two years and return to the good life. But how will you manage when the people you'll see are so poor?"

"The barter system is still used. The patients will bring a chicken or potatoes, or maybe they will perform some work around the clinic, in exchange for medical care. I will live with my parents and share my father's *consultorio*. I will not need much money."

"I didn't know your father was a doctor."

"There is much we don't know about each other, Lydia," he says, peeling a potato.

"Aren't you tempted to work in Lima?"

"Never. I would miss the mountains too much and my people, but that does not mean I don't envy some of the doctors in Lima, the ones who treat the rich and therefore have their own well-equipped hospitals with modern operating rooms. The women who will *dar la luz*—You say, 'deliver,' I think—have luxurious, private rooms."

"*Dar la luz*. To give light. What a delicate and precise description for giving birth."

"Yes, the term does sound biblical. Woman cooperating with God to bring light to His children. The mother squeezes out the baby from the black ocean of her womb and gives it the first pinprick of light, a light that may reveal the goodness and bounty of the earth or one dimmed by cataracts of hardship and abuse."

"You talk like a poet. Where did you learn your English?"

"I had to learn English. The modern medical books are only available in English. Fortunately, there was a British language school in Lima, but teachers concentrated more on literature than on medical terms."

"Please tell me more about your village and family."

"Enough of my life," he says, putting the potatoes on to boil. "Whatever possessed you to come to Peru and to work in Oculto?"

"You have made my work in Oculto pleasant, Rafael. And I love the people. They put me to shame with their generosity."

"But what about your family? You must miss them." He cuts the plain yellow cheese and puts it on the table with the wine.

"At first I missed them very much. I didn't think I'd finish the two years, but we write regularly, and they're already planning my welcome home party."

"What will you do when you return?"

"Go back to school, I think. Maybe study political science or law."

"You would be a good lawyer, Lydia. You like to question, you are persistent, and you care about justice. You also seem very serious to me, not at all like the stereotype we have of North American women."

"You mean that we're loose? That's probably why men stare and make comments under their breath when we walk by. I feel dirty when they look at me that way, and I do take it seriously."

"I'm afraid the behaviors you describe are ingrained. Here men have been trying to impress women with creative *piropos* since the time of the Conquest. Surely, you have heard some beautiful ones; others, I know, are vulgar and are best reserved for farm animals."

"You don't treat women like that, Rafael."

"No, Lydia, I have seen as much machismo as I care to see. I have seen the way men beat their wives when they come home drunk on *chicha*. But you still have not told me why you are here."

"In high school, I wanted to become a missionary nun, and, when I was a senior in college, I nearly joined the Marine Corps. Does that tell you more about me?"

"So the Peace Corps was a safe compromise. I cannot imagine you in the military," he says, joining me at the table. "A nun, maybe, but I didn't know you were Catholic. I thought most North Americans were Protestants."

"They are, but Catholics comprise the largest Christian denomination in the United States."

"And why are you not married yet? There must be many men who have asked you to marry."

"No, not yet."

"Maybe it is because you are too reserved with your feelings."

"Other men have said that about me, too, but I don't see myself that way. It is true, though, that I've never met anyone with whom I wanted to spend the rest of my life." That is, till now, Rafael Serrano.

"And it has been hard for me to find an educated woman who has not wanted to stay near her parents and have a fine house with maids. But then I'm half Indian, and although a woman might want to marry a doctor, she would not marry one whose blood is not one hundred percent Spanish, or criollo, as they say here."

"It's hard to understand how educated people can be so blind," I say, finishing my drink.

"Like in your country, Lydia?"

"*Touché.*"

Rafael gets up and sets the table. "But you wanted to know about my family. My father comes from Lima's criollo society, but he broke with tradition by embracing an Indian wife and Andean ways, unlike those who breed mixed-race children, bragging all the time that their own blood is pure. Criollos can screw Indian women—please forgive this language—you can see how strongly I feel about this, but they must never marry them." I ask myself what it would be like to be this doctor's wife.

"My father," Rafael says, "met my mother while traveling in the sierra. She had begged him to come to her village to attend her dying father, the *alcalde*, the head of the village. My father agreed and remained there, acquiring an appreciation for the dignity, courage, and customs of the native Peruvians. He was the only doctor in the region and still sees patients from isolated villages that few outsiders have ever seen."

"Where were you born?"

"In Pachabuena, a two-day trip from Cuzco. It means 'Good Earth' in English. My parents named me Rafael, after the healing archangel, because they hoped I would continue my father's work."

"I would love to meet your parents, Rafael."

Using cheese, ground peanuts, and peppers, Rafael prepares the sauce for the potatoes. He catches me staring at him and grins. "Lydia, come with me. I want you to meet my parents. I want them to meet you. Can you do it? I hope to leave in three weeks."

"Yes, I'll come with you," I say, without a thought of Peace Corps regulations.

We wash the dishes in water Rafael has heated and rinse them in cold water, leaving them to drain on a newspaper. As I'm drying the counter, he slides his arms around my waist and kisses the back of the neck. I turn in his arms, and we kiss softly, our lips slightly parted. "*Lydia, tú me gustas mucho,*" he says.

"I like you very much, too, Rafael."

A cold drizzle falls as he walks me home, his arm around my shoulders. It takes me forever to fall asleep. I think about his kiss, the trip to the sierra, the future, my family. In the morning, I share my excitement with Susan.

"Girl, you shouldn't do this! I can see it all now. You're going to end up down here for the rest of your life. Is that what you want? You'll die by age forty. Your skin will dry up, you'll get pellagra, beriberi, and who knows what else, and then he'll shack up with an eighteen-year-old mistress, who doesn't care that you're his wife. She'll be set up in some cushy apartment, wear designer clothes, and eat high on the hog, while you take care of your grandchildren."

"Stop it, Susan. You're full of *mierda.* Just listen to you—the one who swoons over any attractive man who pays a little attention to her."

"You're right, Lydia, I'm sorry. But please, give this more thought. I like you too much not to be worried about your getting stuck down here. By the way, what were the names of those little *animalitos* in your stomach?"

"*Giardia lamblia.* Maybe I'm immune now."

"Right, and those weren't parasites either; you just had 'nervous mucous colitis, because you're a nervous, apprehensive, young woman.' Isn't that what Dr. Sutton said?"

"He was inexperienced, Susan. All he could see was a young woman in a strange country. He thought a seventeen-day bout of diarrhea must have been psychosomatic."

*

Three days before our scheduled departure, I receive my travel authorization. I have two weeks. Rafael and I hug in front of sniggering patients. Overland, it will be a long, hard trip. We'll have to go through Arequipa. I think about Claire and the child care center and wonder, once again, what I'm doing.

IX

To Arequipa and Puno

Ay, dear one, dear little one,
if you are sure, come to me.
Through the world I walk alone,
and no one knows me.

Ciro Alegría, *El mundo es ancho y ajeno,*
1941

A T 4:30 a.m. our sleepy *colectivo* driver sullenly
slings our bags into the trunk, collects our tickets,
and motions us to the back seat. By the time we reach
Palpa, an oasis known for its succulent oranges, there
is a pink tint to the sky. We stop for coffee before
continuing southeast to Nazca, skirting the famous
earth etchings preserved on sun-baked sand.

By scraping away the top layer of dark sand, the
Nazca people, who flourished here one thousand

years before the Incas, drew flamboyant figures of a heron, lizard, pelican, fish, dog, monkey, condor, and whale. Archaeologists believe the figures, some measuring four hundred by three hundred feet, were astrological aids that helped track the planting season.

Nearby, in graves dug eight thousand years ago, child mummies wearing perfectly preserved cotton garments have been found. The little mummies sit knees-to-chest, legs tucked under arms, shoulders bent. I've seen them in museums. Seen through a tangle of straight black hair, the wrinkled, leather-like skin on their faces is taut. They look dejected, as if abandoned by their mothers.

The Pan-American Highway heads west toward the Pacific and follows the jagged shoreline, southbound. Thousands of seabirds, mostly terns, swoop to snatch the silvery *anchovetas* swarming near the surface of the cold, churning sea. Pelicans, cormorants, and boobies join the feast. The anchovies not only feed the birds, they provide a living for the fishermen who sell them to fish meal plants for processing, export, and eventual use in pet food. Sea lions loll on the off-shore islands. On the high rocks above them, undisturbed by rain and waves, guano thickens until harvested for fertilizer.

We stop for lunch in the village of Chala, the starting point for the *chasquis*, the runners who relayed fish to the Inca king in Cuzco. Although they had no written language, the Incas did use a coding system that employed knots tied at varying intervals on cords. The *chasquis* used these *quipus* to convey census information to the king, as well as information on crops and harvests.

The Pan-American Highway leaves the coast at Camaná and heads inland to Repartición, where we take a branch road to Arequipa, *la ciudad blanca.* We arrive in the white city as the sun is setting, gilding the mountain peaks in yellow ice, burnishing the buildings made of white volcanic stone, glancing off Tuturutu, the bronze Inca chief who blows his horn on the top of the fountain in the Plaza de Armas.

Once when I was stationed here, having just come from the market, I was standing at the bus stop not far from Tuturutu, carrying packages in one hand and flowers in the other. It was late afternoon, I was weary, eager to return to Ciudad de mi Esperanza, and the buses were mobbed. When one stopped and discharged a couple of passengers, I managed to squeeze into the doorway and worked my way to the back of the bus, where dust from the unpaved streets washed over me. It was then I felt a man's hand on my fanny, but I couldn't turn around to confront him. As if in a conspiracy, a second man, while reaching for the pole to brace himself, rested his arm on top of my bosom. He stared innocently out the window.

Claire would have put us up during this overnight visit, but there would be little privacy, and I want this trip to belong to Rafael and me. I will arrange to see her on my return.

Rafael and I take two cell-like rooms in a sixteenth-century convent. The nuns, suspicious of our relationship, put us at opposite ends of a long corridor. The rooms are bare except for a wooden crucifix, a straight-backed chair, and a bedside table that holds a wash basin and pitcher.

After sponge baths, we dress warmly and walk to the plaza. An old man wearing a *chullo,* the pointed knit hat with ear flaps, sells *anticuchos,* a shish kabob, made of bite-sized pieces of beef heart marinated in a spicy *ají* sauce and grilled on a waist-high brazier. "Do you like *anticuchos* ?" Rafael asks.

"I can't bring myself to eat heart," I say, screwing up my face.

"But you eat steak, right? There is little difference between steak and *anticuchos*, and they are from the same animal. You will try a tiny bite, no?"

I concentrate on the rich flavor, reminding myself that I love liver and onions. The *anticuchos* are delicious, with a pungent taste of cilantro and the lingering bite of red Peruvian pepper. Tearing off small pieces of beef heart from skewers, we sit on a bench opposite the Cathedral, watching people enter for evening Mass. Peruvians have been attending Mass on this site for four hundred years.

Having finished our appetizer, we walk down Calle Mercaderes to the Mónaco Restaurant where my old friends, Diego and Soto, wait tables. They have always been patient with the volunteers, many of whom, despite their training, arrived barely able to ask for a glass of water in Spanish.

We order *crema de tomate*, cream of tomato soup, and *papas a la Huancaína*, boiled potatoes with a sauce of egg yolk, evaporated milk, onion, cheese, and ground hot peppers. For dessert we order flan, smooth and creamy, under its sticky coating of dark brown caramelized sugar. When Diego looks our way to see if we'd like anything more, Rafael gestures for the check, pretending to write on his left hand with the index finger of his right hand.

The city is quiet now, emptied of cars, shoppers, and most workers. Walking under colonial porticoes, we return to the convent of Santa Catalina, where nuns, daughters of Spanish aristocrats who came to Arequipa with dowries of porcelain and silver that still decorate the convent, once made wine and did laundry in exchange for food. Soldiers would leave meat and vegetables on a shelf that swivelled from outside to inside, allowing the nuns to remain invisible while they set out the wine or returned the clean laundry.

"*Buenas noches, mi amor*," Rafael says, kissing me before we enter the convent.

"*Mi amor*," I repeat to myself, curled up under a cold sheet and thick blankets. I shouldn't make too much of these words, but Rafael doesn't use language loosely.

*

Before we board the train to Puno, our eyes rest on the volcano Misti. Cha-Chani and Pichu Picchu compete for majesty against the cobalt sky, but Misti is sovereign. She once released warning wisps of smoke that gave testimony to the tumultuous life in her belly. When I lived here, some men used to call me Misti. Now I understand it was a compliment.

We buy bananas, oranges, and cookies from the food vendors who board with us. After stashing our bags, we make ourselves cozy on worn green leather seats. A conductor chases off the vendors, and the train lurches before gaining rhythm. It wends slowly through the fertile Chilena Valley, where irrigation ditches carry water from the Chili River to crops of onions, their blue-green shoots waving in the wind.

The train ascends to the *puna*, a treeless plateau, two miles above sea level. The air is dry and cold, and the sky is translucent. Flamingos wade in midnight-blue lagoons; a falcon devours its prey on a rock. Grazing on bunch grass, a dozen llamas, with red bows tied to their ears, straighten their long, skinny necks and stare indifferently at our train, a temporary annoyance in their timeless land.

I am dizzy when we arrive at Patapampa, at fifteen thousand feet, the highest point on our journey to Puno. Putting his arm around my shoulders, Rafael says, "Breathe deeply, Lydia, we will soon be at a lower altitude. Look, beyond those mountains lies the Apurímac River. Imagine . . . It will eventually join the Urubamba, one of the main headwaters of the Amazon."

At a lower altitude, we pass mud brick houses. There are no chimneys; smoke escapes through the thatched roofs. The train slows and stops beside a row of tables covered with food. Proud, robust women, wearing white Panama-style hats and white smocks, stand behind the food they sell. After eyeing roasted meat from the train windows, hungry passengers scramble from the cars.

We stop in front of a woman who has displayed her food in an attractive way and buy two slabs of goat meat which she places on brown paper along with ears of cold corn and chunks of goat cheese. The corn has large, tough, starchy kernels, unlike the tiny-kerneled sweet corn I ate every summer in Wisconsin. The goat is crisp, but tender. We eat aboard the train, sitting close together, with a poncho over our legs.

Passengers disembark in Juliaca, and the train turns south toward Puno, arriving after dark. Although we can't see the famous lake, I share with Rafael how, in seventh grade, the boys snickered, and the girls blushed whenever we heard the first two syllables of its name, and how the association with a woman's breasts helped us to remember that Lake

Titicaca, at 12,500 feet, is the world's highest, navigable lake.

We walk across the tracks to the Hotel Ferrocarril, the Railroad Hotel, and take a clean room with two beds, ignoring the raised eyebrows of a receptionist who notices I wear no wedding ring.

"We should get something to eat, Lydia, the dining room will close soon," Rafael says.

"You go, Rafael, I don't feel very good. Would you please bring me a cup of tea? I think I'll lie down for a while."

"I will bring you a special cup of tea, *mi amor.*"

My head appears to be growing larger; I have no other body parts, only this monstrous head with a jackhammer inside, drilling through the lobes of my brain, forcing its gigantic bit through my skull. My mother suffers from migraine headaches. Is this one?

Rafael returns with the tea, sits down on the side of the bed and says, "You have *soroche*, Lydia—altitude sickness. Drink this tea and try to sleep. I promise it will help."

By first light, my head has returned to its normal size. I look across the room and see Rafael in his bed, facing the wall, his black hair sticking out from under the covers. How would he react if I slipped in beside him? Taking the risk, I curl my body around his, spooning him. He stirs and turns toward me. "Ummm, you are cold. Let me warm you. Turn around."

Soon Rafael has an erection. Am I going to sleep with another man? Two men so close together? How terrible is it for a man not to have sex when his penis is hard? But it is Rafael who suggests we get breakfast.

We eat our rolls with *margarina* and *mermalada* and drink huge cups of steaming *café con leche.*

"Before we leave this table, Rafael, I want to know what you put in that tea last night."

"*¿Te gustó?* I hoped you would like it. Lydia, your health was restored by the much-maligned coca leaf."

*

I pull down my bulky alpaca sweater as far as it will go and pull up my ankle socks as high as they'll stretch. Rafael looks trim in a gray wool sweater and navy wind breaker.

I had not expected to see whitecaps on Lake Titicaca, but this lake is huge—3,200-square miles, and, in some places, it reaches depths of nine hundred feet. Small, spongy islands dot the lake. In *National Geographic* I had read about the Urus who live on the islands and make *balsa* boats from the *totora* reeds growing along the banks. The writer had said the Urus are terrified of falling into the water.

Rafael strikes up a conversation with a boat builder who is working on the shore near some abandoned *balsas*. In Aymara, the language of the Urus, the worker tells Rafael the boats take a few days to make and last only a few months before soaking up too much water. Because of his skill and experience, the man has been chosen to build the *balsa* of honor, the one that will carry a pure white llama to an island shrine as a sacrifice to Pachamama, the earth goddess.

Better a llama than the perfect maiden I read about in the same article. She was only fourteen years old and was to be sacrificed but lost the honor when the virgin selection committee found a tiny mole under one of her breasts.

"*Taita*," says Rafael, addressing the elderly boat builder with the familiar word meaning father. "Would you please tell us the story of the sun god?"

As if he had rehearsed this moment, the elder looks out over the vast lake and the floating reed islands, removes the *chullo* from his head, and gestures toward Bolivia. Rafael translates.

There is a holy shrine on the island of Titicaca, across the lake. It was on this island that the sun god hid in a cave during the dark days of the flood. With great brilliance, he finally emerged and restored light to the world. Needing a companion, the sun dedicated a nearby island to the moon and had a statue with a woman's figure, built upon it. The statue was gold from the waist up and silver from the waist down. This island he named Coata, from the word, *coya*, which means "queen."

"Thank you, *taita*," Rafael says, bowing a little.

*

The Puno market women wear black bowlers; some wear two, the new hat on top of the old. They sit on the ground with their herbs and charms displayed in symmetrical piles or in burlap pouches.

"They sell cures for ailments and hexes," Rafael says. A vendor offers a charm for him to inspect. "Andean women buy these when they want to attract a certain man to their bed. This love charm is a *warmi munachi*."

It is a hand-carved, soapstone figure of a man and woman locked in a coital embrace. The tiny figures rest in a nest of colored yarn, and there are red and black seeds in the nest and one large white one, representing an egg. Rafael returns the charm

to the woman who grins and offers it to me. I shake
my head no.

After the market, Rafael invites me to visit a friend
with whom he studied in Lima. I decline, saying I'd
like to rest a while, but after he leaves, I hurry back
to the market woman and buy the charm for five
soles, concealing it in a handkerchief.

Although I've learned to be cautious about taking
pictures of the Indians, I think I can get away with
one of the woman who sold me the charm.
Pretending to be examining an alpaca sweater at a
nearby booth, I slide the camera out of my shoulder
bag, aim, and shoot. The woman hears the shutter
and scowls at me. Shaking her fist, she yells to the
other women, who join in menacing jeers. Some fling
stones at me.

They don't risk the theft of their goods by running
after me. I return to our room and lie down,
breathless. I would have criticized a tourist for doing
the same thing, but I wanted to be able to look at the
picture one day, smile, and be amused by the charm's
power to predict events, but I couldn't explain all
this to the woman whose image I stole.

*

Rafael returns with box lunches. We board a bus filled
with market women returning to their villages. I hope
no one recognizes me.

What are their lives like, these women who wear
petticoats and masculine hats? They have never been
to a city larger than Puno; their worlds have been
confined to valleys carved by glaciers eons ago. What
would my life be like had I been born here?

I'd be working the land, trying to grow a little surplus to sell at the market. I'd be digging and cooking lots of potatoes. I'd be gathering llama dung for fuel to cook the potatoes. I'd have a baby every year and would consider myself lucky if a few of them survived beyond the age of five. I'd have sex frequently because what else would there be to do on damp, frigid evenings? Maybe I'd hate sex because of my husband's ignorance about pleasing a woman. I'd want to keep from getting pregnant, but I wouldn't know how; condoms would not be available, and my husband would refuse to use them if they were. Anyway, I might think we'd go to hell if he used condoms. One of my friends might try to get rid of her baby and would hemorrhage to death because she had been pierced by a foreign object, or get violently sick because some strange herbal liquid had been forced into her uterus to induce a miscarriage. I'd make a lot of *chicha*, chewing the corn kernels till they were soft, spitting them into a bowl to ferment. My husband and his friends would drink most of it, and then he'd want more sex. He'd beat me if I refused. I'd smell musty, wearing the same petticoats and skirts day after day. My skin would be ruddy and chapped, and my unwashed black braids would hang thick down my back. My children would play barefooted in front of our hut when they weren't gathering dung or carrying water. They would have distended bellies. I'd worry about not having enough to feed them but would still give my husband the best food and largest portion before serving them, and I'd eat what was left, or I wouldn't eat. If I ran out of breast milk for the baby, even if I had the money to buy formula, I wouldn't be able to read the instructions on the labels that carry pictures of pudgy, blonde-haired, blue-eyed babies. I might use water that hadn't been boiled to make the formula because I didn't have a spare pot, or I might dilute the formula to make it last. I'd look forward to market day because it would be the only time when I could get together with other women, talk about our lives, and earn a few *soles*, but as soon as I returned to my one-room hut, I'd have to hide my money and start supper. On a special occasion, I'd cook the fattest guinea pig from those that scampered and squealed on the floor of my hut.

*

I gaze out the bus window at an old woman bent beneath her burden of alfalfa. Other women help their men dig potatoes. Golden wheat and reddish-brown *quinua*, a protein-rich grain, ripen in the fields. None of the houses has windows. A young woman standing at her door, wearing a flower in her hat, spins alpaca wool. The flower signals she is looking for a husband.

We get off at Chicuito, a small village with earth-colored houses and a white-washed colonial church. Walking toward the church, we see a man seated before a canvas, holding a palette. He smiles when he sees us and stands in greeting—a tall, stout man with a ruddy complexion.

Raúl has the same surname as Tomás, the artist from Lima, and when I inquire about the coincidence, Raúl says yes, Tomás is his father, but he has not seen him in years. When I tell him his father gave me the painting of the cellist, Raúl says, "Then you must also receive a gift from the son of Rivas Peña. Please allow me to paint you, Lydia."

"Thank you, Raúl, I would love to have a souvenir of my visit to Lake Titicaca," I say, smoothing my hair. "Will it take long?"

"I think I can complete it in one hour, but it will be rough. Would you mind, Rafael?"

"*Por supuesto qué no*," Rafael says. "I would paint her, too, if I had the talent."

Raúl has the outgoing personality of his father, but the work on his easel is more traditional, with more attention to detail. The colors he captures—the vibrant blues of lake and sky, and the sepia of the huts, fences, and soil—are the exact colors we see around us. He directs me to sit on a rock near the shore and to look at the lake.

In an hour, Rafael returns from a walk around the village and plaza where there's a colonial sundial. "Have you two finished? We have a picnic box to share with you, Raúl."

"Yes, I am finished, but I wish I had more time," says Raúl. "I do not want to give Lydia a shabby portrait, especially since she will compare my work to my father's."

Raúl presents me with the hurried water color. He has given me Indian features; my hair is black, and I have Asian eyes and high cheekbones. It's a portrait of two women, but I can focus on only one at a time.

Eating cold chicken, bread, and fruit, we feast on the beauty of the profoundly blue ocean-lake, origin of the Andean Adam and Eve, the mythic ancestors of the woman from whom I stole the image in the market. I tell Rafael and Raúl about my humiliation.

"I'm sorry the women treated you so harshly," Rafael says, "but you knew how they felt about

photographs, Lydia, and you ignored their feelings."
I smart at Rafael's first criticism.

Raúl stretches his long legs in front of him. "*Mi
amiga*, do not punish yourself. The woman in the
market was afraid that your camera would bring evil;
they fear the power of hexes. Peruvians of Spanish
descent also make mistakes here. Not understanding
the Indians, they disparage them, content to blame
their poverty on racial and cultural inferiority,
overlooking the advanced civilization that existed
before the Conquest, but yours was an honest
mistake."

"No, Raúl, I knew I was taking her picture against
her will. I ignored her wishes to have what I wanted,"
I say, shifting to a more comfortable position on the
rock.

"At least you admit your error, Lydia," says Rafael.
"Few will admit to trying to dominate another human
being."

"Yes, that's it," I say, wincing at the truth. "My will
prevailed over hers. Even though it seems like a
stretch of the term, dominance was involved."

"Lydia, you are being too hard on yourself," says
Raúl, "and, forgive me, Rafael, but you are being hard
on Lydia, too. That market woman will forget about
the photo, although she will remember that a
foreigner took it. Your mistake was slight compared
to the abuses of history, Lydia."

"The Indians in the United States suffered
abuses, too," I say. "They were forced from their
homes into reservations that could be compared to
the *reducciones* the Spanish used here to control
the Indians and teach the gospel."

"The Spanish tried to abolish the Indians' way of
life, Lydia. There is no greater abuse," Raúl says,

looking grave. "Before the Spanish, the Indians had land, everyone had enough to eat, all had shelter, and the infirm were provided for. It was an efficient, collective system—but I must not idealize it—there was human sacrifice and little personal freedom. The land, nevertheless, provided all the wealth, and it sufficed for everyone."

"Perhaps," I say, "history is a never-ending struggle between men who believe it's their God-given right to dominate, with arms if needed, and those whose Bible has been written by the sun, moon, and stars."

"Lydia, you are more complex than I realized," says Rafael, smiling at me.

"If there is hope for Peru, *mi amiga*," says Raúl, "it lies in the land. Many say education will solve the problems of the Indians; others believe that they must be assimilated racially and culturally before the problems will diminish. But I believe they must have land. The Indian problem exists because land and the power it represents are still in the hands of a privileged few."

"The capitalists?" I ask.

"No, Lydia," says Rafael, with an edge to his voice I've not heard before. "The people about whom Raúl speaks are not capitalists. Real capitalism requires a spirit of risk, a system of fair play, opportunity, and some distribution of the wealth. When a few control the land, make the laws, prohibit competition, and punish those who challenge them, there is no capitalism; there is only feudalism, and you will have revolutionary movements wherever such a system exists."

"In training," I say, "the instructors told us the Communists were behind the revolutionary movements. Most North Americans think the same."

"Not all revolutionaries are Communists," says Rafael. "In fact, many are Christians who have taken to heart Christ's love of the poor, His criticism of the hypocritical rich, and His admonishment to show our love through the care we give the poor—but enough of this serious talk in the presence of this sacred lake. Let's give thanks, instead, for Manco Capac and his sister-wife, Mama Ocllo, created by the sun god Viracocha to repopulate the earth after the flood."

"What's the rest of the myth?" I ask.

"The two wandered north," Raúl says, "looking for the perfect place to begin their royal family, and when the golden staff they carried sank effortlessly into the soil, they chose to remain in Cuzco, the navel of the universe, through which would flow nourishment to the rest of the empire. They traveled from Lake Titicaca to Cuzco—the route you two lovers take tomorrow."

X

Puno to Cuzco

Little dove with white wings,
generous dove,
tell me, where is your nest?
For I go searching for rest.

Ciro Alegría, *El mundo es ancho y ajeno,*
1941

THE waiting room in the Puno train station is like
the inside of a mausoleum. The cold, stored overnight
in the cement floor, seeps upward, numbing our feet
and legs.

In less than an hour we are in Juliaca. A mist falls
on the vendors, snug in their heavy skirts and shawls.
They sell thick alpaca rugs. My eyes rest on a pure
white one that belongs in front of a roaring fire in a

cozy living room, a buffer between entwined lovers and a coarse carpet.

I would love to have the rug, but it would be an obstacle on this trip; perhaps on the return. Like the portrait Raúl did of me, I'm straddling two identities: the woman who lives and works among the poor, and the young North American who will return to the States with souvenirs made by the mysterious Peruvian Indians.

Leaving Juliaca, we cross a treeless plateau where rough stone walls divide the land, and an occasional shepherd woman tends alpacas or sheep. Two colors predominate in this sparse landscape: earth brown and the limpid blue of the sky, reflected in shallow ponds, upon which float a few intrepid fowl.

By late morning, the sun, on its journey across the Brazilian and Peruvian jungles, edges over the *cordillera blanca*, the eastern, snow-covered mountain range, warming the metal roof of the train. I understand why the Incas had worshiped the sun. It arrives each morning, a gift from *Antisuyu*, the steamy, tropical, eastern quadrant of the Inca empire, the quadrant from which the word "Andes" derives. At these altitudes, the sun brings energy, fecundity, and nourishment.

Hours later, a porter dressed in a crisp white jacket takes our lunch order. I ask for tea; Rafael orders the special, *rocoto relleno*, a sweet yellow pepper stuffed with cheese.

The train follows the course of the Vilcanota River that flows in narrow serpentine swaths around emerald mountains. Terraces collar the mountains to their crests, allowing the Indians to cultivate otherwise inaccessible land. Rock retention walls prevent the soil on each terrace from washing away.

I remember an old song my parents loved, "Stairway to the Stars."

"This is a Peruvian Eden," I whisper to Rafael.

"*Sí, mi amor*, there's more to come," he says, kissing me.

✳

The Cuzco train station is a muddle of harried humanity. Babies peep wide-eyed from slings on their mothers' backs. In their arms, the mothers carry bundles made of home-spun cloth. Those passengers who can afford taxis fight to open car doors against the crush. Children hawk chewing gum and candy. Straining under the weight, Indian men, "strappers," bear bulky burdens on their backs and crane their necks to dodge on-coming traffic. Does each strapper have a family? How many hours a day do they sell their strength? How many coins, tied up in dirty rags, do they bring home at the end of the day?

"*¡Rafael! Rafael!*" shouts a portly man with Middle-Eastern good looks and a brilliant smile. "I don't believe it, how long has it been?" he says, zig-zagging toward us. He gives Rafael a bear hug and then holds him at arm's length, looking into his eyes, as if he were reuniting with a son who has been off to war.

"*Padrino*, it has been too many years," Rafael says. "But look at you. So robust. My godfather must be very successful. And how is my *madrina*?"

"Your godmother is fine, but she will be very upset if she does not get to see you. Of course, you were on your way to see us, no?"

"—Oh, forgive me, Lydia," Rafael says, putting his arm around my waist. "*Padrino*, I want you to meet my *enamorada*, Lydia Schaefer. She is a Peace Corps volunteer. Lydia, this is my godfather, Guillermo Abuad."

"*Encantada, señor Abuad,*" I say, shaking his hand. He has coal-black eyes, covered by thick, unruly brows. I am embarrassed by my disheveled appearance but thrilled that Rafael has called me his *enamorada.*

"*Mucho gusto, señorita Lydia,*" he says, gripping my hand. "You are the first Peace Corps volunteer I have had the pleasure to meet. I am looking forward to hearing about your work. And you, Rafael, are very naughty to have come without informing us. Where do you plan to stay? At a hotel? I won't hear of it. You are coming home with me. I came to the station to pick up this package, and when I started to leave, there you were. ¡*Qué suerte!*"

"What luck, indeed, *padrino,*" says Rafael. "Lydia, is it okay with you if we stay with Guillermo and Gloria?"

"I'd like that very much, providing I can clean up soon."

"Follow me, Señorita. We will make you feel right at home."

We follow Guillermo to his modest Ford. He puts our bags in the trunk and then cautiously navigates the car through congested streets, lined with stalls and vendors selling fruit, vegetables, dried beans, rice, and cheap plastic items. We take Avenida Sol to the Plaza de Armas. Turning right, we pass the Church of La Compañía, begun by the Society of Jesus in 1571.

"The Jesuits," says Guillermo, "wanted their church to be the most magnificent in Cuzco, but the bishop felt it should not be more beautiful than the Cathedral, right across from it. Finally, Pope Paul III got involved and decided the Cathedral should be more beautiful, but his word came too late. La Compañía is like a lovely woman who wears exquisite jewels."

The buildings around the plaza have red tile roofs that undulate over the sagging structures they protect. I imagine colonial women, their black hair covered with lace mantillas, smiling coquettishly at uniformed Spanish officers from the wrought-iron balconies.

The car climbs a steep cobblestone street, bordered by a narrow sidewalk. Pedestrians walk in single file to avoid being hit. The street is cleft with an open sewer, used in colonial times for disposal of nasty liquids.

After a few sharp turns, we stop before a house covered with flowering vines. Guillermo blows the horn, and a stooped, but dignified, Indian man opens the heavy iron gate.

Guillermo parks the Ford inside the gate and gets our bags. César, the old man, locks the gate, and we walk to the front door through a small garden with carefully pruned rose bushes.

A stately woman with short black hair opens the large wooden door. "¡ *Ay, mi Dios, Rafael! ¡Qué sorpresa! ¡Qué felicidad!*"

"*Sí, madrina*, I am surprised and happy to see you, too," Rafael says, embracing her. "You look so beautiful."

"*Ay, por favor, Rafael*, I am now an old woman."

"*No, madrina*, to me you will always be lovely."

"And who is this pretty young woman? I like her already. She is tall—like me—a real woman."

"*Madrina*, this is my good friend—*mi enamorada*—Lydia Schaefer. She is from Wisconsin, in the United States, and is working in Ica as a Peace Corps volunteer."

"Your '*enamorada*.' Ay, Rafael, I am happy to hear you say that word. I thought your head was always too much in the books." Turning to embrace me, she says, "I have heard about the Peace Corps. You must be a good person, Lydia, to come all this way to work with the poor. Wisconsin sounds so far away. Does it snow there all the time?"

"No, Doña Gloria," I say. "It does snow a lot in winter, but summers are lovely, and sometimes the weather gets very warm."

"¡*Gloria, por Dios!*" Guillermo says. "Can't you see you are keeping us outside? Let us inside, so they can rest before telling us about their lives. I have invited Rafael and Lydia to stay with us a few days. I knew you would not mind."

"Mind? Never. Let me take you to your rooms. Because you are not married, you will sleep in two rooms. Here we are *muy Católico*," she teases. "You can bathe, and then we will all enjoy a nice *pisco sour*. Do you like *pisco sours*, Lydia?"

"I'm afraid I like them too much, Doña Gloria."

We climb a wide staircase. The house must be two hundred years old. There are dark oil portraits on the walls and frayed Persian rugs on the wooden floors that creak as we walk down the antique-lined corridor. Doña Gloria opens a heavy, arched door with black metal fittings. The stucco walls are painted white, and the furniture is made of rich, nearly black mahogany. There is a four-poster bed covered with a white chenille bedspread. A crucifix, with a figure of Jesus bearing graphic red wounds in his hands, feet, and side, hangs above the ornate headboard.

I take off my jeans and sweater, put on a long shirt, and find the bathroom at the end of the hall. There's a shower, but no shower stall and no curtain to prevent water from splashing over the rest of the room. A miniature water heater hangs above the faucets, its pilot light burning inside. I turn on the faucet marked C for *caliente* and mix the burning stream with water marked F for *frío*. Shivering, because I can only warm one side of my body at a time, I quickly shampoo and dry off using a luxurious white towel. Now the entire floor is wet, along with the bidet and toilet.

Not wanting to leave the floor all wet, and not wanting to use the fine towel to mop up the water, I peek out the door to see if Rafael is nearby. Instead, I look into the smooth, moon-shaped face of an Indian woman with heavy braids. "*Por favor, señora*, what can I use to dry the floor?"

Her face widens in a smile. "Señorita, do not worry. I will do it."

"No, please, I'd like to clean it up myself."

"*Ay, señorita, no, por favor.*" She takes a broom from a closet and sweeps the water toward the drain.

"*Me llamo Lydia*," I say, introducing myself, extending my hand.

"*Yo soy Avelina*," she says, looking at her feet.

"*Gracias, Avelina, muy amable.*" I tell her she is very kind.

"*De nada, señorita Lydia.*"

I return to my room, brush my wet hair, and put on a navy blue wrap-around skirt and white sweater. After putting on lipstick, I walk down the corridor and catch Raphael entering his room, his lower torso wrapped in a towel. "*Hola—¡Qué guapo!*" I say, thinking how handsome he is. "I need to talk to you a minute before we go downstairs."

"Please come in, Lydia. There is something I want to tell you, too." He lets his towel fall, revealing the back of his long, brown, muscular body and puts on a fresh pair of jeans and a sweatshirt.

"Thank you, Lydia, for being so agreeable. You must realize how surprised I was to see Guillermo at the station. I had every intention of staying at an inexpensive hotel for our two nights here, but I did plan on taking you to meet them. Because I had not seen them in many years, I didn't think it appropriate to ask them if we could spend the night. That was foolish because they are my *padrinos*. Perhaps I have spent too much time in Lima."

"How did they get to be your godparents, Rafael?"

Rafael folds his clean shirts and jeans, placing them on the shelf of a large armoire. "When my father was a young man, he came to Cuzco to intern. He was looking for a place to stay and stopped into the dry goods shop the Abuads own. There he spoke to Guillermo who was managing the shop he had inherited from his parents. Gloria was at home taking care of their son, Pablito, who had been born with serious birth defects. Guillermo went home for the noon meal and spoke to Gloria about my father. Gloria liked the fact that my father was a doctor and thought he could be of assistance to their son. She suggested Guillermo invite my father to dinner that evening. They got along so well that my father stayed with the Abuad family throughout his internship."

"So your families go back a long time."

"It gets more interesting, Lydia," he says, sitting down on the bed. "At the time my father was living with the Abuads, a young woman named Teresa was working as a domestic in the Abuad home. My father was attracted to her, but as I told you, criollos don't dilute their Spanish blood by marrying Indians, and my father was brought up with this prejudice. Well, every morning Teresa would serve my father *café con leche*. She was so sweet and gentle, with hair, according to my father, the color of a raven's feathers, that he feared his heart would stop beating when she raised her eyes to meet his."

"This sounds like a fairy tale," I say, sitting on the stool in front of the mirror.

Rafael gently puts his hands on my shoulders. "One day a runner from Teresa's village came to the house. Teresa's father had had an accident and was close to death. Teresa asked my father to accompany her to the village, but they arrived too late for my father to save him. So now, my sweet Lydia, you know how my father came to Pachabuena and married his sweetheart Teresa."

"Hearing you talk about your parents with such love makes me miss my parents."

"Your parents had to be brave, letting you come to Peru, and they had to trust you. Peruvian parents would never allow an unmarried daughter to travel so far from home and stay away for such a long time."

"Even a daughter who is twenty-three?"

"Even one who is *that old*," Rafael says, taking the comb from my hands before kissing the top of my head. "But I shall always be grateful to your mother and father."

"And I'm eager to meet yours, to see where you got your good looks," I say, tilting my head up to kiss him.

"We would make pretty babies," he says casually.

"—So after your birth, you were baptized, and the Abuads became your *padrinos*?" I should tell him I loved what he just said.

"Well, not right away. The trip from Pachabuena to Cuzco is a difficult one, but when the rains stopped, my parents brought me to the Abuad home, and the next morning I was baptized in the Church of La Merced. My father had always loved the statue of the Archangel Rafael there. The plaque under the statue describes St. Rafael as God's physician and the patron of travelers. It also states that he is the protector and guardian of Christian marriage. That was good enough for my parents, and I was baptized Rafael."

"Your parents seem devoted to each other."

"My father always said that the best example he could give me was to love my mother. They respect each other, always treating one another with kindness and consideration. They touch frequently, and when their hands do not touch, their eyes do."

"Speaking of eyes, sometimes the intimate way you look at me makes me uncomfortable. It's not as if you're being seductive, but the effect is the same. I feel undressed."

"Perhaps it is your soul I see, Lydia."

"Maybe that's it, the way you're looking at me now. Where did the Abuad family originally come from?" I ask, avoiding his eyes.

"From Palestine. Guillermo came here with his parents, brothers, and sisters in 1949, shortly after Israel became a nation. They had been successful merchants in Palestine and owned much land, but they left it all to start a new life. Two of Guillermo's uncles settled in Chile. Years later, visiting his relatives there, Guillermo met his first cousin Gloria, and they fell in love."

"But Gloria said she and Guillermo were Catholic. How can they be Catholic and Palestinian? Do they speak Arabic?"

"Gloria and Guillermo speak Arabic with each other, and, although they consider themselves Roman Catholics now, they were brought up in the Orthodox Church in Palestine." Running his fingers through my damp hair, Rafael says, "You look very pretty Lydia. I want to show you off to the Abuads. Let's go downstairs and have that drink."

"You go down. I want to do something with this hair."

"Let me braid it for you. My mother always liked it when I braided her hair. She said that the hands of her son, a future doctor, did precise work." How would those hands feel caressing my breasts?

Rafael leans outside the window and snips a section of vine from the wall, strips it of its leaves, and cuts it in half. After combing the hair back from my face, he parts it in the middle. He deftly weaves my hair, tying the braids with a piece of vine before winding them on top of my head. Finally, he reaches for the red carnation in a vase on the vanity and fixes it above my left ear. "You look like a Goya painting, Lydia. All you need is a fan and a lace mantilla."

"Where did you learn about Goya?"

"I won a scholarship to study in Madrid for one semester. When I couldn't concentrate on my medical books, I'd concentrate on the paintings in the Prado. You, *mi querida*, look like the Clothed Maja. I cannot compare you to the Unclothed Maja, but I can imagine."

"Was that a *piropo*?" I ask. "I thought you didn't like them."

"It's true. I don't like to flatter, but I was not flattering you."

"We'd better go down for that drink now," I say.

Guillermo stands when he sees me. "¡*Qué guapa, Lydia*! I see why you call her your *enamorada*, Rafael."

"But I have a good teacher, *padrino*. Our taste in women is very similar," Rafael says, giving his godfather another hug before kissing his godmother.

Family photographs decorate the mantle, among them one of Gloria holding a baby dressed in an elaborate baptismal dress. "That is me holding Rafael," she says, pointing to the picture. "And the one next to it is Guillermo and me with Rafael's parents."

"Are these your children?" I ask, pointing to a picture of a handsome youth and a darkly beautiful girl, a miniature Gloria.

"Yes," says Gloria. "That is a picture of Vicente and Sophia. Vicente is studying architecture in Chile now, and Sophia, having been influenced by her *padrino*, Dr. Miguel, is studying medicine there."

"So Rafael's parents are Sophia's godparents?"

"Yes," says Gloria. "That is how we do things here. We like someone, and then we want to keep them close, so we make them *padrinos* or *madrinas* at baptisms, confirmations, or marriages. Then they are in the family. We can go to them when there are troubles, and they know they can always come to us."

There is another picture on the mantle, one of a baby with thin arms extending rigidly from his body. His head stretches to one side, as if a powerful muscle is pulling it away from the camera.

"That is our Pablito," says Guillermo. "He has cerebral palsy; he is also mentally retarded and cannot speak or walk. We took him to many doctors, but they all said there was nothing they could do for him. They told us to put him in an institution, but we refused to send him away."

"Did he receive any special education?" I ask.

"No," says Gloria. "There was nothing like that here. Even now there are no programs for children who have problems like Pablito's. He is twenty-nine years old— three years older than Rafael. You will meet him before you go, Lydia. He is a good boy. I blamed myself for a long time because I thought I had done something wrong in my pregnancy, but we are resigned now. We try to keep him comfortable and give him all the love we can. Avelina has been a big help. She loves Pablito like a son."

Avelina, the woman who cleaned up after my shower, enters with a pitcher of icy *pisco sours,* a tray of cocktail glasses, and a dish of green olives. Guillermo pours and offers a toast. "To our handsome, intelligent godson. May he grow in wisdom, compassion, and skill, and may he not forget his godparents when they are old, feeble, and in need of his services." We clink glasses, saying *salud,* before sipping the frothy, tart cocktail.

Doña Gloria says there must also be a *brindis,* a toast, for me, Rafael's *enamorada.* "Welcome to our home, Lydia," she says. "We do not know you very well, but we trust Rafael's judgment. If he has chosen you, we shall love you, too."

While they catch up on family history, I look around the room, keeping tuned to the conversation. Thick, hand-hewn beams support the vaulted roof. We sit in leather chairs with heavy wooden armrests and legs. A hefty chest, one that might have held Inca treasure long ago, holds our drinks.

Rafael looks worried and is leaning over in his chair, listening to Guillermo. "Times are dangerous. Vicente and Sophia study in Chile because of the unrest in the universities here. Farm workers are organizing to protest forced labor. They are following Diego Torrente who is said to be a Castro sympathizer."

"The students were talking about him in Ica," I say, sitting down beside Guillermo.

"Two weeks ago," says Guillermo, "Ricardo Bonilla got nervous when he saw a group of *campesinos* approaching his house. He had heard that Torrente supported violence to end the old ways. The peasants had no weapons, but Bonilla, thinking the peasants wanted to take his land, killed seven of them with the help of his guards."

"My God, that's terrible," Rafael says. "Is anyone trying to stop the violence?"

"I'm negotiating with you to come to the table," says Gloria. "We are going to eat good Arabic food, and you are not going to mention violence," she commands.

Avelina brings a brimming bowl of stuffed grape leaves. The brownish-green leaves have been tightly rolled around a savory rice and ground meat filling and resemble those I have eaten at Greek celebrations in Milwaukee. There's also roasted chicken basted with olive oil, lemon, rosemary, and garlic. White rice and a tomato and cucumber salad with yogurt dressing complete the meal. Guillermo pours white Chilean wine, and we toast again.

"Tell me, Rafael," Doña Gloria asks, "what are your plans? When will you see your parents?"

"I want to show Lydia around Cuzco first, and then we'll begin the journey to Pachabuena. We can take the train to Machu Picchu, and from there we'll go by foot."

"And after your visit to Pachabuena, you will both return to Ica?" asks Gloria.

"*No, madrina.* Unfortunately, Lydia must return without me. I will stay and work with my father, but I wanted them to meet Lydia, and she has never been to this part of Peru before, so I convinced her to travel with me."

"I did not need much convincing," I say.

"She has only eleven days of vacation left, and then she must return to her work in Ica. I will escort her back to the train in Machu Picchu. She assures me she can make it back to Ica on her own."

"*Por supuesto,*" Gloria says. "Lydia is a Peace Corps volunteer. She is not afraid to travel by herself."

Avelina removes the plates, and Guillermo pours more wine.

"How did you and Rafael meet?" he asks me.

"I was working in a medical post in Ica after the flood," I say, "and—"

"—*Sí, sí*—that was a dreadful flood," Guillermo says. "Many died. We read about it here."

"Well," I continue, "Rafael came to work in our clinic. He was our only doctor."

"And we are grateful that you have come to Peru, Lydia," Gloria says. "You are a strong, brave woman, *una mujer de consequencias.*"

We return to the living room. César puts more wood on the fire, and Guillermo serves small glasses of brandy. He and Gloria ask about my family and invite me to stay with them on my return from Pachabuena. "Maybe then you will have good news for us," Guillermo teases, before kissing me goodnight on my cheek and promising to accompany us on our tour of Cuzco tomorrow.

In bed I read from Prescott's *Conquest of Peru* and fall asleep dreaming of the Inca, the chosen women, and the Temple of the Sun.

XI

Cuzco

Had you seen . . . the devilish Cruelties of
those that called themselves Christians: had
you seen the poor creatures torn from the
peace and quiet of their own Habitations,
where God had planted them, to labour in
a Tormenting Captivity . . . , your compassion
must of necessity have turned into
Astonishment: The tears of Men can hardly
suffice; these are Enormities to make the
Angels mourn.

From a letter to Oliver Cromwell by John
Phillips, accompanying his 1656 translation
of Bartolomé de las Casas' *Brevísima
relación de la destrucción de las Indias*,
1552

Roosters crow somewhere on the hill above the Abuad house. I slide my limbs over the soft sheets and consider the relationship between people and their wealth. The Abuads have money, but they don't flaunt it. Having worked hard for it, they feel no guilt in enjoying the money they've earned through honest labor. Do they give to the poor, inconspicuously, like Scripture advises, not letting one hand know what the other is giving? I recall a teacher back home who said that wealth is God's blessing for keeping His commandments, and that the poor suffer because they either have not accepted Jesus as their Savior or are lazy.

After putting on the same outfit I wore last night, I go down to breakfast. Avelina is busy heating milk and putting out rolls, margarine, jam, and boiled eggs.

"*Buenos días, Avelina.*"

"*Señorita Lydia, buenos días. ¿Cómo amaneciste?*" How did you greet the break of day? How did you dawn? In the United States we ask people how they have slept, not what mood they're in upon arising. Maybe it's a good thing.

"*Muy bien, gracias, Avelina.*"

"*¿Quieres café con leche?*"

"*Sí, por favor.*" She pours a small amount of cold, syrupy coffee into my large cup and adds steaming milk.

"Has Rafael come down yet?"

"No, señorita, he is still sleeping."

"Do you have any children Avelina?"

"No, señorita, I came to this family when I was very young. They were good to me and taught me right from wrong. I did not go out to meet boys like some of the girls who came from the villages, so I never married."

"Did you ever want to have a family?"

"*Ay, sí*, but I had much work to do, and I did not want to leave Doña Gloria and Don Guillermo. They had always warned me about the bad things young men and women do when they get free time—about the drinking—and you know what I mean. Now I am too old to have children, but the Abuads are my family. I do not know what I would do if I did not have them."

"You work hard, Avelina. I see you clean, do laundry, cook, shop, and Doña Gloria says you also look after Pablito."

"Pablito is like my son. I am the only one who understands him. I make his meals and feed him. I grind up all of his food so he can swallow easily, and I change his diapers. My bed is in his room."

"Do you ever take a day off?"

"Where would I go Señorita? I am an old woman. I am afraid to go in a bus or cab, and all of my family are gone. Sometimes, in the evening, after all of the dishes are done, and Pablito is sleeping, César and I sit in the garden and talk about our villages and of our childhood. That is enough for me."

"Avelina, are you telling Señorita Lydia bad things about me?" Rafael gives her a kiss on the cheek and playfully tugs her braids.

"*No, doctor Rafael.* I say only good things about you. But you did stay away from us too long."

"From now on, Avelina, I promise to visit you more often. Now may I please have my *café con leche*?"

He bends to kiss me on the forehead. "And how is my Clothed Maja this morning?"

✳

Scattered dark clouds portend the rainy season. We follow Waynapata, a steep cobblestone lane, and wind down Culebras, the street of the serpents, before entering the Plaza de Armas. Passing both the Cathedral and La Compañía, we come to Marquez Mantas Street and the less pretentious Church of La Merced, the Church of Mercy.

We enter La Merced, stepping over a wooden threshold worn to a smooth patina after four centuries. After our eyes adjust to the darkness, we walk down the center aisle and genuflect before entering the pew behind an aged Indian woman wearing a tattered gray sweater. Her thick gray braid follows the contours of her curved back. A well-dressed man and his young son kneel across the aisle. A matronly, well-groomed woman kneels at our right. Behind us we hear footsteps and the creaking of brittle wood as the faithful enter the pews.

With its gold leaf and silver tabernacle, the altar radiates a tarnished opulence of a bygone era, an embarrassment to contemporary Catholics like me who have overlooked Jesus's praise for the woman who washed His feet with precious oils. He had admonished His disciples, after they bemoaned the waste, that "the poor you will always have with you."

A gnome-like deacon in a black knit hat and a white alb shuffles into the sanctuary, approaches the altar, bends low, and strains to see if the Mass book is opened to today's Scripture readings. Satisfied, he pads back toward the sacristy.

There is a tinkling of bells, and a priest, more decrepit than the deacon who follows him, enters.

His accent reveals Spanish birth and education: "*En el nombre del padre y del hijo y del espíritu santo.*" Mass begins in this church as it has every day for four centuries.

Walking toward the communion rail with Rafael, I pray God will bless our relationship. At the end of Mass, the priest makes the Sign of the Cross and says, "Go in peace to serve Christ and one another."

We exit down a side aisle, past intricately carved altars dedicated to Mary or to a saint. Through compassionate eyes, the saints, dressed in cloth robes of royal blue and purple, look down upon frail humans who need their faith to survive. The faithful pray for cures, emotional solace, or for the intentions of family members and friends. After putting a coin in a slotted container, they pick up a long wick and light a candle to their favorite saint. The flames are tangible symbols of their uplifted prayers.

With his sandy hair, faded red cape, and white robe, the statue of Archangel Rafael is the most visually pleasing. His white wings stand out proudly from his strong body. He looks down lovingly at those who seek his favor. Not a fighter like Michael, not a messenger like Gabriel, he is the healer, and there is nothing more dear, in a poverty-stricken country like Peru, than a healing angel.

"He looks so kind," I whisper to Rafael.

"I am happy with my patron saint," says Rafael.

As we turn to leave, I notice that people have gathered at the foot of a large crucifix. They are gazing at the suffering Christ, prayers visible on their lips. His sorrowful eyes ask why they've sinned. *Milagros*, small silver models of hearts, legs, heads, and other body parts made whole through prayer, have been pinned to the black velvet fabric behind the crucifix. Believers approach the crucifix, touch Christ's feet, and then touch their fingers to their lips.

As a child, adults taught me that faith was a gift; we should be grateful for it because we did nothing to earn it. Atahualpa, the last Inca, was betrayed and executed by Pizarro because he didn't have the faith of the conquistadors and rejected the cross. Although he believed there was one primary God, Viracocha, the creator of all life, he also believed in minor gods and couldn't understand how the three persons of the God of the Spanish—Father, Son, and Holy Ghost—could be equally divine.

Atahualpa had kept his part of the bargain, filling rooms with gold and silver, in exchange for his freedom, but he persisted in refusing conversion until he learned he was to be burned alive. How could he enjoy life after death if his body were reduced to ashes? He converted just before the Spanish broke his neck with an iron collar, becoming at baptism, Juan de Atahualpa. The Spanish, having been influenced by the Inquisition, had referred to the Indians as "Moors" and were just doing their duty.

*

The Cathedral rests on the site of the palace of Viracocha, the eighth Inca who took the name of his people's lord and creator. The main altar is covered in silver-plate; the tabernacle is gold. Age-streaked mirrors hang from the altar's heights, reminders to sinners who see their reflections that it is time to go to confession.

The chairs in the choir area have hand-carved arm rests, their weight supported by naked Pachamamas, voluptuous goddesses, responsible for earthly bounty. Although the Spanish priests disdained native religious beliefs, they accommodated some to accelerate conversions.

To the right of the main altar hangs a large oil painting of the Last Supper by Peruvian artist Marcos Zapata. He combined Indian and European influences; the Paschal supper includes a platter with a roasted guinea pig, *cuy*, the affordable meat favored by the Indians.

A priest is saying Mass at a side altar dedicated to *Nuestro Señor de los temblores.* The crucifix, blackened by candle smoke, depicts Our Lord of the Earthquakes wearing a decorated skirt like those used by Inca royalty. On the Monday after Easter, it is this statue that men carry around the Plaza de Armas to bring good fortune to those who view it.

The shrines lining the side aisles of the Cathedral are dedicated to Our Lady of the Snows, Our Lady of the Assumption, and the Virgin of Pains, whose eyes have just watched her Son's crucifixion. Rich and poor see their own suffering reflected in the images of Christ, Mary, and the saints, as if the statues were saying to them, "Look, we understand your plight, but life is like that. We suffered, too. Bravely accept your crosses; God will give you the strength to bear them."

Those who doubt or despair receive inspiration at the shrine of a glorified saint—radiant in white, triumphant—one who has seen God. There *is* heavenly reward for enduring injustice.

"I need some fresh air," I say to Rafael.

"*Bueno*, it's nearly time to meet Guillermo and Gloria for lunch. Maybe today you'll order *cuy*, Lydia."

We take a cab up a steep hill leading to the ruins of Sacsayhuamán, the Inca fortress. The *picantería* is hardly noticeable from the road, but the restaurant is crowded. Most of the men and some of the women are drinking *chicha*.

"*¡Aquí, Rafael, Lydia!*" shouts Guillermo, gesturing for us to join him and Gloria at their table near the window. "How was your morning? Did you have enough churches for one day?"

"Yes," I say, "and what I'd really like now is a cold beer."

"Are you sure you would not prefer some *chicha*?" asks Gloria.

"If you don't mind, I'd prefer the kind of beer I used to drink in Milwaukee, but I will take your recommendation on the food."

"Then you must have the *cuy*," says Guillermo.

"If it's good enough for Jesus, it's good enough for me," I say, reminding them of the painting I saw at the Cathedral.

The waiter brings *chicha* for them and a *Cerveza Cuzqueña* for me. The cold beer bites and washes away the taste of ancient church air.

Waiting for lunch, I learn that Sacsayhuamán was more than a fortress. Despite the zig-zag walls that required those who scaled them to expose their backs to the enemy, scholars now say it was also used as a place of religious worship.

It took thirty thousand men to build Sacsayhuamán, and some of the stones weigh over one hundred tons. No one knows where they found the stones, or how they transported them.

My guinea pig, often called *conejo chactado*, or flattened rabbit, has been grilled under stones, as if ironed. It still has its head, legs, little feet, and claws. Served on a large platter, it is garnished with yucca, a stringy tuberous plant, and marinated vegetables. Guillermo eats *adobo*, a spicy pork stew, and Gloria and Rafael have ordered *anticuchos de corazón*, the marinated pieces of beef heart Rafael and I had eaten in Arequipa. I cut off a thigh and leg from the guinea pig. "Use your fingers, Lydia," says Guillermo. "It is much easier." The bones are delicate, and the meat tender and delicious.

Satisfied and drowsy after our large meal, we leave the restaurant and drive with Gloria and Guillermo up the road to Sacsayhuamán, which in Quechua means "happy falcon." At the entrance is a plaque bearing the words of Pedro Sancho de la Hoz, a conqueror who recognized the incomparable feats of the race the Spanish wanted to dominate. In 1534 he wrote the following in his journal:

> Not the bridge in Segovia, nor other build-
> ings made by Hercules or by the Romans
> are as worthy of verse as this. . . . On top of
> the round yet rugged hill you see from the
> city, there is a very beautiful fortress made
> of earth and stone, with large windows that
> look out upon the city. Within it are many
> rooms and one main tower in the center
> made from cube-like stones, one on top of
> the other. The rooms and dwellings are
> small, and the rocks from which they were
> made have been carefully wrought and so
> well fitted, one with the others, and it ap-
> pears no mortar was used. The rocks are so

smooth that they seem like polished slabs.
There are so many rooms and towers that a
person cannot see it in one day, and many
Spanish who have seen it and have walked
in Lombardy and in other foreign realms,
say they have never seen another structure
like this fortress, nor a castle more strong.

*

The rest of the afternoon we wander through the
ruins and onto the plain that Manco Inca crossed to
recapture Sacsayhuamán from the Spanish. Manco,
named after the first Inca, held it, using it as his
staging area and threatening the enemy in Cuzco,
until Juan Pizarro, Francisco's brother, retook it with
a small band of cavalry men.

Sitting on a large, smooth boulder, we watch the
sun set and hear in the distance someone playing
the *quena*, an Andean flute. The stones will be here
till the end of time, indifferent to our human dramas.

*

School girls in freshly laundered uniforms giggle
when Rafael and I pass them on our walk the next
morning. Merchants sprinkle water on the sidewalks
to control the dust before sweeping them with hand-
made brooms.

The church of Santo Domingo encloses the ruins
of Coricancha, the Temple of the Sun, believed to
have been built by the first Inca. An earthquake
destroyed Santo Domingo in 1650, and, in 1950,
another quake destroyed the rebuilt church. The
people who dug it out in 1950 were stunned to find

Inca walls that had withstood both quakes. Rafael is my guide to a history and lore I might have ignored had I not met him.

Pachacutec, the ninth Inca, embellished the original Temple of the Sun by covering it with seven hundred solid-gold plates. Artisans used emeralds to decorate the plate depicting the morning sun and its rays. Silver plates, bearing the face of the moon goddess Mamaquilla, sister-bride of the sun, covered the walls of the Temple to the Moon, within the larger temple.

A gold model of the sun god had been found during the excavation in the fifties. The statue represented a boy of approximately ten years who stood with his right arm up, his fist nearly closed. He held up his index finger and thumb like he was about to give an order. Minor gods, assistants to the sun, had their places of worship within the temple; thunder and the stars were represented; so too, the rainbow.

The living revered the remains of dead Incas and every day offered them food and drink. An Inca did not represent divinity; he was divine.

Mamaconas, cloistered women married to the sun, said to have had intercourse with him, lived in Coricancha. Educated by older, wiser women, who had been similarly honored, they learned the precious art of weaving the elaborate fabrics used in clothing the Inca.

It was from the Temple of the Sun that Atahualpa's followers retrieved the wealth he had promised Pizarro in exchange for his freedom. The Spanish melted the precious ransom and shipped it to Spain.

*

Before walking back to the Abuad home, we eat *mixtos*, grilled ham and cheese sandwiches, at the Tupac Amaru, a restaurant named for the last Inca. Apart from the restaurants, store owners have closed their shops and have gone home for the three-hour siesta.

The only sound in the house comes from a grandfather clock. "Everyone is resting," says Rafael. We tip-toe up the stairs.

"A siesta sounds good to me, too, I whisper. What do you have planned for the rest of the day?"

"We should buy our train tickets to Machu Picchu, so we don't have to stand in line tomorrow. Are you excited?"

"Yes, I'm excited, but if I had to return to Ica tomorrow, I'd still be satisfied—except for not having met your parents, of course—Thank you, Rafael."

"I still forget how remarkable is the history of my people, Lydia. Thank you for helping me rediscover it."

Avelina approaches with a glass of juice in her hand. "Pablito is thirsty. I made some papaya juice for him. Would you like some?" she asks.

"Avelina," says Rafael, "do you think we could see Pablito? It has been a long time since I last saw him."

"I do not think Don Guillermo and Doña Gloria would mind. You are part of the family, doctor Rafael."

"Thank you, Avelina," Rafael says, as she quietly opens the door to Pablito's room.

Despite the open windows, I smell urine. On the bed I see the outline of a figure, topped by a thatch of thick black hair. Avelina goes to Pablito's side, pulls down the blankets to reveal his face, and offers the juice to him. He sips awkwardly on the straw, and

Avelina wipes the juice dribbling down his chin. As Rafael draws closer, Pablito jerks his head around to look at us. He is startled, like an animal aroused from sleep. He knocks the juice out of Avelina's hands, and it spills over the bedding. His mouth contorts, and he moans in fear, but Avelina whispers into his ear, stroking his hair, telling him everything is fine; we are friends and will not hurt him. She tells him our names and asks if he remembers Rafael.

Pablito's spastic limbs relax, the muscles around his mouth soften, and a smile spreads over his face. Rafael approaches, brings his face close to Pablito's, and speaks to him, as he might speak to a child who has just had a nightmare. Pablito responds with soft animal noises, like the ones coming from a box in the corner. It holds four adorable puppies that Avelina removes and places on the bed. The puppies tumble over Pablito, making him laugh, and he tries to touch each one.

We leave this man-child who is as vulnerable as the puppies. His senses, like theirs, register only pleasure and pain. No one will ever measure the dimensions of his mind or understand what transpires within.

"I'm really tired, Rafael, I think I'll lie down for a while," I say.

"*Bueno, mi amor.* I think I'll read."

How neat and ordered is my little room, how unlike the chaos that rules Pablito's mind and body. Opening the shutters, I see tiny birds swinging back and forth on delicate branches of ash trees. In the garden are white lilies, *azucenas*, and yellow, pink, and mauve roses. I turn down the bedspread, lie down and watch the movement of the leaves until I fall asleep.

XII

Machu Picchu

Under the weight of these four centuries,
the Indian has been bent, but the dark
depth of his soul has hardly changed. In
the craggy sierras, in the distant gorges,
where the rule of the white men has not yet
reached, the Indian still guards his
ancestral code.

José Carlos Mariátegui, *Siete ensayos de
interpretación de la realidad Peruana*, 1928

AT 5:30 a.m. we walk to the market near the train
station. Stout Indian women serve rice and bean
breakfasts to workers—the weary strappers—human
beasts of burden. A man in an old, heavy sweater, his
breath visible, squeezes juice from green oranges into
glasses he has washed in a bucket of cold, greasy

water. From a different vendor we buy oranges and small bananas, called *niños*, because the fruit resembles the size and shape of a little boy's penis.

Just inside the bustling indoor market stand huge baskets brimming with fragrant rolls. We buy sweet rolls for breakfast and plain rolls and cheese for our lunch.

Standing in line to buy tickets at the train station are tall, blonde, European students wearing backpacks and hiking boots. They wait next to short, dark, traditionally dressed Indians. Like the Indians, the students are somber, as if preparing for a spiritual journey.

The train lurches and slowly begins its halting ascent over a multitude of switch-backs, changing tracks and directions until we see below us the tall steeples and brown houses of Cuzco. Miniature ceramic churches decorate some of the red tile roofs of the houses we pass, protecting the occupants from evil spirits, from the trains behind them, and from the abyss in front. Tiny Peruvian flags fly above other roofs, positioned between ceramic bulls and condors, the country's national symbols. All that remains in the small gardens are a few dry corn shucks. They will not go to waste; nothing here does.

Oblivious to the passing voyeurs, a man shaves, looking into a broken mirror nailed to the side of his adobe house. A young girl in a torn red dress slops a hog. A woman drapes her laundry on a stone fence. She moves slowly, deliberately, as if she knows she will never be done with this task, that speed cannot help her. How does she get her family's thread-bare clothes so clean? Where does she draw her water, and how far does she have to carry it? As a child I watched my grandmother add blueing to the last rinse in her washing machine to make the clothes white. The machine had a hand wringer into which she fed the dripping clothes, turning the crank with her other strong arm. I wanted to help, but grandma refused, fearing I'd get my fingers caught. Men and women all over the world engage in the same mundane activities; what differs are the tools available to them, and the time required to complete each task.

At the first stop, swarms of women push green onions through the open windows. A young girl, with eyes that tell me she won't eat if I don't buy a knit hat from her, stands behind her mother who sells colorful fabrics. The students lean out the windows to take pictures of a swaddled baby with unruly pitch-black hair and chapped cheeks. He rests, wide-eyed, upon a pile of rags on top of the track used by trains returning from Machu Picchu.

The train follows the course of the Urubamba, the mighty river that runs north to feed the Amazon in Brazil. Forests give way to lush green foliage and spikes of red and yellow flowers.

Rafael takes off his sweater. "The Spanish pursued the last Incas by following this river," he says, standing to put the sweater on the rack above us. Enjoying the sun's warmth, and accommodating my legs so I won't disturb the sleeping, silver-haired, light-skinned man in the seat facing us, I rest my head against the back of the seat and listen.

Pizarro's Spanish rivals, also in search of power and riches, sought Manco II who was trying to preserve the remains of the Inca empire. They found him at Vitcos, an outpost, perhaps, of a deeply hidden city. After feigning loyalty to the Inca, the Spanish killed him and his son. Manco II's brother inherited the title, but he became very sick. The Spanish friar, who had been allowed to remain in Vitcos after the murders, could not cure the brother, so the Indians, distrusting all the Spanish by now, killed the friar.

As retribution, the Spanish viceroy sent a contingent to destroy Tupac Amaru, next-in-line to be Inca. According to oral history, Tupac Amaru did not have the war-like nature needed to defend the empire against the Spanish, having been educated by, and cloistered with, the Virgins of the Sun.

Seeing the hopelessness of his situation, Tupac Amaru fled into the jungle with his pregnant wife. The Spanish finally captured them next to a campfire, near the quiet tributary they had descended by raft. With them was Punchao, the gold idol that contained dust from the hearts of dead Incas, salvaged from the Temple of the Sun in Cuzco.

The Spanish took Tupac Amaru back to Cuzco where they forced the gentle Inca to watch the torture of his wife. Then they mutilated and beheaded him. Although they buried Tupac Amaru's body in the high chapel of the Cathedral, to show their supremacy, the Spanish stuck his head on a pole and displayed it in the plaza for all to see. That evening the plaza resounded with the moans of the Inca's followers.

The Indian people gradually lost the will to defend their land. They were already used to following orders affecting every detail of their lives— where they lived, when and whom they married, the gods they worshiped, when they worked or rested, whether today they would work for the Inca, or for the Sun, or on public works, or even in their own gardens. The authoritarian Spanish took the place of the Inca rulers, but their rule was far more harsh.

Two hundred years later, for leading an uprising against them, the Spanish captured a descendant of Tupac Amaru. The rebel leader, who had chosen his ancestor's name, was drawn and quartered in the Plaza de Armas in Cuzco.

*

The sun's rays reach through the window, glinting off the fine hair on Rafael's golden arms. He is dosing. I think back to the martyrs of the Church—St. Cecilia, St. Lawrence, St. Sebastian—about all the self-sacrificing saints we read about in grade school. I had wondered, then, how long I would last were I burned or gouged. Not very long, I told myself. I was not only interested in the courage of the saints, but also in the torturers themselves. How did they bring themselves to inflict pain on other human beings? How did the Spanish reconcile torture with Christ's message to love the stranger? When I'm sure he's awake, I share these thoughts with Rafael.

"Dear, sweet Lydia, please look out the window and enjoy the beauty of this place. Do not entertain these dark thoughts." He stretches his legs into the aisle to avoid waking the elderly man.

"You're right," I say, taking his hand. "It's just that Peru has so many extremes."

"What do you mean?"

"The rich are not just rich, they're filthy rich, and the poor live in conditions that would kill the average North American. And that's just for starters," I continue, turning to face him. "Take the geography. Look at the way that water pounds the boulders. A person falling into that river wouldn't have a chance. So much water, yet on the coast it never rains. And those mountain peaks make me question my faith. Maybe God doesn't care about our well-being. Maybe after creating us, He leaves us to our own devices. Maybe that's why torturers and tyrants win."

"If this is how you react to the Andes, I'd better not take you to the jungle," Raphael says, amused.

"Since you think I'm so funny, yes, the jungle is another example of the extremes I'm talking about. It entwines and strangles, and, from the pictures I've seen, it looks like it could digest people and places."

"And that is exactly what happened to Vilcapampa, the lost city of the Incas." Rafael draws me to him, and I place my head on his shoulder.

"I thought Machu Picchu was the lost city of the Incas."

"Maybe," says Rafael, pulling in his legs. "Hiram Bingham, thought he had discovered the lost city when he discovered Machu Picchu, but some think it is still out there, deep within the jungle."

I lean into his body. "What do you think?"

"I believe the Spanish never found the lost city of Vilcapampa. They never saw Machu Picchu either."

Rafael explains that those who wrote about that period made no reference to it, not even the writer Garcilaso de la Vega, the well-educated son of an Indian princess and conquistador, who described the Conquest in detail in his *Royal Commentaries*. And the friars, who kept detailed records, wrote only of their attempts to get to a place known as Vilcapampa to convert the heathens there. They referred to Vilcapampa as the "University of Idolatry."

Hundreds of years later, archaeologists naturally thought Machu Picchu was the lost city; it was a perfect refuge, lying between the Apurímac and Urubamba Rivers, located high above a jungle, impenetrable during the rainy season. The city had been built just beneath the peak of Machu Picchu, two thousand feet above the Urubamba River.

I take Rafael's hand and squeeze hard. I am in love with this half-caste doctor, caught up in the grandeur of Incan history, of his history.

Workers had to hang out over the gorge to build the walls that fortify Machu Picchu. The treacherous Urubamba formed the first barrier for potential intruders, and its gorge protected the city on two sides. The back side could only be reached by a narrow ridge that was guarded by men who were skilled at using the *bola,* a sling used to throw stones at rapid speeds with astounding accuracy. Enemies, even those with muskets, would have to contend with the storm of stones pelting down on their heads.

Then there's Huaina Picchu, the precipice that rises on sheer walls of granite to further protect the city. From its summit Indian scouts could signal to those living in the sanctuary the presence of invaders. Anyone foolish enough to scale Huaina Picchu from the river would have to cross a razor-thin ridge, easily defendable by Inca warriors.

Machu Picchu was designed to withstand any assault, but it doesn't appear that one ever took place, at least not by the Spanish, an amazing fact when you consider that it is less than one hundred miles from Cuzco. One false move crossing the Urubamba, and an enemy would have been swept downstream, tossed from boulder to boulder, churned in whirlpools. Because the river is dangerous, even in the dry season, the Indians crossed on rope bridges at its narrowest part. The Spanish would have been terrified to use the bridges that hung sixty feet over the river and swung precariously back and forth.

Bridge keepers, the *chaca camayocs*, given their mission by the Inca himself, kept the bridges repaired. Men who still fill this role are responsible for yearly repairs. Enormous quantities of thin ropes are braided to form the cables that may be as thick as tree trunks. An entire community will participate. If a bridge must be replaced, the men begin by floating small ropes across the river. Holding on to these guide ropes, they haul the heavy cables across and anchor them to rocks that will form the hand and floor rails. To prevent people from falling through the sides of the bridge, short ropes are tied at even intervals between the hand rails and the floor cables. Finally, using branches and twigs, the bridge keepers weave the floor of the bridge. With everyone working, it takes about fourteen hours.

"If there were no bridge," Rafael says, reaching for the water canteen, "people would cross in a basket suspended by rope cables controlled by pulleys. They still cross this way in some places."

"No thanks," I say.

Below us the foaming waters of the Urubamba pound huge gray rocks the size of small houses. I remember the gentle flow of the Menomonee River in Milwaukee. On hot summer days, my friends and I used to bike to the river, taking bag lunches. We would remove our shoes, roll up our pants' legs, and step from one smooth flat stone to another, crossing the river, escaping imaginary bad guys. The sun cast dappled light on our heads and hearts, but before we headed home, we had to remove the dreaded bloodsuckers that clung to the flesh between our toes.

*

At noon, a vendor wends his way down the narrow aisle of the train car, selling sandwiches made of cheese, wilted lettuce, and dry white bread. We offer to share our lunch with the old man.

"I sure appreciate your sharing your food with me," he says. "I'm a little short of cash right now."

"Think nothing of it," says Rafael.

"This is Rafael Serrano, and I'm Lydia Schaefer," I say.

"I'm Norman Kowalski," says the man. "From Manitowoc, Wisconsin. I usta' be a farmer. Glad to meet ya' both. Are youse' married or just good friends?"

"Good friends," I answer, aware of how direct North Americans can be. "I'm from Wisconsin, too. Milwaukee."

"No kiddin! I usta' enter my steers in the Wisconsin State Fair in Milwaukee."

"I used to sell cream puffs in the dairy building at the State Fair." I say. "My grandfather had a stand there every year."

"I remember them cream puffs. Say, they was awful good. Who'd of thought me and you would meet on a train to Machu Picchu!"

He eats juicy orange segments between bites of cheese and bread. "This Peruvian cheese sure ain't like our cheese in Wisconsin—Hey, have you folks been to Iquitos? I just got back, but I didn't much like suckin' oxygen on that plane. We flew right between some of the tallest mountains I ever seen. They was all covered with snow. Looked like you could reach right out and touch em'. I was nervous, I'll tell you, but the pilot was real good."

"What did you do in Iquitos?" I ask.

"You're gonna' have a hard time believin' this, but I went water skiing on one of them tributaries of the Amazon. The people who owned the boat told me there was piranha in the river, but that I didn't have ta' worry unless I cut myself. I was real careful, but I still fell. That water was the color of Coke—you couldn't tell what was underneath. I tried ta' swim back to the boat, but the current was too fast. It swept me downstream. And all the time I'm wondrin' what would happen to my body if the boat don't catch up with me. If the piranha don't get me first, I might wind up in the Atlantic."

"We're glad you returned safely, Señor Kowalski," Rafael says, offering him more cheese.

"Betcha' can't guess how old I am," the old man says, his blue eyes gleaming.

"Sixty-five?" I ask, obliging him. He pats my hand, pleased.

"I'm seventy-eight! And I got a lot a' world ta' see yet. My wife died two years ago, bless her soul, and I'm gonna' see all them places I read about in *National Geographic.* Already been travlin' six months."

"Where are you going after Machu Picchu?" Rafael asks.

"To the Galapagos, if I can get some money transferred from the States. I've always wanted to see them big turtles close up and them blue-footed booby birds."

Two hours after lunch the train pulls into the station that serves the ruins. We wish Norman Kowalski a pleasant visit and board a rickety school bus that will carry us to the ruins, over fifteen harrowing switchbacks.

The gravel road drops straight off on my side of the bus, and I imagine the headline in the *Milwaukee Journal*: Milwaukee's first Peace Corps Volunteer Plummets to Death from Heights of Machu Picchu.

Hiram Bingham, who is credited with discovering Machu Picchu, wrote about the two Indian peasants who had guided him to this site. Wanting to avoid paying taxes to the Peruvian government as well as military conscription, they had secretly lived at Machu Picchu, farming its terraces. Perhaps they had worshiped in the Temple of the Sun, slept in the high priest's dwelling, and bathed in ceremonial fountains, but they never got credit for the discovery, although I suspect Bingham must have offered an enticing reward in exchange for their guide service.

We pay the entrance fees and follow a footpath to the ancient city. Nothing could have prepared me for the visual shock of these ruins, perched like a celestial illusion upon a saddle of land between Machu Picchu and Huaina Picchu.

We walk up chiseled stairs to the Funerary Rock upon which mummies had been prepared for burial or display. Just below the Caretaker's Hut we sit on a small ledge. I feel I've entered another dimension, more of heaven than of earth, and I wish for a photographic memory, one that, upon command, could retrieve every detail. Below us spills the once-hidden city, a warren of roofless rock structures, personal dwellings, sacred sites of worship, and terraces wedged between two daunting peaks. Huaina Picchu's steep eastern-facing slope is furry with shrubs, but its north slope is dark and foreboding, its craggy granite visible.

The one hundred-fifty stone steps we descend are smooth and whale-gray, as if ocean-tumbled. Near the bottom, Rafael points out the ten steps carved from a single rock.

Hiram Bingham thought Machu Picchu's Temple of the Sun might have served as a model for the Temple in Cuzco, making parts of this site nearly one thousand years old. He believed Machu Picchu could also have been the birth place of the first Inca, Manco Capac.

Most of the human remains found at Machu Picchu were female, bodies of the Virgins of the Sun, maybe those who fled Cuzco when the Spanish invaded and first desecrated the Temple there. The bodies might even have been those of the virgins with whom Tupac Amaru, the last Inca, lived.

We sit down on the last step and gaze up at Huaina Picchu. "Is it true that only the Inca and his sons could enter the home of the chosen women?"

"Not exactly," Rafael says. "Inca priests and some nobles were also allowed to enter the *accla-huasi,* their sanctuary."

"Did the Inca sleep with them?"

"I'm not sure, Lydia," he says, smiling, shaking his head in mock surprise. "Each Inca had his own legal wife, who was also his sister, but we do know many of the Incas had illegitimate children."

"Let me see if I have this straight. The Virgins of the Sun were supposed to be married to the Sun, and the Inca was considered the son of the Sun. Wouldn't the Inca have been committing incest by having sex with his father's wives? But then, what the heck, he was already having sex with his sister."

"By having children with his sister, the Inca kept the wealth and control of the empire in the immediate family," Rafael says, leading me to the large plaza that divides the residential section of

Machu Picchu from the religious area. From there we climb to a rock platform commanding a spectacular view of the mountains to the west.

"Those peaks are so high they can also be seen from the Cuzco valley. That one is Salcanty," he says, pointing, "and over there is Soray."

"Salcantay . . . Soray . . . ," I say, drawing out the last syllables. "I love how they sound."

"Were there Indians in your part of the United States, Lydia?"

"Yes, many. In fact, Milwaukee and Wisconsin are both Indian names, and there are many other places with Indian names like Menomonee, Oconomowoc, Waukesha, Minocqua, Mukwonago."

"And the name of the city Señor Kowalski was from?"

"Yes, Manitowoc, too."

"Please don't expect me to pronounce them."

"I won't if you don't expect me to pronounce the Quechua I hear you using."

"They are all related, you know."

"The Indians?"

"Yes, the Indians throughout the Americas."

Above us stands the *Intihuatana*, the Hitching Post of the Sun, carved from a single boulder with a narrow, perpendicular outcropping used to measure the sun's shadow. I run my hands over its smooth angles. The Inca and his priests impressed the people with their divine powers when they performed their ceremonies here.

At the winter solstice, they "caught" the sun, preventing it from moving farther north. The people celebrated the sun's return, but the horrified Spanish would not permit this idolatrous practice. They

smashed the *Intihuatanas* in the Cuzco area. I imagine
a travel advertisement for Machu Picchu:

> "Attention! Jaded tourists! Find refresh-
> ment in an ancient Inca Empire. Tended
> by Virgins of the Sun, you will have breath-
> taking views, unforgettable sunsets, *chicha*
> cocktails served at the Intihuatana Plaza,
> where, on the winter solstice, the Inca will
> tether the sun. At sunrise you will drink
> *café con leche* outside the Caretaker's Hut,
> and your eyes will feast upon the ruins
> bathed in ethereal pink clouds."

*

The sun ignites the western sky, and a nippy wind
blows. Already most of the tourists, those not
spending the night in the small, State-owned hotel,
have hurried to catch the last departing bus and train.

"*Vamos, amor*," Rafael says. "I have more to show
you before we settle down for the night."

We walk down the terraces and cross the sacred
plaza to an area lined with small, roofless houses with
trapezoidal doors and windows. Here the stonework
is more rustic, and adobe appears to have been used
to hold the stones in place.

"Is this were the common people lived?" I ask.

"I think so, although it might also have been the
place where business was conducted. I think there is
even a jail here."

"I'm a run-away Virgin of the Sun," I shout, taking
a foot path between the stone houses, dodging in
and out of doorways.

"Lydia, where are you? I'm the Inca, and I'm going to find you," Raphael calls in a sing-song voice. "When I find you, I'm going to have my way with you."

"Then I surrender," I say emerging from the maze. "Your wish is my command."

I pull him to me. I want to consume him; I want, just once, to drop all restraints. Then, a guard blows his whistle. All visitors must leave the ruins.

We watch the tourists depart and wait till nightfall to cross the plaza. Rafael nudges me into the ruins of a house with a thatch roof. In the dwindling light, I see that some of the stones are rectangular, others polygonal, but all fit against each other without mortar. The entire front wall has been made from one boulder, and four niches have been carved on its inside surface. I sit on a long stone bench opposite the door.

"We'll spend the night here," Rafael says, unpacking our gear.

"Who lived here?" I ask, assembling our food.

"A high priest, perhaps, given the workmanship, but the bench and the niches make me think it might have been the room where the mummies of Inca royalty were displayed."

"Ummmm," I say, getting up, imagining a neat row of little mummy bundles, like a collection of antique, porcelain dolls.

When it's too dark for the guard to see the smoke, Rafael makes a small fire, and we prepare dehydrated soup, eating the rest of our bread and cheese, saving our fruit for breakfast. Unable to get comfortable on the mummy slab, I join Rafael on the ground, and we sleep bundled in the extra clothes we carry with us.

I dream I'm in a hotel room, frantically preparing for a trip. When I open the door to the closet, the suitcases tumble down on me. I can't stuff things into them fast enough. My good friend Susan is with me, but she's packed and organized. A bus driver leans on the horn, and volunteers board the bus. It leaves without me.

XIII

To Pachabuena

If the true autonomy of the Indian were to
dawn one day, through the gospel of Jesus,
we would witness the renewed evolution of
an oppressed and humiliated race.

Clorinda Matto de Turner, *Aves sin nido,*
1889

"*L*YDIA, *despiértate,*" says Rafael, heating water
for coca tea in the faint light of dawn. I stretch,
loosening the kinks from the night on the damp
ground and go outside to pee, envious on this cold
morning of the ease with which men handle this
business.

Nearby is a fountain with icy water pouring from
three spouts. As I splash it on my face, I feel

connected to the women who centuries ago stood in this exact spot to gather water.

"I see you found the fountain," says Rafael, yawning and smiling at the same time. His hair is ruffled from sleep, but he has no morning stubble. He is unconscious of his good looks.

"The water was too cold to bathe, but it sure woke me up."

"Don't worry about bathing now. There is a surprise later."

We eat fruit, drink tea, and pack. In the gathering pink light we climb to the Hitching Post of the Sun. Snow shimmers on the mountains to the west.

"*¿Lista, Lydia?* We have a long day ahead of us."

"Ready," I reply.

After climbing to the Caretaker's Hut, we look back at Huaina Picchu, the jagged "young peak." Then Rafael takes the narrow trail on the south side of Machu Picchu, the "old peak." Crossing terraces still planted in maize, sweet and white potatoes, broad beans, and peppers, we begin our ascent through moist clouds. I hug the granite cliff, aware of the cloud forest tumbling luxuriously below us.

The clouds lift when we reach Intipunku, the Gate of the Sun, where we turn to gaze back at the now-golden ruins. It would not seem strange for the Inca to emerge from his dwelling of fitted rocks, wearing a plumed head-dress and a silver shield on his chest. His ear lobes, stretched by heavy gold bodkins, would rest upon his shoulders, and he would carry a gold shield in one hand and a gold spear in the other. The garters on his legs would be decorated with feathers and tiny wooden bells.

After three hours, we reach Huiñay Huayna, a poor, weathered village. Rafael approaches a stooped Indian woman who is leading a goat by one hand and a dirty little girl by the other. He asks where we might find food and explains he is returning to Pachabuena, the place of his birth.

Squinting from under her battered fedora, she gives Raphael a toothless smile. She examines me and beckons us to follow. We pass mud-brick houses, shielded from the dirt road by a rock wall, and enter a courtyard where several children play in the red soil. They wear tattered clothes. Their bare feet are like hooves, and their globe-like cheeks are red and cracked from the dry cold. Given the travel photographs I've seen, it would be difficult to distinguish them from children in Nepal or Tibet.

In her hut, a large blackened pot of potatoes boils on a fire fueled with llama dung. I feel something brush against my foot and jump.

"Don't be afraid, Lydia, it's only a *cuy*," says Rafael, steadying me with his hand on my arm.

I look down at the floor, my eyes adjusting to the darkness. Andeans don't like windows because they let in the *serena*, the dew-laden night air they believe to be harmful.

The woman chases and catches one of the guinea pigs scurrying over the floor. It squeals as she carries it to the courtyard. I don't watch the kill, and I don't watch her skin and clean it. So much for my Cornell training.

After cutting the meat into chunks, she adds it to the pot of potatoes, also throwing in yucca, red peppers, salt, and cilantro. Stirring the pot, she sings a Quechua tune in a whiny, child-like voice. I ask Rafael to translate.

"It comes from a carnival song," he says. "For three days, before the start of Lent, people forget their troubles by singing, dancing, and drinking a lot of *chicha*. Many of their songs deal with love—and with sex," he says, squeezing my hand.

> Remember little dove,
> how there, in the path,
> under the stems of the *ichu*,
> we would cover ourselves?
>
> Little white dove,
> flying in the *llano*,
> once you tried it,
> you wanted it ten more times.
>
> Little white dove,
> what a hard heart you have.
> Seeing I adore you,
> you make me cry.
>
> Tiny pebble,
> from the river bed,
> after that *cholita*
> I will scurry.
>
> What do those girls want,
> standing on the corner?
> Baby seeds?
> I have them; let them buy.
>
> You say yes,
> I say no.
> So, just keep those desires
> to yourself.

The woman covers the pot and whispers to Rafael. "She wants to know where our children are," he explains. We enter the bright courtyard in front of the hut and sit down on two crude stools.

"What did you say?"

"I said we are still waiting. I don't want to complicate things."

"What did she say to that?"

"She says she will pray that very soon you have a strong baby boy."

Although she is probably no more than ten years older than I, she has already lost most of her teeth, and her skin looks like it would crack and bleed from the slightest caress. There are no creams, no dentist, no tooth paste, no doctor.

"Is she married?" I ask.

"Probably not in the way you mean, Lydia. She may live with a man, although it is possible she was married religiously as well as civilly. There are times when the priests and civil authorities get all of the unmarried couples together to perform both ceremonies."

"Then a ceremony is not important to the women?"

"Some are recognizing that they have no rights unless they are formally married. They also learn that their children have no rights either. Although a women may keep the property she has inherited from her mother, she does join the husband's household, and it is only the legitimate son who inherits land from the father."

"What happens if the husband dies?"

"The woman may return to her own clan, to her *ayllu*."

"It's not considered wrong to sleep together before marriage?"

"On the contrary, it's natural. It's not as if young people sleep with many different partners; it's more like a trial marriage, and sex and children are a normal part of that relationship."

I wipe my forehead with a dirty arm, and Rafael takes out his handkerchief to wipe a smudge from my face. "And if the man abandons the woman after she's pregnant?" I ask.

"I have never known a woman who asked as many questions as you, Lydia. Well, the woman is in a bad situation because another man will not want to assume responsibility for her children. It's especially difficult if her family is far away. It will be hard for her to feed her children because people here depend upon each other to get work done, and men trade their labor," Rafael says, making designs in the dirt with a stick.

"A single woman," he says, looking up at me, "although knowing how to weave and cook, is not in the position to exchange plowing services, for example, a job that is always done by men, because it takes great physical strength."

"She would live a hand-to-mouth existence."

"Absolutely, unless she had grown sons who would assume the labor exchange. Now you see why these families want to have sons." I sigh at the unfairness of it all.

The little girl whom the Indian woman was leading on the path stands at a polite distance. She is pretty in a ragamuffin way. "*Ven, ven,*" I say to the child, gesturing for her to join us. "*¿Cómo te llamas? ¿Cuántos años tienes?*"

"*Me llamo Lucia*," she says, holding up five fingers to tell her age.

"*Lucia, ¡qué nombre bonito!*" I say. "Look, I have something for you." I take out a small notebook and ball point pen from my pack. She shyly takes her gifts. Then she touches my face and hair and asks my name. I write it in the notebook. She studies the letters, taking the syllables apart. "Ly-di-ah," she says softly. Then I show her how to print her name.

Her mother fills tin plates and brings them to us in the courtyard. I turn aside to wipe the spoon on my shirt. The stew has a gamey smell, but it satisfies our hunger, and everything was boiled, so we shouldn't get sick.

We thank the woman for her hospitality. Rafael offers money, but she won't accept it. As we walk back to the trail, we hear her high-pitched song:

> Look, look at those two,
> at what they are doing.
> Don't they know that is how
> crying babies are made?

We turn around and wave goodbye to Lucia and her mother. "What does the name of their village mean?" I ask.

"*Huiñay* comes from the words, 'to plant the earth,' and *Huayna* can mean 'young' or 'small.' The words together tell us to keep the earth young by planting it."

"People who live here are poor and cut-off from the outside world, yet they are very poetic."

"We all need poetry in our lives, Lydia." Yes, Rafael, you are my poetry.

At a barely visible fork, Rafael chooses the overgrown path, deftly bending or breaking the brush as he walks by so it won't snap back at me. We come to a steep flight of narrow steps.

"This is a short-cut, but it's very steep. Please be careful," he says.

There are hundreds of steps. After the first twenty, I hear my heart pounding in my ears. I try to breathe deeply, but chains seem to bind my chest. We rest for five minutes, Rafael sitting on a stone two steps above me.

"You are doing fine," he says, supporting my head with his knees.

"Then why do I feel as if my heart is going to explode?"

"We will be at Phuyupatamarca soon, and then we can rest again."

"Phooyoowhat?"

"It means 'village above the clouds.'"

"In other words, we keep climbing."

"Yes, but from there it is only a little further to the pass, and then it is downhill to Pachabuena."

Continuing upward toward the pass, my lungs protest, wanting to burst from my chest. I collapse on the mossy ground when we reach the top. A cloud obscures our view of the valley below us, but soon the sun opens a narrow window, permitting a glimpse of the emerald land and a glistening river. "Is Pachabuena in that valley?" I ask.

"Yes, but before we descend, I want to show you the surprise I promised this morning."

I hear water and walk toward the steam rising from the ground. Hot, sulphurous water pours down a turquoise, mineral-encrusted channel to a small pool. I bend to touch the water.

"¡*Cuidado! Lydia*, it's very hot," Rafael warns. "Come over here to this pool where cold water mixes with the hot."

We undress and slip into the pool. "You are very beautiful, Lydia," Rafael says. "You look like an Inca *coya*."

"A shy queen," I say.

The bath is narrow and deep. We rest our heads on the stone ledge and let our bodies bob in the steaming, bubbling water. I have never been further from Milwaukee.

Refreshed and relaxed, we climb out and recline on top of our clothes. My drying body prickles in the sun. I roll on my side to look at Rafael who appears to be sleeping, his hands cradling his head. The skin on the inside of his arms is a smooth, olive color, and he has very little hair under his arms. The bones of his chest are outlined under tightly drawn, copper skin. My eyes travel upward from his finely shaped toes to the soft pouches that hold his seed and the penis that rests on his thigh. The arrangement looks vulnerable, caressable, not menacing, as my cousin's of many years ago. Nor does it offend like the sight of the little man who had exposed himself a year ago in Ica.

"What do you see?" Rafael asks, moving languorously, squinting out of one eye.

"A very handsome man," I say.

"And you, *mi amor*, have breasts that speak to me of the harvest," he says, turning toward me. "They are cream-colored like the wheat. They are like small, firm bundles of straw. Your nipples remind me of mountain peaks, dark, pointed, challenging any man who would try to conquer them."

"You're making fun of me."

"No, Lydia, but I am trying to sound like Pablo Neruda, my favorite poet. I cannot, however, achieve his eloquence."

Raphael's kiss is moist and sweet, and as he eases on top of me, it becomes more familiar, more urgent. The air is fresh and fragrant, and a light breeze glances off our warm bodies. I look up at blinding white clouds and reach my arms out to them. We remain immobile for a few minutes and then slowly rock. A condor soars overhead. I have read of eagles mating in mid-air, free falling, unaware of the doom below. It was like that.

*

"Now you are my wife," Rafael says, again on his back, utterly relaxed, "as is the custom here." There is warm affection in his voice but no trace of humor.

"A common-law marriage for a good Catholic girl? I'll have to think about that," I say, turning toward him. "—Rafael, I saw a condor while we were making love."

"I know."

"I've never seen one before."

"It was a happy omen."

"I saw its shadow on the rocks before I saw the bird."

"They come magically, unexpectedly, riding air currents from below."

"It didn't flap its wings; it dipped them in graceful arcs. It was black with a white ring around its head."

"Some condors live for fifty years. I hope we have fifty years, Lydia."

"What are those red flowers?" I ask, pointing to the rocks above us?

"That is the *pisonay*. The Indians here believe that flower also grows on the sun, where they are much bigger than here on earth—but why do you change the subject?"

"Rafael, the way you're talking to me now makes me very happy and very confused. I don't want to ruin this moment by saying the wrong thing."

We drink from the cold water canal and climb through to the pass before beginning our descent. The foliage becomes more luxuriant; there are ferns and orchids, and as we near the bottom of the trail, we hear the Aobamba River.

"It's not much further. We will be there by nightfall," says Rafael.

A man, bent over by the large bundle of straw he carries, approaches us on the trail. "*Qampas hinallataq*," he says, and Rafael answers him in Quechua.

"What did he say? What did you say?"

"He said, 'do not lie, do not steal, do not be lazy,' and I said, 'to thee likewise.'"

"That's a strange greeting."

"It's really a beautiful, ancient Quechua greeting, Lydia. It conveys the values of our people."

"I'm sorry. It is beautiful." I can only imagine the reaction I would get if I greeted a stranger that way in the United States.

XIV

Pachabuena

I had to leave my mother and my home
to go in pursuit of you.
"Perhaps," I said, upon seeing her hut,
"I shall find my fortune here."

From "Colección tierra firme," *La poesía
quechua,* translated into Spanish by Jesús
Lara, 1947

THE bottom land beside the Aobamba River is dark
and fertile. Men and women are planting corn in
the diminishing light. Five men walk backward in a
precise line, making holes in the soil with *chaqui
tacllas,* their pointed foot plows; five women, like
dance partners with mud-caked hems, face the men
in another line. They walk forward, bending
rhythmically, placing seeds in the holes their partners

have dug, in a timeless ritual that gives reproductive power to women.

"It looks like a ballet," I say.

"Andean men and women have been planting like this for centuries," Rafael says, hurrying his steps. "Male and female labor is complementary. They depend upon each other; there's no confusion over who does what job. It's a system that would be hard to change. Even their gods have different functions."

Rafael explains that while men will occasionally worship Pachamama, when it's time to plant the corn, it is the women who usually pray to her. Men have their own gods like Illapa, the god of thunder. The early priests forced these practices underground, but it wasn't clear to the Indians why a rock, for example, shaped like the head of a person, could not be an *apu*, a physical form of a spirit god, when bread and water were turned into the Body and Blood of Christ at Mass.

As we pass, the farmers look up from their work and recognize Rafael. Faces that were expressionless register delight. Rafael makes the rounds, clamping each man on the back in the male *abrazo*, calling each by name. The women bunch around Rafael but eye me suspiciously. With their heavy skirts, concealing bodies stretched to accommodate many babies, they don't appear to have waists.

Rafael hastens me to a whitewashed house where a woman is staking gladioli lining the path to her door. "¡*Mamá*!" Rafael shouts, running to her. Tears well in her eyes. "¡*Rafael, mi hijo, gracias a Dios!*" She kisses his face many times. I am intruding.

"*Mamá*, I want you to meet Lydia," Rafael says, slowly releasing his mother.

Wiping the tears from her cheeks with the back of her hand, she moves toward me, also receiving me with an *abrazo*. "*Mucho gusto doña Teresa*," I say.

"*Bienvenida, Lydia. Adelante, por favor,*" she says, taking me by the hand, leading me through the door. "The two of you must be hungry. Let me bring you something to eat."

"*No, mamá,* just some water," says Rafael. "Later, we will all eat together. Now I want to hear about you and father. Where is he?"

"*Siéntese, por favor, Lydia,*" she says, pointing to a chair. "Your father," she says, turning to Rafael, "is visiting a woman who will soon have a baby, but she is very weak and has already many children. Your father does not think she is strong enough to have another.—But now is the time to celebrate. Our son—a doctor—has returned home. How long have I waited for this day!"

"Will we see Dr. Miguel tonight?" I ask.

"Yes, Lydia, he will be home for dinner."

Rafael's mother is about five feet-seven inches, taller than most Indian women, and in her late forties. Years of physical labor have honed her body to a perfect balance between flesh and bone; her arms are tan and muscular. She wears a slim, dark skirt and a white blouse. There are silvery strands in the glossy black hair braided and coiled on her head.

While his mother pours water, Rafael reaches for one of the orange and green fruits in a bowl on the table. He breaks open a *tuna,* the fruit of the cactus flower, offering a sweet, fleshy section to me.

What does Doña Teresa think about my presence here? She must see the way I look at her son, at his black eyes and perfect lips, and she must know we are lovers. After so long a separation, she could not want this reunion diluted by the presence of another woman.

"*Mamá*, how have you been? I have not had a letter from you for many weeks. I was worried," says Rafael.

"Do not worry, son. I have good health, thank God, but I am worried about your father. He works too much and sees many patients, traveling by himself to distant villages. My heart is grateful that you are here to help him."

The Spanish-style house is of modest size. The inside walls are white, and dark wood beams support the roof. A single yellow rose in a small vase is on the window sill, and a wrought-iron cross hangs above the hearth. Although two worn upholstered chairs are near the fireplace, the rest of the room is sparsely furnished. Books line the wall opposite the fireplace. An open door leads to an inner courtyard and laundry area.

Many of the medical works have English titles, but Peruvian literature abounds, including books on the history and traditions of Peru by Ricardo Palma and the poetry of the radical—or so we were told—César Vallejo.

"Rafael, perhaps you should take Lydia to your room," says Doña Teresa, a little more formally than I'd like. "She can bathe and rest before your father returns."

On the way to his room, Rafael shows me the immaculate three-bed infirmary. His father's consultation room adjoins the infirmary and has its own entrance from the street.

Rafael's room is small and neat. An alpaca rug covers the wood floor, and an alpaca blanket covers the bed. On the walls are photographs of Rafael taken in Lima, Spain, and at San Luis Gonzaga University in Ica. A soccer ball decorates an alcove.

"Your parents don't mind my sharing this room with you?" I ask, settling down on the bed.

Rafael sits beside me. "*No, mi amor.* I have already whispered to mother how strongly I feel about you. Please don't worry. Love happened to them the same way it is happening to us. Of course, they will want us to get married. Both of my parents are religious, and I know yours are, too. Also, our children must be legitimate in the eyes of the State."

"Then you weren't teasing about marrying me after we made love?"

"No, Lydia, I absolutely want to marry you, if you will have this half-breed doctor."

I walk to the small window and watch his mother cutting yellow roses in the courtyard. "You have made me very happy, Rafael. I want to say yes, but I'm afraid there are too many obstacles."

"None we can't overcome, Lydia," Rafael says, joining me, putting his arms around my waist. "I'm so afraid that once you leave here, you will cling to your own life, to your family and friends. Do you remember when you told me that you wanted to marry someone who shared your ideals? I am that man."

"But I'm surprised that someone with your background would act so impetuously," I say, turning to face him.

"Someone with my background is frequently called upon to make life and death decisions without much time for reflection."

"Is that what this proposal means to you? A life and death decision?"

"I could be a romantic and say that, yes, I will die if you don't marry me, but I know that won't happen. Yet, marriage to you would bring such joy to my life that, by comparison, without you, I might as well be dead."

"But you're no fool, Rafael," I say, leaving his arms, walking toward the bed where I empty my knapsack. "What chance do we have of making a marriage work? We come from different worlds, and I want to return to mine, to my family. If you place yourself in my position, you would understand how sad your parents would be if you moved to the United States, if you had children there—grandchildren they'd rarely see."

He studies a family photo on the chest of drawers. "I know it would be a big sacrifice for you and them."

"We've had so little time together, Rafael. We hardly know one another," I say, putting my brush and comb on the chest.

"Perhaps, but I do know you well enough to trust your basic goodness, to know you would never intentionally hurt anyone, especially your husband."

"And then there's the question of religion. I don't know what you really think about it, or how you would react if I insisted on bringing our children up Catholic. Getting married in the Church, in a ceremony your parents approve of, and actually raising our children Catholic are two different things."

"Lydia, believe me, I am familiar with the Catholic education you have been given," he says, sitting down on the bed, "but what do you really know about my spiritual side?"

"That's just it. I don't know much, except that you love your neighbor in a way few do."

"And is that not what we're called to do?"

"You've turned the question around. I know you love your neighbor, but you don't seem to believe in the Catholic Church. Yes, you appreciate certain traditions for their beauty or history, like a rich cultural practice, but you disdain others. Although I'm uncertain about some teachings, I was brought up Catholic, and I would want our children to be Catholic and not just in name only."

"What does the word 'catholic' mean to you, Lydia?"

"Universal."

"Then I am Catholic. I believe in the dignity of all people. I believe conditions that diminish the dignity of any human being also diminish my own dignity."

"Like John Donne."

"Yes, I share in the destiny of the poor. We all do, whether we realize it or not. I believe in Christ's command to love, but this message is frequently lost in an effort to preserve dogma and ritual in a Church out of touch with the people it claims as its own."

"But the Church is changing, Rafael. Priests are living and working among the poor, sharing their poverty."

"Yes, there have been many positive changes. I have met some of these priests, and they are much-loved by the people. Still, they are men who live without women. How can they understand the troubles of husbands and wives?"

"I can't talk about this any more," I say, standing up. "I'm tired and I need to clean up and rest. My head is spinning."

"I'm sorry, Lydia. I have given you too much to think about, and we have just arrived. Come, I'll show you where we get our water."

A pipe captures the water that flows from a spring behind the house and carries it to a cement trough in a rustic little hut next to the main house. The frigid water circulates around the perishable food that sits on steps of varying heights in the trough. You control the flow of water by turning the knob at the head of the spring race, and when the standpipe in the deepest part is removed, the water drains into the garden. Rafael fills two pitchers, pours the water into a kettle, and heats it over a wood hearth.

"I hope a sponge bath will do," he says. "We have a cistern that collects rain water for showers, but it must be empty now because we are at the end of the dry season."

"I've had a lot of practice with sponge baths."

"You go first, *mi amor*, I will be in our room."

Exhausted but clean, we sleep until Doña Teresa knocks on the door and calls us to dinner.

*

"I'm nervous about meeting your father," I say, sitting up in Rafael's small bed.

"*No te preocupes*. He will love you," Rafael says, stroking my hair.

I brush my hair into a ponytail, put on my wraparound skirt and a red sweater, and look out the window. An armed guard, wearing a disheveled khaki uniform, is leaning against the house across the narrow dirt road. After throwing his cigarette butt in the gutter, he looks up at our window and sees me through the straight black hair that covers his eyes. I call Rafael to the window. Although he frowns, he dismisses the guard's presence.

*

Dr. Miguel Serrano sits before the fireplace with a book in his lap. "*¡Papá!*" says Rafael, going to his father.

"*¡Mi hijo!*" Dr. Miguel rises to embrace his son and holds him as if part of his own body has been returned to him. His eyes closed, the doctor seems to be offering a prayer of thanksgiving.

"*Papá*, I want you to meet Lydia, *mi enamorada*," Rafael says.

"*Encantado, Lydia.*" Dr. Miguel takes my hand in his and gently pulls me toward him, kissing me on the cheek.

"*Encantada, doctor Miguel*," I say, looking into his friendly blue eyes. He is shorter and a little heavier than Rafael and has wavy white hair.

Drawing up two more chairs from the dining room table, he gestures for us to join him. Doña Teresa enters, carrying a tray with glasses of *chicha*.

"Well, children," the doctor says, "you have not told us yet, but do we have a little *covivencia* here?"

"Miguel—*por Dios*—you are being rude. We have just met Lydia," says Doña Teresa.

"It's all right, *mamá* . . . *Sí, papá*, we are living the way the two of you first lived, before you saw the priest and the civil authorities. The religious ceremony will follow for us, too, if Lydia says yes."

"Excuse me," I say, "what is this *covivencia*?"

"It is the word," Doña Teresa answers, "used when a man and woman live as husband and wife without the blessing of the Church and without recognition from the State. Now if you will excuse me, Lydia, I must get dinner."

"May I help?"

"No, Lydia, thank you. Today you do not help. I want my husband to get to know you. We all have much to learn about each other."

Taking his wife's cue, Dr. Miguel directs his questions to me: Are my parents Catholic? How did they feel about my going away for two years? If Rafael and I marry, would I have to return to Ica? When would I return to Pachabuena? Do I want children? Could I give up the United States? Would I work with Rafael?

Rafael breaks in, "*Papá, por favor*, Lydia is tired, and she has not yet agreed to marry me."

"No, it's all right, Rafael. I want to answer your father. My father would do exactly the same if the situation were reversed. I don't have a medical degree, Dr. Miguel, but I've assisted Rafael for a few months at the clinic in Ica, and we work well together."

"*Ah, bueno.* Then you would work with him, at least until the babies come, yes?"

"*La comida está servida*," Doña Teresa announces, bringing steaming dishes to the table, assisted by a dour, young Indian woman who doesn't look at me. Doña Teresa introduces Saturnina as one of the family, but Saturnina doesn't act like family when, serving Rafael, she brushes her breasts against his shoulder.

There's stewed chicken with white potatoes and tender orange sweet potatoes, a corn pudding, and bowls of fava beans and *quinua*.

"You're a good cook, Doña Teresa," I say.

"Soon, perhaps, you will call me *mamá*, but I am old-fashioned; we will wait for that until you are married in the Church."

"When will the priest come next, *mamá?*" asks Rafael.

"If the rains hold off, Padre Martín should arrive Saturday afternoon to celebrate evening Mass. As is his custom, he will leave for Sacotambo at dawn on Sunday."

"Please—Doña Teresa—Dr. Miguel," I say. "I need to tell you something. You have been gracious to me. Thank you. I am honored that your son wants to marry me, but he is 'jumping the gun,' as we say in the United States. I need time to think about it, and we do have time, Rafael," I say, putting my hand on his.

Dr. Miguel handles his utensils with the deliberate care of a surgeon. His hands are large and carefully manicured, like the hands of the cello player painted by Rivas Peña. "I understand, Lydia. I, too, would be happy if you and Rafael would wait, and I think my wife feels the same. All his life Rafael has been impulsive, but I must say, he has made good decisions so far, and I like his choice in women, too," he says, grinning at me.

"My husband is right, Lydia," Doña Teresa says, leaning forward with her elbows on the table, with just a bit of cleavage showing above her white, scooped-neck blouse, "when he says I would prefer that you and Rafael wait, but I understand Rafael. Having lived away, he knows how different are the worlds you come from, but he has already become a part of your world. Although he has been gone a long time, I know my son. There are no women here for him. Perhaps he is being selfish. He believes that if you marry him now, you must return to Pachabuena."

"—Excuse me for interrupting," Rafael says, abruptly standing up and looking out the window, "but why does a guard stand across the street from our house?"

Deep lines appear between Dr. Miguel's eyebrows, and he takes a drink of *chicha* before responding. "The political situation in the mountains has worsened since you went away to study, Rafael. There is much unrest among the *campesinos*; they now follow a man named Diego Torrente."

"We have heard of him," says Rafael. "The army considers him a Communist, but most of the university students I knew in Lima worshiped him, and Guillermo and Gloria also talked about him when we stayed with them in Cuzco."

"Torrente," Dr. Miguel continues, "has taken refuge in this area. The Guardia Civil watches our house because the authorities think he may be injured, and that he may come here for medical help. I did not want to worry you and Lydia."

"Why are they so afraid of Torrente?" I ask.

"Because Torrente wants to return the land to the people," Dr. Miguel says, propping his legs on a stool. "And land is wealth in Peru. Without it you have nothing to leave your children; you are dependent on others for food; you have no prestige in your community. True, there are communal lands that one may work, but it is not the same, and the powerful *hacendados* are taking those lands away, too. They know they are wrong, but they do not want to be reminded by a rebel, and they do not want to give up the land that is the source of their wealth."

"If that's the case, the struggle may never end," I say.

"Remember, Lydia," Dr. Miguel says, wrapping his sweater about him, "famine was unknown before the Spanish came. A Peruvian Indian could never hope to better his position, but he would never go hungry, not like today."

"We see many malnourished people in our clinic in Ica," I say.

"Exactly," says Dr. Miguel, "and now, rebel groups led by Torrente have seized the large estates owned by *hacendados* whose only claim to the land is a fraudulent title, given by a Spanish king hundreds of years ago. The *hacendados* say the land is rightfully theirs because it has been passed down from generation to generation. The poor people fear the land owners because they exercise influence over the Guardia Civil, so much influence that the Guardia recently suspended civil rights in this area."

"But," I say, "I thought President Belaúnde wanted to change land ownership patterns."

"He does," says Dr. Miguel, "but these things do not change overnight. If only the *campesinos* had waited."

"Waited for what, *papá?*" asks Rafael.

"Shortly after President Belaúnde's inauguration, about three hundred *campesinos* from all over the region invaded the estate of Don Ignacio Santander. But Don Ignacio had been warned; he had his private army ready. Unfortunately, the *campesinos*, with only hoes for weapons, did not have a chance. Don Ignacio's guards killed eighteen of them, and now the Guardia will not rest until they catch Torrente, whom they call the 'intellectual leader' of the rebellion."

"It is very sad," says Doña Teresa. "The Guardia do not respect the rights of the poor people; they break into their homes and drag out the young men, forcing some into the military; others are never seen again. So far we have been lucky in our village, but women are afraid because they might lose their husbands and sons, and young women are not safe either; the Guardia think it is their right to rape them."

"It seems incredible that such things could be happening today," I say.

"Lydia," Dr. Miguel says, "the people here are poor. They have no power, and the mountains and rivers cut them off from the outside world. People in Lima do not know what happens here, and I don't think they would care if they did know."

Saturnina clears the table and serves coca tea. Dr. Miguel asks Rafael to put more wood on the fire.

"Thank you, Doña Teresa; thank you, Saturnina; that was a delicious meal," I say.

"You are welcome, *hija*," Doña Teresa says. With all my ambivalence about joining this family, I still like that she has called me "daughter."

"*Bueno, Rafael*," Dr. Miguel says, "when will you begin to work with me?"

"As soon as possible, *papá*, but I would like to spend some time with Lydia, too. Perhaps she can work with us."

"Of course. I must visit a woman tomorrow who is about to deliver her sixth child, but she has already lost two babies, and I am worried about her."

"I would love to go with you, if you don't think I'll be in the way," I say.

"In the way? Never," says Dr. Miguel.

"Now you both go to bed," says Doña Teresa. "Your father and I have much to discuss."

Before we fall asleep, I ask Rafael to tell me about Saturnina. "She looks at you in a very possessive way, and she doesn't seem to appreciate my presence here," I say.

"Saturnina has been in the family a long time, Lydia. She came to us when she was eight years old, after her parents died of tuberculosis. She had been a serious child, melancholic, so they named her for the early evening, when the sun sets and darkness descends, the time, according to local myths, when 'the sun swims under the earth.'"

"She doesn't act melancholic when she's around you."

"That is because she is in love with me, and she does not want you to have me."

"I've just learned something else about you, Rafael," I say, kissing him soundly. "You have a good opinion of yourself."

"*Duerme con los angelitos, mi amor,*" he says. Yes, thank you, Lord, I am sleeping with one of your angels tonight.

XV

Life and Death

From now on, my country will be
Humanity.

Flora Tristán, *Pérégrinations d'une paria,*
1837

TRYING not to wake Rafael, I slip out of bed, dress, and go outside. Against a sky the color of the Virgin's veil, cumulus clouds, like a regatta of sailing ships, course over Pachabuena. Farmers are walking to their fields, their breath visible in the clean, cold air. Apart from Rafael and his parents, few inhabitants of the valley have ever left their birthplace.

Shivering, I return to the house, grateful that Saturnina has brought warm bread and *café con leche* to the table. The sun pours through the windows, dousing the room in yellow light.

"*Buenos días, mi amor*," Rafael says, entering the dining room, stifling a yawn. "I saw you outside, deep in thought, but I did not want to disturb you."

"¡*Doctor Miguel! ¡Doctor Miguel! ¡Venga!*" A man wearing Andean knickers, a poncho, and a *chullo* over his head and ears, shouts outside the window.

Dr. Miguel runs to open the door. "¿*Qué pasó?*"

"Enrique Chuspi—He is bleeding!" shouts the man.

"Where is he?"

"On the path from Sacotambo. He was returning from the market and was attacked."

"Quick, Rafael, we must go to him!" says Dr. Miguel. "Teresa, *mi vida*, please take Lydia with you to visit Amparo. Do you know where she lives?"

"*Claro qué sí mi amor*, I know where Amparo lives. Lydia and I will take good care of her, but you and Rafael must be careful. Please watch out for the Guardia."

The spouses kiss before Dr. Miguel and Rafael run out the back of the house. Rafael saddles an old horse and helps his father mount before swinging up behind him. As they take the dirt road toward Sacotambo, I say a prayer for their safety.

"Lydia," says Doña Teresa, "as soon as you finish your breakfast, we must go to Amparo. It is a long walk, and we may need to spend the night."

After gulping down my coffee, I return to my room to get a change of underwear and socks and grab my toothbrush. Doña Teresa has changed into slacks. Her braids, tied together at the ends with a bit of red ribbon, fall to the middle of her back.

Saturnina gives us food for the trip, and Doña Teresa carries a small leather bag, explaining that *parteras* usually attend women giving birth in this region. Although the midwives are experienced, their hygiene is often lax, and complicated births frequently result in the baby's death or in the death of the mother from hemorrhage.

Dr. Miguel has worked hard to teach pregnant women and midwives that evil spirits don't take newborns from their mothers, but tetanus infections do, caused by dirty scissors or razor blades used to cut the cord. Andean women call the infection the *mal de los siete días* because the infection causes the children to die when they are seven days old.

"Do you think the baby will come while we're there?" I ask.

"My biggest fear, Lydia, is that the baby will come before we arrive. Amparo lost her last baby less than a year ago. She has had her children too close together, and her body did not have time to recover between pregnancies. If she has complications, like a breech birth, or if she hemorrhages, I am afraid both mother and baby will die."

"Do we have everything we need?"

"Yes, everything, considering the circumstances. Dr. Miguel gave instructions to Amparo and her husband the last time he visited, hoping all would be ready when he returned."

"And if there are complications?"

"We pray. That is what people do here; there is nothing else."

We follow a path along the river's edge. Looking up at the mountains, I see a condor soaring and remember my first, sweet union with Rafael.

"What made those openings in the mountain side?" I ask, pointing to small excavations high above us.

"They are *colcas*. My ancestors used to store their

crops in those caves to keep them safe from animals. Do you see the gray mounds next to them?"

"Yes," I say, shielding my eyes from the sun.

"They are tombs with mummies buried inside."

"People went to a lot of trouble to bury their dead."

"It had to be done properly because it was a family's responsibility to insure that the dead would enjoy a happy afterlife, and that the animals would not get to the bodies."

After walking a long time in silence, I bring up a topic that has been troubling me. "Doña Teresa, I hope I don't offend you, but why don't couples like Amparo and her husband use birth control?"

She smiles patiently and sighs. "Lydia, I have often asked myself the same question, and I will be happy to share my thinking with you."

"Being a Catholic, I know the Church opposes contraception, and, until coming here, I unthinkingly accepted that position, but now, after working at the clinic, I can't believe it's wrong to use birth control to save the lives of women and babies."

"You are still young, Lydia; it is good that you have grown in understanding."

"Before coming to Peru, I had never understood women's suffering; I had never seen malnourished babies. Just before I left Ica, a woman brought a dying baby to us. She had tied a cord holding a llama fetus around her child's neck."

"Yes. She was hoping the fetus would restore her baby to health. I imagine such things have been shocking for you."

"I felt powerless and angry."

"From the little I know of your country, Lydia, it seems you have seen much more than most North

Americans your age, and you have compassion for the poor. You are learning that women and children have unique burdens here. Many women, even those who are pregnant and nursing, get what food is left after feeding their men and children, and, on some days, mothers must decide which children will eat and which will not."

"Then why isn't more done to control births?"

"You are well-meaning, Lydia, and I do not want to be harsh, but you must learn to use more than your own values and experiences to judge other people. In your country you have a high standard of living. You have clean water and food that is abundant and safe. Parents are not worried about their children dying from respiratory infections or diarrhea. Here the common cold can kill. Water can kill."

"But isn't that even more reason for limiting births?"

"Be patient, Lydia. I am still explaining," she says gently, switching her medical bag from one hand to the other. "Parents think they can compensate for the deaths of some of their children by having as many as possible. And most women do not wait for their bodies to get strong before again becoming pregnant."

"But what about the young girls? Don't they want a better life?"

"Andean girls get little education; there is no expectation for them to finish school. Most are illiterate. They learn only what is passed down to them from their mothers and grandmothers. Many still believe they were born with a certain number of babies inside of them; they think they will have babies until each one in their belly has been born. They get pregnant when their reproductive organs are not yet mature, which not only leads to premature births and deformities, but is also dangerous for the young mothers, too."

"Then the answer lies in education," I say, avoiding a large stone in the path.

"It goes beyond education, Lydia. I hear that in your country you have a government that provides for people when they are old or sick. Here, it is the children who take care of aging parents; having many children is like having old-age insurance. And, Lydia, it is easy to forget this, but sometimes children are the only source of joy in a life that is otherwise bleak."

Doña Teresa walks swiftly, deftly, over the rocky path, while I struggle to keep up. "Is *machismo* also to blame?" I ask.

"It is true that men are considered more macho if they have lots of children, especially male children. By not challenging these attitudes, the Church condones them. The Church should be teaching that men show strength when they are considerate of their wives, and that a female child is as sacred in the eyes of God as a male."

"Do you think priests really believe that females are worth less than males?

"It's not that it's conscious, Lydia, but I do think there is an unexamined acceptance of the superiority of males."

"But priests revere Mary."

"Yes, but although they honor Mary as the mother of Jesus, the hierarchy does not extend this respect to women in society. Instead, we are told that if we bear our burdens, we will be rewarded in the next life. We are told to imitate Mary by not complaining. Yes, Peruvians honor Mary, but what do we honor about her? We honor her patience, her long-suffering, her willingness to bear burdens, her acceptance of her Son's death on the cross, not her intelligence or courage."

"Yet she would have been her Son's main teacher."

"Of course, but priests and the hierarchy find comfort in their interpretation of Mary for another reason. Because they fear their own sexuality, they are fearful of women as sexual beings."

"But, before coming here, I read the book *Aves sin nido*. It was fiction, of course, and written in the 1890s, but the author wrote of the hardships suffered by the children of priests, the 'birds without nests.'"

"Clorinda Mato de Turner was a brave writer. She not only criticized the clergy, she exposed the brutal treatment of the Indians. She was especially compassionate toward Indian women. But do not think that, because a priest has had sex with a woman, he does not fear his own sexuality. Oh, no. He fears it because, having committed a sin of the flesh, he has become an ordinary man, no longer belonging to a superior class."

"And a women has caused his fall from grace."

"Yes, that is how I think they see—with ancient, blind eyes. Even today the Church has refused to acknowledge the female disciples of Jesus, preferring instead the image of Eve, the temptress, or the image of woman as a child. The clergy forget that after the Resurrection, Jesus first appeared to Mary Magdalene, a woman who had sinned in the flesh. It was she who announced the good news of the Resurrection. Forgetting this and other examples, priests treat women like children who must be obedient and tolerant of their husbands' affairs. They foster the belief that women should have many children, and that it is their destiny to suffer in childbirth." Doña Teresa takes a handkerchief from her pocket to wipe pinpricks of perspiration from her forehead.

"From what Rafael has told me, you still practice your Catholic religion."

"After everything I've just said, it must seem a contradiction to you. Yes, I still love my religion, although I recognize the accident of having been born to it. I am a woman of this land, of the people. Were Christ here today, He would be walking among the poor, not the hierarchy. We, the people, are the real Church."

We cross a narrow bridge and walk down the dirt road into the tiny village of Chipay, stopping at a hut where women crowd around the door. They step aside, allowing us to enter. Amparo's husband greets us and says Amparo is in labor.

"Are the pains coming regularly?" asks Doña Teresa.

"*Sí, doña,*" the husband says, "and Amparo is in much pain, but I gave her basil tea and have been rubbing her belly."

"That is good, Don Luis, and do you have ready everything that Dr. Miguel left with you?"

"*Sí, doña,*" he says, bowing a little.

Amparo rests on a small bed in the dark room. On a crude table next to her are a candle and matches, basin, soap, razor blade, alcohol, gauze, and towels.

"Has Amparo eaten anything solid since the pains began?"

"Only teas with sugar, like your husband told me, and there is water boiling."

"Thank you, Don Luis, now it is all right for you to return to your work. This is Señorita Lydia. She is from The United States and will be my assistant."

The man looks up and smiles. His remaining teeth are deeply stained. I extend my hand to him, but he shies away, surprised by my gesture.

"*Gracias doña, gracias señorita Lydia,*" Don Luis says, backing out the door. Andean commoners, when departing the presence of the Inca, had to walk out backwards. They also bore burdens when entering, sometimes a heavy rock on their backs, a symbol of subservience.

Doña Teresa bends down to greet Amparo, whose name in Spanish means "shelter." Amparo smiles weakly, and then her face contorts in pain.

"Amparo, this is Señorita Lydia. She will help me. You will be fine."

"*Mucho gusto, señorita,*" Amparo whispers in high-pitched, Quechua-accented Spanish.

With no job to do at the present, I step outside and see the husband in a corn field, praying before a thick, phallic-like stone. He sprinkles a liquid around its base, sets a cup before it, and burns what appear to be coca leaves.

"He is praying to Pachamama," says Doña Teresa, coming up behind me. "For the safe delivery of their child."

"What was he sprinkling, and what was in the cup on the ground?"

"He sprinkled *chicha*, and in the cup was *ticti*, the thick material from the corn that remains after making *chicha*. He is returning to Pachamama some of the bounty she has given him."

"Does he think the stone is Pachamama?"

"No. To him the stone is a *huaca,* a holy thing that embodies a descendant of Pachamama."

"Ayiiiiii!" A scream erupts from the hut. We run to Amparo. Doña Teresa scrubs her hands, puts on gloves, and checks her dilation.

"She is ready. Lydia, bring me that pitcher."

"Amparo," Doña Teresa says soothingly, "I am going to wash you with water of rosemary. It will feel cool."

"*Sí, doña, gracias,*" Amparo says.

"Lydia, what is in that pot over the fire?" asks Doña Teresa.

"It's chicken broth," I say, smelling it.

"Good. Give some to Amparo." I hold Amparo's head as she sips. With no warning, she pushes my arm away and tries to get out of bed, spilling some of the hot broth on my arm.

"*Es tiempo,*" she says.

"It's time. She wants to kneel," explains Doña Teresa. "Gravity will help the baby descend."

Doña Teresa asks the neighbors to close the door before she removes Amparo's plain gown and places towels on the floor at the foot of the bed. Amparo kneels over the towels, gripping the rail with such force I think it might break.

"¡*Ya viene!*" she screams, bearing down, tensing every muscle as the baby descends. I wipe the perspiration from her face with a cool rag. How can this small, frail woman endure this pain and kneel at the same time? Amparo pushes again, but the baby does not appear.

"Lydia, help me move Amparo to the chair. She is too weak to kneel," Doña Teresa says. "Stand behind her and hold her under her arms so she does not slide off."

"*¡Puja! Amparo, ¡puja!*" Kneeling before her, Doña Teresa urges Amparo to push.

"*No puedo*," Amparo says weakly.

"You must, Amparo," Doña Teresa encourages. "Your baby needs a little more help to enter the world." To strengthen the mother, a neighbor enters and offers Amparo a punch of milk and egg, but there is no time for that.

Amparo takes one great breath and pushes until the top of the baby's head is visible. Using her fingers to gently spread the tissues so they don't tear, Doña Teresa eases the head out of the vaginal opening. The baby's head, black hair glistening with its mother's protective fluids, turns to the side, leading the way for one shoulder, then the other, then the rest of its tadpole body. Amparo has given light.

"*Es hembra*," Doña Teresa says, raising the baby girl to Amparo's arms and breasts.

"I will name her after you, Doña," Amparo says, smiling.

Doña Teresa suctions out the mucus from the baby's nose, mouth, and throat before placing a drop of silver nitrate into the baby's eyes.

We move Amparo and the baby to the bed. Doña Teresa ties the cord with clean thread at a distance the width of four fingers from the baby's belly; then she ties the cord close to Amparo and cuts it between the two knots, using a sterilized razor blade.

"If the baby had been a boy," Doña Teresa confides, "I would have left a longer length of cord on the baby's side."

"Why is that?" I ask.

"Because people here believe that a long length of cord will make the baby's penis grow nice and long.

If the baby had been Amparo's first, she would save the cord to use for its curative powers."

"Would she put it around someone's neck like they do with a llama fetus?"

"No, but after it has dried, it might be grated and mixed in a glass of liquor to cure alcoholism or another illness."

Doña Teresa uses iodine to clean the end of the cord adhering to the baby and places sterile gauze over it.

Amparo is still bleeding. Doña Teresa passes the crying newborn to me and massages Amparo's womb, loosening and freeing the placenta. Fortunately, it is intact, and a neighbor carefully places the placenta in a bowl. It's a holy substance, having belonged both to the body of the mother and the body of the baby.

Amparo tells Doña Teresa she wants to dispose of the placenta in the river, so she will become less fertile. Later she will wade in the river to cool her ovaries. Doña Teresa cleans Amparo with cooled, boiled water and puts antiseptic on the small tear in her vagina.

The neighbor women remove the blood-soaked towels while I smooth Amparo's hair and wash her face. The baby suckles and Amparo rests, drained, content for now.

Don Luis enters. "*Permiso, por favor,*" he says, removing his hat.

"You have another daughter, Don Luis," says Doña Teresa.

Don Luis looks disappointed, but he manages to ask about the baby's health.

"Your baby girl is fine," says Doña Teresa.

"My woman?"

"She is weak, but she will be all right, if you do not make her have another baby. But, if you must have another baby, you need to wait a long time until Amparo is strong again—at least two years."

"But Doña Teresa, how can we control these things? It is in God's hands," the husband says sheepishly.

"It is also in your hands, Don Luis. You must talk to Dr. Miguel. He will show you how you and Amparo can wait."

"*Sí, doña,*" says Don Luis, unbelieving.

The sun is setting. It's too late to walk home, so we sleep on the floor next to Amparo's bed along with the four youngest children. The oldest son sleeps outside with his father.

Saying goodbye in the morning, Amparo addresses Doña Teresa as *comadre*. Together the two women have birthed baby Teresa, and there will always be a special bond between them.

I follow Doña Teresa down to the river path, loving the way she walks—her back straight, her head erect.

"Lydia," Doña Teresa says, slowing her pace, "I like you very much, and I liked the way you worked with Amparo. Please forgive me if I say something that makes you sad. I have watched you. You are not like the gringas I have heard about. You seem to love my son very much, and I can see how much he loves you. I believe you would make him a good wife and partner, but can you give up your family and country to live here with us?"

"I'm not sure, Doña Teresa."

"Come sit beside me on this rock. I love the view of the river from here," she says, gracefully lowering herself, patting the smooth space next to her where she wants me to sit. "If I were your mother, Lydia, I would try to convince you to come home. A mother looks forward to her daughter's wedding and wants to be helpful when the grandchildren come. If you stay here, your parents will lose much. How would your father take the news?"

"He would be very sad, but he would not want to burden me with his sadness. You would like him. He loves to laugh and has a special way of making people happy."

"I am sure we would love your parents, Lydia, but you must think this decision through carefully. Today is Wednesday. My husband has already sent word to Padre Martín. And the people will want to celebrate your wedding with a *pachamanca*."

"Doña Teresa, I respect you and Dr. Miguel, and know I would grow to love you. If Rafael and I marry, I promise to be a good wife. I would never want to hurt him or you."

"He is our only child, Lydia," she says, leaning over to wet her handkerchief in the shallow water of the river. She wrings it out and wipes her face. "And you already know that large families are the rule in the Andes. I wanted more children, but it was not to be. I do not expect you to understand how it is to love a child so completely that you would gladly die for him; you will know soon enough. For me, there would be no effort in dying for him, no sacrifice. While he was away, my first prayer in the morning was for him, and my last prayer before falling asleep was for him. I think I would die if I were to lose Rafael."

"And you would feel his pain if he were married to the wrong woman. I understand, but I think I am the right woman for your son. When I'm working beside him, I feel as if God had placed us together, that our union was always in God's mind."

"We cannot predict the future, Lydia. All we can do is gather as much information as we can and try to make the best decision. And even after we do that, there are times when we must set aside all the logical arguments for or against something and do what our hearts command. I shall pray that God guides you and Rafael," she says, taking my hand. "*Vámanos, hija.* I am worried about our men."

XVI

The Decision

God does not permit evil so that good may
come of it.

Bartolomé de las Casas ("Apostle of the
Indies"), 1542, in William Prescott, *History
of the Conquest of Peru*, 1874

T HE house appears empty when we return. I had
been so absorbed in the birth of baby Teresa and in
my conversations with Doña Teresa that I had given
little thought to the safety of Dr. Miguel and Rafael.

A heap of bloody clothes lies on the floor in the
corner of Rafael's room. I hurry to the infirmary and
find Dr. Miguel and Rafael examining the man they
rescued yesterday. He is sleeping, and his head and
arms are wrapped in bandages.

"Ah, here you are *mi amor*," says Rafael, holding his arms out to me. "I was beginning to worry, but *papá* reminded me you might have had to spend the night, and I remembered how strong are the two women I love the most."

"I saw the blood on your clothes and thought you were injured," I say, grateful for his arms.

"I will leave you two *amantes* alone," says Dr. Miguel. "You can share your adventures, and my wife and I will do the same."

We heat water and bring it back to our room. As I bathe, Rafael watches my every move. "Rafael, you're making me nervous."

"*Querida*, after what I have just seen, I want to enjoy your graceful, healthy body. Do not deny me this pleasure."

"Please tell me everything," I say.

"Thank you for filling me with life, Lydia."

"It wasn't I who filled you with life, Rafael. You entered the world that way."

"But without you, my heart would contract; there would be no room for joy."

"I'll never get used to the way you talk, but I do love it, and I love you. Now lie down beside me and tell me about yesterday."

"Enrique Chuspi, the injured man, carried messages from village to village, like the *chasquis* who used to run for the Inca. There was a rally in Sacotambo, and people from many villages had gathered to listen to Diego Torrente who was calling for the workers to participate in a general strike. Enrique was afraid because he saw the armed guards nearby, but his curiosity and Torrente's convincing words kept him there."

"But how can a strike help the people? Won't it just make things worse?"

"It can't get much worse. Most of the men who live around Sacotambo work at the hacienda of José María Castillo. He has been gradually claiming more communal lands for himself and has been ejecting the *campesinos,* so that later they cannot claim title to the lands."

Rafael reaches for the blanket and covers us. "Do you remember when we talked with our artist friend Raúl about the labor taxes the landowners were demanding from the *campesinos?* Even women are not spared this tax because they are still forced to do domestic work in the landowners' houses. On top of this, for the people to have access to the diminishing communal lands, the State requires that they do construction work on roads or repair irrigation canals."

"Torrente sounds like a courageous man, but what are his chances, considering the centuries of tradition?"

"I'm not sure. The workers are not used to standing up to authority. Yet, Torrente pushes them by insisting that the communal lands are theirs, and that they should pay no labor tax on them. He also demands that the landowners return some of the land, so the Indians can continue to work it collectively."

"But what happened to Enrique?"

"He was returning to Pachabuena and was followed by the Guardia. They took away Enrique's machete and demanded that he turn over what little money he had, making it appear like a robbery. Then they attacked him with the machete, and all Enrique could do was to ward off their blows with his arms.

He suffered wounds that went to the bone, and his head was also opened to the skull. We closed the wounds, made a stretcher, and brought him back with the help of other *campesinos.*"

"My God, Rafael, how can this happen in 1963?"

Rafael sits up against the back of the bed. "Look, Lydia, the feudal European land system still dominates in the Andes, and it will continue until there is land reform. People must eat, and because the *campesinos* have little money to buy food, they must grow it. To grow food, they need their own land. I agree with Torrente, but I hate to see this conflict end in bloodshed."

"But why did the guards attack a *campesino?*"

"To frighten others from joining the movement."

"Who are these guards, anyway?" I ask, sitting up against the headboard, placing my hand on Rafael's thigh, "And why aren't they on the side of the people?"

"Some are hired by the landowners, but those in the Guardia—at least the ones who do the dirty work—come from the poorest backgrounds. Before joining the Guardia, they had no future, but when they get a clean uniform and training with a gun, they feel important—big men—no longer *cholos.* They are dangerous because they've been conditioned to obey, not to think before hurting their own people. And make no mistake, Lydia, the Guardia leaders, those that have come up through the ranks, are influenced by the rich landowners."

"But how do you know the men who attacked Enrique were not thieves?"

"Thieves do not call their victims *comunista,* Lydia. No, they were guards who followed the orders of the ones who have the most to lose if there is a revolution."

"The *hacendados*?"

"*Sí, mi amor*," he says, pulling me down beside him. I rest my head in the hollow of his shoulder. Turning toward me, Rafael asks, "Do you want to be my wife, Lydia?"

"I feel as if the rest of my life hinges on this moment, on what I say to you now. I don't want to lose your love, but to keep it I will have to give up everything else I care about—my family and home."

"I thought, perhaps, you had already become part of my family," he says, kissing the top of my head.

"Yes, your parents have accepted me in a way I didn't think possible, but your mother is worried that I might hurt you. What if, after we marry, I decide I can't live here anymore? The truth is, Rafael, I don't know if I can turn my world inside out for your love."

"But I would turn mine around for you," Rafael says, moving on top of me, his arms supporting his upper body.

"Would you leave your family and village to live in the United States? Would you go that far?"

"That's not a fair question, Lydia." He rolls off me.

"Why isn't it? Do you think you would be giving up more than I?"

"But my people need me, and my parents have waited for me to return."

"And mine? Do you think that because I'm a woman it should be easier for me to leave my family and my country? I'd never ask you to give up your family for me—I hate being the one who must choose."

"Don't be upset Lydia," he says, propping himself up on an elbow, looking at me. "Just tell me you will be my wife."

"—There is something else, Rafael, but I'm not sure of my thinking on the subject.

"We must be honest with each other, Lydia."

"All right. I'll try," I say, sitting on the edge of the bed, "but you're not going to like what I have to say . . . There seems to be a dark and violent side to life in Peru . . . How can there be so much evil in a country where most people claim to be Catholic?"

"If you think the Christians in the United States are free of this 'dark and violent' side, it's only because, until now, you've lived a sheltered life," Rafael says, his voice rising.

"I think I've lived here long enough to trust my own experiences."

"I'm sorry, Lydia. This is the last thing we should be talking about now, but if we are to have a life together, it is important that you understand my culture."

"Then perhaps you need to enlighten this poor gringa."

"No, my beauty, I will not lecture you, but the contradiction you have noticed demands a response. Maybe the Church in Peru has found it easier to live with the strong men who call themselves patriots and Catholics than with the strong men who call themselves Communists and atheists."

"'Strong men, Communists, atheists!' It's all too much," I say, putting on my shirt.

"*Mi amor*, you grew up expecting people to behave decently, the way your parents behave, the way you behave. No one prepared you for the way most people in the world live. I have known much love, too, but I have come to expect evil. Expecting it, I am on guard; expecting it, I might prevent it. Stay and work with me, Lydia."

"You make any life together sound like battle."

"I'm sorry—and I thought you were the serious one. No, we will love too much for that. We will laugh, sing, and dance with our children, and, when it is time, we will weep in each other's arms."

"I must return to Ica—you know that," I say reaching my hand out to him.

He pulls me down beside him. "Yes, I have counted on that, but when you finish your work there, you will return to me, to our mother and father."

"But I need to see my family in the States."

"You will go home first. Yes, see your family. Tell them about us; tell them how much I love you. No, I will write a letter. When they read it, they will be convinced of my love and devotion. They will let you return to me."

Soon Rafael is asleep. I should finish out my two years, go back to Milwaukee, return to school, maybe medical school, and see if this love lasts. I turn my face toward his. Dear God, he is beautiful. If I say no to him, am I saying no to God's design?

*

After a supper of hearty vegetable soup, we sit around the fire. Dr. Miguel wears a white *guayabera*. With his thick white hair and proud bearing, he resembles a Spanish diplomat. Doña Teresa has woven a blue ribbon into a single braid and wears a white flouncy blouse and a full skirt that comes to her ankles.

"Well, children, what are your plans?" Dr. Miguel asks.

Rafael looks at me for my answer, and I, heart pounding, nod yes. I wonder how I could have had any doubts when I see the tender love in his eyes. Without taking his eyes from me, Rafael says simply, "*Sí papá.*"

"*¡Bueno, bienvenida a la familia, Lydia!*" Dr. Miguel says, welcoming me to the family, getting up to hug me.

"*¡Qué felicidad!*" says Doña Teresa. Rafael pulls me to my feet and kisses me.

"We must toast," says Dr. Miguel, "and I have just the drink."

Returning with a dusty bottle, he says, "I have been saving this brandy for such an occasion. It is from Ica, Lydia. Many years ago I brought it back from the coast, carrying it on buses, trains, and even on burros. Tonight we shall see how good is the brandy from Ica."

We sip the smooth, golden liquid late into the night. Dr. Miguel and Doña Teresa share stories of their romance and of their hopes for the people in the sierra. Just as Rafael and I leave for our room, his mother, with a raised eyebrow and a knowing smile, says, "Remember Rafael, to wait until after all of the ceremonies."

"*Sí, mamá.* We will try."

In our room I ask Rafael what his mother had meant. "She knows that we have made love, but she was reminding me, according to ancient Andean

customs, that now we should abstain to prepare
ourselves for the wedding."

*

Oct. 11, 1963
Pachabuena, Peru

Dearest Family,

The daughter who writes this letter will
never stop loving you. She will carry forever
the joyful memories of her childhood and
the secure, comfortable world you provided
her. Now she is the woman you prepared
her to be.

Mom, Dad, Johnny, by the time you get
this letter, Rafael and I will be married. My
heart is at home with him, and I can't
imagine my life without him. You would like
Rafael's mother and father. Doña Teresa is
a midwife. She is bright, capable, and
down-to-earth. Rafael's father is a medical
doctor, with a sense of humor you would
appreciate, Dad. They plan on writing to
you.

It breaks my heart to realize I must leave
you to have Rafael; that my father will not
give me away; my mother will not help me
with my wedding dress. I offer you the
consolation of my happiness, and I promise
to come home after I've finished my Peace
Corps assignment, perhaps with Rafael. But
I don't want to mislead you. We will be
returning to Pachabuena, his village in the

Andes, so he can gradually take over his father's medical clinic.

Please be happy for me dear ones.

Loving you always,
Lydia

October 11, 1963

Dear Mr. and Mrs. Schaefer:

Who is this bold young man who steals your daughter, who denies you her grace and goodness, her deep faith, and generous heart? He is a doctor to the poor, the son of a doctor of Spanish ancestry, and of a noble mother of Indian blood, a man privileged to work with your daughter, to look into her heart and see there the qualities you inspired.

Forgive me, please, as I reach out to your beloved daughter Lydia to possess the greatest happiness I have ever known. I promise to love, honor her, and keep her from harm. Were we in the same country, I would have come to you to ask for your blessing. But I believe there is a divine force at work, one I am unwilling to question or defy.

I regret the pain I will cause you, and hope you will not look too unkindly upon me. Perhaps, one day, God willing, you will accept me as your son.

Rafael

*

The day before the wedding we visit the man who will build the oven for our *pachamanca*. Señor Juan Mamani tells us how proud he is to be entrusted with the job. First, he digs a hole four feet deep and three feet wide, explaining that the proportions of the hole are important in determining the taste and texture of the food. *Pachamanca* comes from the Quechua words *pacha*, for earth, and *manca*, for kettle.

Señor Mamani places large, flat stones on the floor of the hole and leans smaller ones against the sides of the hole to construct the oven walls. Tomorrow morning he will burn dry eucalyptus branches inside the oven to heat it. The oven will be ready when the stones have turned white.

The *papas de regalo*, the potatoes set aside for special occasions, will be placed in the oven first. There will also be sweet potatoes and pineapple-shaped potatoes. A layer of stones will be placed over them, and then comes the meat that will be marinated today in oil, garlic, *ají*, and salt. Because Dr. Miguel will be paying, we'll have lamb and pork instead of guinea pig. The meat will be covered with stones, and then a third layer of sweet and salty corn cakes, wrapped in shucks, will be added. A last layer of stones will cover these ingredients and will be crowned with the native plants *marmakilla* and *walmi walmi*. Finally, come the beans, protected by more plants, before a blanket is placed over the oven mound. The blanket protects the food from the layer of earth that will finish the oven. After two hours, the succulent food will be removed, layer by layer, into awaiting receptacles.

"*Muchas gracias, señor Mamani*," I say, "for making the oven and for teaching me about it."

"*De nada, señorita*," he says and then whispers something to Rafael.

"What did he say, Rafael?"

"He asked if you were a *palla*, a woman of royal blood."

"What made him say that?"

"He said that you walk with your back so straight, and that you are very tall."

"You told him yes, of course?

"Yes, I did. Now let's go home and see to your dress." Two women at a fruit and vegetable stand giggle as we pass.

"Rafael," I say, squeezing his hand, "look at the doorway of the church. It's the same guard we saw when we first arrived."

"Don't let the *desgraciado* bother you, Lydia. He's just a miserable person who cannot stand for others to be happy."

"You have made me very happy, Rafael, but I feel the way I did before leaving for Peru, the way I would feel if I had to cross one of those rope bridges."

"I'll be with you on that bridge, Lydia."

"*Pachabuena, pachamanca, palla*, . . . everything is strange, and it's all happening too fast. If we were in Milwaukee, we would have been engaged at least six months before any of this would have happened. My parents would rent a place for the reception, hire a caterer to cook and serve the food, a bartender for the drinks, and musicians for dancing. I would have been fitted for my gown months ago, and my parents would pay a florist to arrange and carry flowers to the church. There would be a rehearsal at the church the night before, followed by a dinner, and the day of the wedding there would be a reception costing thousands of dollars."

It is already late afternoon, and the mountains have cut off the light from the setting sun. The temperature has swiftly dropped. Rafael puts his arm around my shoulder. "Except for the money and the length of the engagement, it will not be much different here, Lydia. We already have the 'caterers,' and there will be many volunteers to serve the *chicha* and *aguardiente*. The flowers are free, and my father will give a little something to the local musicians. And tonight, *mi amor*, you will be fitted for your dress. You will never forget the reception, but it will not cost thousands of dollars. I hope you aren't disappointed."

"How could I be disappointed? How many girls from Milwaukee have a *pachamanca* to celebrate their wedding?"

"It's a tradition that unifies us, especially the people who will work hard to provide the food."

"But why are they working so hard for us when we're not family?"

"The *pachamanca* makes us family, Lydia. It's a celebration of the fruits of hard work, but more than anything, it honors the harmony and communion between the people and Pachamama, Mother Earth. And you, I, and our future offspring are part of that harmony."

"You make it sound very solemn."

"Not at all. Everyone will drink *aguardiente* and dance the *huayno*.—Look—there is a long line at the infirmary. This is a good chance for me to help my father." Ignoring custom, he holds me to him and kisses me. "I will see you at dinner, *mi amor*" he says, running off.

*

That night I dream Rafael and I are on our honeymoon on a tropical island. The reception is at an elegant restaurant with panoramic views of the turquoise water, but the windows near our table are shuttered. Suddenly I'm swept off a cliff and fly over the sea, fearful I'll never return to land. Someone grabs hold of me and leads me back to shore. He and I embrace in the shallows of the warm water, and I awake, aroused.

XVII

The Union

The violet among flowers
The cross among emblems
My land among nations
You among women

Ricardo Palma, attributed to Simón Bolívar,
Tradiciones Peruanas Completas, 1875

THE white-washed Church of San Damián stands
at the end of the main dirt road in Pachabuena.
Behind it is the cemetery, where the graves are
marked with rough-hewn crosses, and tin cans are
filled with freshly cut flowers. Yellow and black
calandrias sing in the top branches of the dark green
lúcumo trees that provide shade for the dead. The
late afternoon sun bestows butter-soft light, filtered
through silvery eucalyptus leaves.

Doña Teresa's cream-colored wedding dress, with its delicately embroidered bodice, fits me well, although the hem reaches only to the top of my ankles instead of brushing the floor. Saturnina, friendlier now that Rafael's marital fate has been decided, has woven a crown of tiny white flowers for my hair. Because my father won't be here, I will walk down the aisle alone.

Women in wide-brimmed, Panama-style hats wear blouses woven with colorful ribbons and their best *polleras*, the long, full skirts made wider by layers of petticoats. Beads of water cling to the just-combed, straight black hair of the men who enter the pews, their heads bowed. They wear knickers and immaculate home-spun shirts and sandals cut from discarded rubber tires.

The altar has been decorated with brilliant red *pisonay* flowers and with *azucenas*, pure, white lilies. The fragrance of eucalyptus fills the church. Musicians play the panpipe, harp, and the *churrango*, a kind of mandolin.

Father Martín Goigoichea, from Barcelona, Spain, stands at the communion rail, facing the congregation. Rafael stands to his left, wearing a white *guayabera* and dark trousers. Upon seeing me enter the back of the church, he mouths the words, *te amo*, and smiles reassuringly. His parents, standing at Father Martín's right, smile too, but there's sadness in Doña Teresa's eyes.

Father Martín begins the Nuptial Mass and wedding ceremony: "May the God of Israel join you together and may He be with you."

I am getting married and my family isn't here.

The priest reads the epistle from St. Paul's letter to the Ephesians: "Brethren: Wives should be submissive to their husbands as though to the Lord; because the husband is head of the wife just as Christ is head of the Church , . . . Just as the Church submits to Christ, so should wives submit in everything to their husbands."

I love Rafael, but I'm not good at submission. Our marriage will be a union of persons equal in worth and intelligence.

"Husbands, love your wives, just as Christ loved the Church . . . . In the same way, husbands, too, should love their wives as they do their own bodies . . . . Now no one ever hates his own flesh; no, he nourishes and takes care of it , . . ."

We shall nourish each other.

Father looks at Rafael before beginning Psalm 127: "Your wife shall be like a fruitful vine in the recesses of your home. Your children like olive plants around your table."

I see Rafael at one end of a long table and I at the other, both with gray hair. Our children and grandchildren sit, heads bowed, during the blessing. Then laughter and gaiety.

After reading the Gospel in which Jesus tells the Pharisees that divorce is not permissible, Father Martín leaves the pulpit and stands before us at the center of the altar. Looking again at my future husband, he says, "Rafael, do you take Lydia, here present, for your lawful wife, according to the rite of our holy Mother, the Church?"

Rafael is looking at me with such tenderness.

"I do," he says.

"Lydia," the priest says, facing me, "do you take Rafael, here present, for your lawful husband, according to the rite of our holy Mother, the Church?"

"I do." *Yes, again and again, yes.*

Rafael and I join hands. His voice is clear and strong as he seeks my eyes and repeats the marriage pledge: "I, Rafael Joaquín Serrano Supay, take you, Lydia Catherine Schaefer, for my lawful wife , . . . till death do us part."

My voice is shaky at first, but I breathe deeply and recover. Speaking up, I firmly commit myself to Rafael.

His expression grave, the priest looks at the wedding guests. "I call upon all of you here present to be witnesses of this holy union which I have now blessed. 'Man must not separate what God has joined together.'"

Father Martín takes from Rafael the ring that had belonged to Dr. Miguel's mother. "Bless, O Lord, this ring, . . . so that she who wears it, keeping faith with her husband in unbroken loyalty, may ever remain at peace with You according to Your will, and may she live with him always in mutual love , . . ."

And, Lord, may he be also loyal to me.

Rafael places the gold ring with its ruby center on my baby finger, saying, "Take and wear this ring as a sign of our marriage vows."

The priest invites the people to say the Our Father: "*Yayaku, hanak' pachapikak . . .*"

Priest: "May you be blessed in your children, and may the love that you lavish on them be returned a hundredfold."

Congregation: "Amen."

Priest: "May the peace of Christ dwell always in your hearts and in your home; may you have true friends to stand by you, both in joy and in sorrow. May you be ready with help and consolation for all those who come to you in need; and may the blessings promised to the compassionate descend in abundance on your house."

Congregation: "Amen."

Before Communion, Father Martín bestows the Nuptial blessing: "Oh God , . . . You put in order the beginnings of the universe and formed for man, made to Your image, an inseparable helpmate, woman. You gave woman's body its origin from man's flesh, to teach that it is never right to separate her from the one being from whom it has pleased You to take her . . . ."

Now the priest looks at me: "May this yoke that she is taking on herself be one of love and peace. May she be faithful and chaste, . . . Faithful to one embrace, may she flee from unlawful companionship. By firm discipline may she fortify herself against her weakness. May she be grave in her modesty, honorable in her chastity , . . ."

What does he mean by "her weakness?" May Rafael also flee from "unlawful companionship."

Priest: "May she be rich in children, may she prove worthy and blameless , . . ."

Congregation: "Amen."

We kneel to prepare ourselves for Holy Communion and repeat the centurion's prayer of the Gospel: "Lord I am not worthy that You should come under my roof. Speak but the word and my soul will be healed." I watch as Rafael receives the Host on the tip of his tongue. With all his criticisms of the Church and all his scientific training, he still believes.

At the end of Mass, Father Martín says: "May the God of Abraham, the God of Isaac, the God of Jacob be with you, and may He fulfill in you His blessing, so that you may see your children's children to the third

and fourth generation , . . ." We say the final amen
of the wedding mass.

My mother-in-law Teresa gives me a bouquet of
lilies to place before the statue of the Virgin. I should
be asking a blessing, but I'm thinking how much I
miss my parents.

"From now on, I will wipe away all your tears, *mi
amor*," Rafael says, giving me his handkerchief.

Followed by the guests and the musicians, we walk
from the church to a clearing near the river and stand
under an arbor thickly woven with flowers. In the
Andean tradition, we exchange gifts that signify our
mutual value to each other. Rafael places a woolen
slipper on my right foot, and I present him with a
hand-loomed shirt made of fine wool.

The villagers crowd around us offering
congratulations, and the musicians play a lively
huayno. Soon Señor Mamani supervises the removal
of the food from the *pachamanca* oven. It is plentiful,
spicy, and heavy, and people eat most of it with their
hands. Biting aguardiente flows "to cut the grease"
from the meat.

While we dance, Rafael grins flirtatiously as he
twirls a small lasso above his head, approaching me
with small skips and hops, inviting me to come closer.
I glance at him, coyly encouraging him, pinching up
my dress a bit at the knees. Guests encourage us with
shouts of *k'atiy!* Some drunken men are singing and
slyly glance at us, poking each other. When I ask
Rafael what it's all about, he says they're singing a
Quechua tune about a hummingbird who teaches a
groom the secrets of sipping flowers.

*

In the middle of the night, to the sound of distant
thunder, we savor each other's bodies, dreading the
separation, trying to stave off future longing. Rafael
whispers lines by Pablo Neruda.

> I could write the saddest verses this evening.
> I loved her, and at times she also loved me.
> In nights like this I held her in my arms.
> I kissed her many times beneath the infi-
> nite sky.

XVIII

The Separation

When Misti ignites,
think of me because I am
always thinking of you.
How far will my widowed heart have
traveled for your love?

From "Colección tierra firme," *La poesía
quechua*, translated by Jesús Lara, 1947

ON our last evening together, my new family and
I sit before the fire, reviewing the plan for the next
few months. Rafael will return with me to the train
station at Machu Picchu. In Cuzco I'll spend an
evening with Guillermo and Gloria and then fly to
Arequipa, where I'll inform the Peace Corps of my
marriage. I'll take a *colectivo* to Ica and finish my
term before visiting my parents in the States. Then

I'll return to Pachabuena. If anyone had predicted that my going to Peru with the Peace Corps might end this way, I would have laughed.

*

The plane flies over the Valley of the Volcanoes. Misti stands vigil over the white city, her perfect, pyramidal peak sheathed in snow.

I take a cab from the airport to the Peace Corps office. Irving Worthington is traveling, so I write a succinct letter, assuring him and Peace Corps director for Peru, Harold Rugger, that my marriage will not prevent me from fulfilling my obligations. As I pick up my bag to leave, I hear a welcoming voice.

"Lydia girl!"

"Joey!" Joey Amado, the friend from Peace Corps training I thought I'd never see again, struts into the office like someone who knew he'd be there all along. We hug, and I feel like I did when, as a child, my mother embraced me after I had trudged home from school in an unexpected snow, without a scarf, mittens, or boots.

"Oh, you are a joy to behold," he says. We sit on an orange vinyl-covered sofa with cigarette burns.

"How long have you been in Peru?" I ask. "Have you been cleared? Why did it take so long?"

"Whoa, Lydia, one question at a time. I've been here about ten days. Yes, I've been cleared. Having friends like you and Susan helped me to keep fighting, and—get this little friend—they made me a volunteer leader."

"That's great news, Joey," I say, hugging him again.

"I knew you had a knack with prayers," he says, kissing my cheek. "They've given me the use of one of those pretty baby blue Jeeps. Why don't we have lunch, and then I'll take you to Claire's. She's living by herself, and I understand your bed is still free."

We drink cold Arequipeña beers and eat *lomo saltado* at the Mónaco. When the restaurant clears, I tell Joey about Rafael, his family, and about the marriage. As usual, Joey, who learned his pragmatism on the streets of Los Angeles, boosts my confidence.

"Don't imagine obstacles, my friend," he says, pressing my hand. "Rafael sounds perfect for you, and don't be afraid of bureaucrats like Worthington or Rugger. Sure, your parents will be disappointed, not because you married, but because you'll be living so far away. Shoot, Lydia, you'll give them grandbabies, and, who knows, maybe one day you and Rafael will live in the States."

"I hate hurting them, Joey, and I don't know if I can adjust to life in Pachabuena."

"It's too late for those thoughts, Lydia. You'll be just fine in that village. Look how much you've already adjusted to. By the way, tonight is the feast of *Nuestro Señor de los Milagros*. Because you're a good Catholic girl and know all about these things, I'd like you to teach me about what promises to be the biggest parade of the year."

"It will be a procession in honor of Our Lord of Miracles, Joey, not a parade, and as far as my being a good Catholic girl, I think that status has changed."

*

Seeing surprise on the face of an old friend is one of the few advantages of not having a telephone. Claire is doing laundry at the cistern in the backyard, moving the surface algae aside to fill her basin with the clear water below. I come up behind her and ask, "Señorita, if you have a moment, and if it is not too much trouble, could you teach me the stroll?"

"Oh my God, Lydia!" Claire shouts, knocking the basin into the cistern. She gives me a bear hug with her wet arms and hands. "Have you transferred back? Oh, I hope so."

"No, Claire, I'm here just for tonight. Can you put me up?"

"Is the Pope Catholic? Come inside. I'll fix you some of that 'espresso' we used to drink, and we can talk."

Claire boils water on the alcohol stove, puts heaping spoons of Nescafé and sugar into our cups, and when the water is boiling, pours a tiny amount into each cup. Using a teaspoon, she blends the coffee and sugar into a thick paste before adding two more inches of boiling water to each cup.

Claire strolls through life, not because she's lazy, but because she's optimistic. In the States she had worked as a medical technician, but in Peru the Peace Corps wasn't sure what to do with her, just like they didn't know what to do with a speech therapist. In recent months I heard she had proved her worth by heading up an emergency child immunization project in Pucallpa, a rough and tumble frontier town near the Brazilian border.

Although I'm eager to share my news about Rafael, I let Claire talk first, but my mind wanders, remembering how my newly engaged friends in college had showed off their diamonds. The rest of us feigned excitement, made a fuss, hovered, all the time apprising our own progress toward marriage.

The engagement ring was *the* benediction, the ultimate validation of worth and beauty.

*

I nap until Joey picks me up for the procession which begins at dusk. Hundreds of men and women have gathered in the Plaza de Armas. They are barefoot, a sign of humility, and carry purple candles that signify their repentance. Singing hymns, they line up behind twelve men who carry a flower-strewn litter that bears a tall wooden crucifix and a portrait of Christ. The portrait somehow managed to escape damage during the earthquake that destroyed most of Arequipa in the 1600s.

The women will wear their purple dresses, cinched with white knotted cords, throughout October. Each knot symbolizes one of their petitions to the Lord of Miracles. Dear Lord of Miracles, keep Rafael and his family safe. Bring me back to him. Comfort my parents.

*

The alarm rings at 4:00 a.m. Claire rolls over and continues to sleep, secure in her single life. I dress quietly, gather my things, and dash off a thank you note. Joey is at the door by 4:30.

Except for the lethargic sound of the windshield wipers, we drive in sleepy silence. At 6:00 the drizzle stops, and the sun rises behind us, glancing off the peaks of Misti, Cha-Chani, and Picchu Picchu. The rays cast a rosy hue on the boulders lining the highway, making visible the *apachetas*, the stacks of small stones set near the road to indicate the presence of an *apu*, a mountain spirit.

At 7:00, Joey pulls into a gasoline station and after filling up, we visit the restaurant next door: *El Orgullo del Camino*, the Pride of the Road. I pee into the hole in the ground in the ladies' room and join Joey for instant Nescafé and freshly made *empanadas*, trying not to think about the source of the meat in the tasty fried pies.

I volunteer to drive the standard shift Jeep, but Joey says he isn't tired. "You're going to get tired of my telling you, Lydia, how indebted I am to you and Susan for having stood by me during that deselection mess."

"You are our friend."

"But you had a choice."

"Everyone wanted you to make it."

"But you and Susan were the only ones who did anything."

"Do you think they gave you a hard time because of your color?"

"I'm not sure. I know whites were deselected, too, but it's hard, with all the ugly experiences I've had, to think race wasn't an issue."

"I'd like to say I understand, but I don't."

"I do think you come closer than most. Even though you don't know much about my background, you don't see my color first. If I'm going to be disliked, I'd rather be disliked because I'm a democrat, or because I prefer poetry to newspapers, than because I'm a person who happens to have brown skin."

"You're right about my not knowing much about you."

"I'm from a place called Watts, named after a wealthy Pasadena realtor. My family is still there. I've got one brother in prison, and I have little contact with my father. I decided if I didn't get out, I'd just be another statistic, in jail or six feet under. The Air Force gave me my first break, and now the Peace Corps. You already know that I'm the world's best carpenter, the world's best photographer, and that I love to dance, especially to Latin music. What more is there?"

"What was the Air Force like, Joey?"

"You mean for a Negro? It was 1945; the war was just ending. I was part of a segregated unit stationed at Eglin Air Force Base in the Florida Panhandle. I wanted to start an NAACP chapter. Would you believe I was actually arrested for being an agitator? Our unit had formal instruction on where we could and could not go off base, while the German prisoners of war at the base could visit town freely. Even now I can't think of the South without remembering that humiliation."

"But you said the Air Force gave you your first break."

"Education, travel, and a profession were no small things, Lydia."

"Tell me about your mother," I say, shifting positions on the hard seat.

"I still write to mom and help out financially when I can, although helping her on a Peace Corps salary won't be easy. She is my inspiration."

The last time I had taken this road trip was with Rafael, and it had changed my life. My relationship with Joey will be lifelong, too. There are people who never leave us; they insinuate themselves, becoming lodestars on our journeys.

The highway turns sharply to the north, and there, as our reward after the bleak, twelve-hour drive, is the Pacific. The largest and deepest ocean in the world covers one-third of the earth's surface and washes the shores of Antarctica, Easter Island, Samoa, Fiji, and Bora Bora. I want to go to all those places, but now I never will.

*

Perhaps we'll arrive in Ica in time to have supper with Susan. You did what? she'll ask and reiterate and exaggerate her concerns about my marriage: babies lost in childbirth, a philandering husband, my increasingly decrepit health, and premature aging.

With my directions, Joey cautiously steers the jeep through the crowded street market. Vendors and customers stare at the brown and white gringos in the baby blue jeep. When we arrive in Oculto, the people are restrained in their greetings. Susan stands outside the clinic with a group of women dressed in black. They part down the middle as we pull up. Susan smiles but suppresses her excitement upon seeing Joey, informing us that Pilar Medina, one of our new, young assistants has died.

Pilar was a serene girl of sixteen who had silently suffered nausea and cramps for several months. Because her stomach was growing rapidly, neighbors thought she was pregnant, but the doctors at the local hospital took X-rays and said she had an ulcer. Finally, during my absence, practical nurse Ruby took Pilar to Lima, where exploratory surgery revealed a massive, malignant tumor. I had just missed the funeral.

"Welcome home, Lydia," whispers Susan. "I missed you." She sidles up to Joey. "Joey, you old fart, you made it, and you could not have come at a better time."

*

Joey helps in the clinic for a few days before heading back to Arequipa. Because four people in the *barriadas* have recently died of diphtheria, the Peace Corps doctor visits to give us booster shots.

Mothers continue to bring in malnourished babies. One woman has given birth to fifteen children, but only five have survived. Seeing so many of these weary women and their sick children is getting to me. I lie awake at night trying to reconcile the religious dictates of my church with the suffering I see—suffering few of the hierarchy in Rome have seen. How can I obey their laws when I'm working with Rafael? I know I'll distribute contraceptives if I can get my hands on them.

The Church says its position on birth control corresponds with Natural Law, but how natural is it for a poor woman to deplete her body with each pregnancy? How natural is it for infants and children to die before the age of five? How natural is it for illiterate women to use the rhythm method, to consult calendars to determine their fertile times, before telling their husbands it's okay to have sex?

The Church fears that contraceptive use will weaken and devalue the married relationship, but love-making between husband and wife should be a redemptive act, regardless of whether or not it leads to procreation, an act that generates more love, and, when needed, reconciliation.

The Church says that before we blame hunger and disease on the proliferation of births among the poor, we must first deal with the social sins that cause hunger, malnutrition, disease, and the inequity in the distribution of land and wealth.

In the confessional, if I were to mention that I was distributing contraceptives at the clinic, a priest would tell me I was committing the sin of pride, while causing others to commit grave sin. What would my personal heresy mean? Would I be excommunicated if I were to make my position public? At least I would no longer be a hypocrite.

*

On the evening before Joey's departure, while we're walking home from the clinic, a young man kicks a mangy yellow dog that has crossed his path. The dog, whose thin, depleted teats hang close to the ground, yelps in pain. The youth laughs and kicks her again. I hate him and everything he represents. Torturer. Oh, God, I want to go home. How can I live in this country?

"¡*Malcriado*!" I scream. "¡*Hijo de puta*! Son of a bitch, asshole! Does kicking that dog make you feel big? You little shit. How would you like to be kicked, huh?" I slowly circle him, targeting his legs with quick, small kicks. He dodges, unsure of what to do. Will he hit me? "Big man, tough guy, picking on a weak dog," I snarl. Joey calls for me to stop, trying to pull me away, but I persist, moving in on the youth. "Come on, kick me you fucking twerp," I taunt. People gather. The men snicker and urge me on; the women look bewildered, embarrassed for me. Joey pulls me away. "Lydia girl, that's enough. Let's go, I'm buying you a drink."

An hour later we're at Huacachina, sipping sweet-tart *pisco sours*, munching peanuts, rocking on the hotel's veranda with the green lagoon just feet away. Because we're gringos, with a little money in our pockets, we can shake off the dirt and misery when they're too much for us.

Joey takes my face in his hands, locks his eyes on mine, and says, "Lydia girl, don't let anybody take your day from you. No one. No stupid, macho kid. No Peace Corps bureaucrat. No suffering individual. No one. You don't have to be miserable, denying yourself pleasure in order to help the needy. You don't have to wear a hair shirt all day, every day. Enjoy this moment and the friends who love you. Enjoy thinking about your husband, and for crying out loud, enjoy this *pisco sour*. It's costing enough!"

XIX

Kennedy's Children

Look, there are hunters who with evil end
might catch you in their enticing, lethal nets,
and when they catch you, will cruelly martyr you.
Don't let them hunt you. Flee this danger.

Mariano Melgar, "Yaraví IV," 1814

November 1, 1963,
All Saints Day,

Rafael, healer,

Heal my lonely heart. Are you real? Is
Pachabuena? Are we married, or have I
dreamed it? But the patients ask for you,
and I remember our days together, our love-
making and know you wait for me.

I'll need your reassurance during the

months ahead. Please write. I fear the
mountains, rivers, and gorges that separate
us, reminders of the obstacles we chose to
ignore when we married. Hold me in your
mind and heart, my sweetest love. I miss
you more than I ever thought possible.
Yours,
Lydia

*

Befuddled and not having faced this situation before,
the Peace Corps has requested information about
Rafael. Does he pose a security threat? Only to the
established order, I think, as I assemble answers to
their questions.

*

On November 22, as Susan, Ingrid, and I are leaving
the movie theater Dux, we run into a swarm of
people shoving each other to read an announcement
on a blackboard set up on the sidewalk. We can see
over their heads and read, "*Kennedy mató por un
balazo.*" We try to break free of the crowd, but many
stop us with tears in their eyes to offer condolences.
They know Kennedy had sent us to Peru; to them,
we are "Kennedy's children."

Other red-eyed volunteers have already gathered
at the Mogambo. The owner puts plates of french
fries on the table and serves us soft drinks. He refuses
our money, pointing to the picture of Kennedy on
his wall.

The next morning there is a black wreath and a
picture of President Kennedy on the clinic door. The

mestizo women in the *barriada* wear black; the Indian
women, illiterate and in their separate worlds, dress
as usual, but they know a good man has died, and
that he was the leader of our country. Everyone
speaks in hushed tones, and a funereal air descends
upon the clinic and upon each house. Some of the
women asks if they can name the clinic after the fallen
president. In less than an hour, in bright red paint
above the door are the words: *Posta Médica John F.
Kennedy.*"

*

It takes weeks for the shock of President Kennedy's
death to subside, and the women still wear black.
Although the university students who sit with us at
the Mogambo regret the assassination, many hold a
skeptical view of Uncle Sam's benevolence to poor
countries. They think us naïve not to recognize the
U.S. government's role in supporting oppressive
governments.

Opposition to the Belaúnde administration gets
a boost when student members of the Communist
Party circulate a letter attributed to Diego Torrente.
The letter condemns President Belaúnde's plan to
improve the lives of the Indians through an agrarian
reform program that promises land to those Indians
who are willing to buy it, in installments, from the
landowners. Although some Communists support the
Belaúnde approach, as a first step and a good-will
gesture, Torrente insists it's preposterous for Indians
to pay landholders for what already belongs to them.

In his letter, Torrente invites students to become
revolutionaries, instead of "radical talkers," and urges
them, if they really want to do something, to come

to the countryside to help unionize the peasants. He persuades them with descriptions of the flagrant abuse of the Indians. In one incident, because a peasant had lost a cow, the landowner put a saddle on him and made the peasant work on all fours for an entire day. Torrente tells how Indians have been beaten for small infractions and of landowners' refusals to let Indians leave their situations because of their "debts."

The Indians, according to Torrente, should not trust the landlords to implement land reform because they will use bribes to influence the officials overseeing the reform. If bribes don't work, the landowners will use eviction. Once off the land, a peasant can't press for his rights.

Torrente's movement incorporates the elevation of Quechua language, music, and dress. No more will the word *Indio* be an ugly epithet; it will be a word connoting pride and unity. Torrente uses the Quechua term *manan* to say absolutely no to the practice of *yerbaje,* the tax paid to landowners in the form of livestock for the "privilege" of using pasture lands.

Schools need to be built, Torrente says. University students can help with construction and teaching, and he ends his letter by explaining that the term *Indio* has more to do with social class than with blood, and that the students can put on an "Indian heart," even though they might not have Indian blood. The words, *dignidad o muerte* appear before Torrente's signature.

✳

My period is late. Dr. Suárez tells me that this time the delay is due to pregnancy and not to the effects of high altitude, as he had explained when I first moved from Arequipa to Ica after the flood. He had recounted, then, how disappointed the Spanish settlers were that the cows they had brought from Europe failed to bear young. They had no way of knowing that their animals had temporarily ceased to ovulate because of the change in altitude. Cows-schmows, I think. I have a baby growing inside of me, and I must get word to Rafael.

"You look content for a girl who's on the coast with a husband in the sierra," Susan says, watching me seal the letter.

"Those words sound like lyrics to a song," I say, looking up. "Maybe you could write one, Susan, but you must add that the 'girl on the coast' is pregnant."

"Lydia, please, you can't be serious. What were you thinking? You guys ever hear of birth control?"

"Susan, don't you understand that condoms aren't available in Pachabuena, that I'm a good Catholic, and that, subconsciously, I wanted to return to Rafael as soon as possible?"

"How about you were just plain stupid! Now you *will* have to leave the Peace Corps early."

"Not that early, especially when you consider how many volunteers leave before the end of their first year."

"Oh, Lydia, no, please. I'm not ready to live here without you. You're my buddy. Why is it guys always come between good women friends?"

"Sit down here with me, Susan," I say, pulling out the second chair from under our kitchen table. "Rafael hasn't come between us; we'll both love you. Maybe you can be our baby's *madrina*."

"Oh, Lydia," she says, sitting down. "I know I should be happy for you, but I'm too worried. What kind of medical care will you get?—Hey, you could go back to the States to have the baby."

"Rafael's a doctor, his father's a doctor, and his mother is a midwife. I think I'll get better care in Pachabuena than if I were in the States."

"What about your parents?"

"They're the ones getting the bum deal. My mom will be devastated if she's not with me when the baby's born."

"Maybe they can visit, or maybe you and Rafael can travel there with the baby."

"And maybe he and I are part of Peru's oligarchy," I say, reaching across the table to hug her.

"Lydia," Susan says, returning my hug, "let's put these problems aside for a while and go to the Chifa for dinner; we'll order fried wontons and cold beers.

"*Con mucho gusto*," I say.

*

Harold Rugger sends a letter coolly thanking me for my service to the poor of Peru. Because I've nearly finished my term, the Peace Corps will pay for my return to the States; I should be prepared to leave in two weeks. I'll still receive the relocation allowance of $75.00 for each month I've served.

In a second letter to Rafael, I explain my plans to visit my family and, with the relocation money, to return to Peru well before the birth of our baby. I begin to sort my belongings into stacks—items that will accompany me to the United States, those to be given away, and those few things I hope will find their way to Pachabuena.

The week before my scheduled departure for the States, Susan asks me to accompany her to the clinic to find a medicine for a sick neighbor. I walk into a going-away party. Native dishes cover the examination table, and *pisco* circulates freely. On the record player is the popular hit, *Cuándo llora mi guitarra*, "When my Guitar Weeps."

The next morning there is a letter from Guillermo and Gloria asking me to come to Cuzco immediately.

XX

Diego Torrente

. . . for truth, time, and for justice, God.

Clorinda Mato de Turner, *Aves sin nido*,
1889

I write to Harold Rugger, Peace Corps director for
Peru, telling him I must postpone the "processing
out" formalities, and that I no longer hold him
responsible for my well-being. Susan will see to my
belongings.

A large plastic *Papá Noel* decorates the entrance
to the Arequipa airport. In Cuzco, Guillermo and
Gloria meet my plane and whisk me to their home,
eluding my questions. Gloria serves an abundant
evening meal, but I have no appetite. They show no
enthusiasm when I announce my pregnancy.

"Lydia," says Guillermo, "something dreadful has happened in Pachabuena, but before I tell you, I want you to know that Rafael is safe."

"What happened, for God's sake?"

"From what Saturnina has told us, some peasants took Diego Torrente to Pachabuena after he had been shot while escaping the Guardia. Dr. Miguel and Rafael operated on him and removed the bullet from the infected shoulder wound. Later, while Rafael was visiting the sick in another village, the Guardia came to the clinic and demanded that Miguel turn Torrente over to them. When Miguel refused, the captain ordered one of the men to shoot him for treason. In trying to protect Miguel, Teresa was knocked unconscious with a rifle butt."

"Oh, dear God, and Rafael?"

"He returned to the house to find his father had been executed," says Gloria, "his mother barely conscious, and Torrente gone." Tears spill from Gloria's sorrowful eyes. "Two of the Guardia stayed behind, waiting to apprehend Rafael, but the villagers rescued him. Carrying their tools and *bolas*, they surrounded the guards, pressing closer and closer, shaming them in Quechua. The young recruits ran off, and a small band of villagers escorted Rafael to a hiding place, assuring him they would look after his mother."

"Tomorrow you will take the train to Miabamba," says Guillermo. "Someone will meet you there."

"Rafael?"

Guillermo gets up from the table and walks over to me. I rise to enter his embrace. "No, he will not be there, but you will be closer to him," he says, soothingly

"Isn't Miabamba near the jungle?"

"Yes," says Guillermo, releasing me. "From Miabamba, you will be taken to Rafael. It will be a difficult journey."

"But Guillermo," says Gloria, ushering us into the parlor, "while it is true Lydia is a strong young woman, she is now pregnant, and I worry for her safety and for the baby. Is this plan wise? Perhaps Lydia should stay with us. We could try to get word to Rafael. We could hide him here, too."

"*Mi vida*," Guillermo says, going to his wife, "I understand your concerns, but with the heavy concentration of the Guardia here in Cuzco, and with so many informants about, it would be impossible to keep his presence a secret. We would endanger Lydia and our family, too. Rafael is alone now, and he may have to hide for a long time. He needs his wife, and they will be safe in the *montaña*."

"Guillermo is right, Gloria," I say. "I'll be fine. I must go to Rafael, but what about Teresa? Who will take care of her?"

"Saturnina will stay with her," says Gloria. "It would be good for you to rest now, Lydia."

*

In my dream, I am looking for my parents in our Milwaukee apartment. My mother is sleeping, but dad is gone. I enter my bedroom and see an array of black triangles on the bed. The triangles become wings, and the wings become bats. They fly at me. I fend them off with my arms. Somehow I'm lifted up near the ceiling, still struggling against the bats. I try to call for my daddy, but my voice, paralyzed with fear, can only manage a faint, "da-da-da-da."

*

In the morning, I dash off a note to Susan, telling her I don't know how long I'll be gone, but that I'll try to get word to her. I also write my parents, telling them my trip home will be delayed, and I give them the Abuad address in Cuzco. I dress warmly because the rainy season has begun. The Abuads take me to the train, making sure I will have plenty to eat on the journey.

The train careens from side to side, and the little lump of life in my womb seems to careen, too. After losing my breakfast, I decline to drink the tea a woman offers me from a container that has never seen soap.

I fall asleep and have another nightmare. This time I'm soaring through the air, holding a baby boy in my left arm, using my right arm as a rudder. Swooping low, we skirt Indian villages and flocks of alpacas before soaring high above icy mountains. I feel the queasiness in my belly and fear we'll be impaled on a peak. The arm holding my baby grows weak, but when I try to draw him closer to my body, he slips, inch by inch, till he falls.

*

The train follows the Urubamba River on its way to the Apurímac, named for the Andean River Oracle who speaks to the Indians. The Apurímac flows into the Ucayali and the Ucayali into the Amazon.

At widely separated train stations, women who resemble North American Indians sell bananas, sweet potatoes, tobacco, coca, and peanuts. The station in Miabamba is no more than a cement platform covered by a tin roof. A German-speaking man is bargaining with another European over the price of a thick boa constrictor coiled in a cage. Blue and orange-beaked toucans perch on the shoulders of an Indian man. A photographer dressed in safari gear argues with a guard. I look up and down the platform for someone who might be looking for me. A petite woman approaches, smiling.

"Are you Lydia?"

"Yes, thank you for meeting me."

"I am Helena Ahabi. Gloria and Guillermo are my friends. They asked me to look after you. Please follow me. I will take you to our home."

Helena doesn't have a car, but I have little baggage. Rain has turned the dirt streets into a brown ooze that seeps into my shoes. The wooden houses have a mildew-green patina, and window cases display pots and pans, canned corn beef, Vienna sausages, fruit cocktail, Kotex, and U.S.-made peanut butter, precious at $3.00 a jar. Emaciated dogs sniff at garbage.

Of Palestinian descent, like Guillermo and Gloria, Helena and Felipe Ahabi operate the Canaan Hotel, the only hotel in Miabamba, that is, they rent rooms above their dry-goods store. Bolts of fabric cover the long tables in their store. The only way a Miabamban woman can have a new dress is to sew it herself or have someone else make it.

Felipe is balding but compensates with a thick, black, carefully groomed moustache. He inquires about the Abuads, saying it has been years since he has seen them. Helena shows me to a small room painted chartreuse. There is a musty upholstered chair and a single bed covered by clean, worn sheets. Next to the bed is a night stand with a chipped enamel basin and pitcher. An antique armoire hides one wall, an object of luxury, perhaps, from Helena's former life. There are no screens on the windows, but a mosquito net hangs from the ceiling over the bed. The bath, shared with other roomers, is down the hall.

There is no restaurant in the hotel, so Helena asks if I'll be eating at the one next door. I tell her I'm tired and prefer to stay in my room, even if it means not eating. She brings me a tray of chicken and vegetable soup and a perfect piece of papaya with a slice of lime.

Loud music from the bar across the street jangles the night. I sit at the window watching heavily made-up women, wearing tight skirts and tops, go in and out of the bar with disheveled men. One of the women knocks loudly on the Ahabis' door, demanding a room, but Felipe flings open the shutters on his bedroom window and tells her to sin some place else. Muttering obscenities, she staggers off with her changeable partner.

Needing something to help me sleep, I knock on the owners' door and ask if they have a beer I could buy. They apologize for the racket in the street and give me a warm bottle of *Condor y Torro*.

I sit against the headboard, gather the mosquito net about me, drink my beer, and swat at the circling mosquito that wants her blood meal. An image from the early years of television comes to mind. In each performance of "The Life of Riley," things would get so dismal that William Bendix would say, "What a revoltin' development this is!"

Drowsy, I slip the empty bottle outside the net, and, despite the heat, pull the sheet over me. As a child, during Milwaukee's hot summer months, I had done the same thing, because if someone were to break into our house, I didn't want to be killed "in cold blood," another line I must have absorbed from television's early detective shows.

I dream I'm late for a flight. I run after the plane and jump onto the back of the fuselage as it takes off. The wind tears at my body, prying away my hands, and my stomach heaves during my plummet to earth.

I awake to the sound of rain on the tin roof, but it stops after five minutes. Birds call raucously. Helena knocks and enters with a tray of *café con leche*, a roll, and a banana. "A truck will pick you up in forty-five minutes," she says.

"And it will take me to Rafael?"

"No, I am sorry, Lydia. The road ends at Mancate. From there you must walk, but the driver will escort you. Be sure to carry something warm with you because the road goes very high."

"Thank you, Helena. I'd like to pay for my room now."

"*De ninguna manera, doña Lydia,*" Helena replies. "You are our friend now, too." I thank her for generosity and smile, hearing myself addressed as Doña for the first time.

A battered truck, loaded with workers in the back, stops in front of the Ahabi house. The driver leans on the horn. Grabbing my bag, I thank my hosts and claim the seat next to Lucho Ortega, the muscular driver who flashes gold fillings when he smiles. Lucho revs the engine, and we get underway to the current radio hit, "Magia blanca." I will need white magic, I think.

"Where are the men going?" I ask Lucho.

"To the land of the *hacendados*. The workers come from far away to earn money to feed their families."

"And these *hacendados*, did they inherit the land way out here?"

"No, Señora," he grins. "They go to court and make a claim to the land. Because no one has worked it before, they become the owners. Of course, the judges always like a little gift."

An hour out of Miabamba, we come to a roadblock. "La Guardia," Lucho says.

"What could they want?" I ask.

"Have you heard of Diego Torrente? They look for his supporters."

A guard holds up both hands, gestures for us to stop, demands Lucho's papers, and orders all the men off the truck. The workers face the truck, place their hands against it, and spread their legs so they can be searched. Another guard climbs into the bed of the truck and rifles through their belongings. A third man comes over to my side of the cab and orders me to get out and assume the same position as the men. "Why?" I ask. He grabs me by my hair, pulls me out of the cab, and forces me up against the truck, pressing his pelvis to my rear. His fingers dig into my arms.

"I like spirited women," he says, grinding against me. "I think you could make me very happy. You would make my friends happy, too. It has been a long time since we have had anything this good."

The workers turn and watch the guard who bullies me. As if on signal, they unzip their pants, take out their penises, and pee against the truck, using the ancient Inca gesture that communicates disdain. "I piss on you," they say.

"Before you get any ideas," I say to the guard, wanting to turn around and kick him in the groin, "you'd better take a look at my passport. Look at the official seal of the United States of America. I am on official business, and my government knows where I am. Do you want to start an international incident?"

"But, Señorita," he snarls, "maybe they will never find you."

I answer loudly enough for the other guards to hear. "You can be sure they will search for me if I don't get to my destination and make the report they are waiting for."

His buddies signal him to leave me alone. "Get out of here, gringa bitch," he says.

I can't risk slapping his face or swearing at him. For the first time, I know what it is to be the victim of arbitrary power. And it hits me that, as a women, I'm especially vulnerable to that power.

Resuming the trip, we pass through moist banana groves, where we drop off some of the workers. The others get out at a higher elevation, near a coffee plantation.

By late morning, we begin the serious climb toward the Maldonado Pass. The truck groans, but Lucho knows his machine well, operating the shift as skillfully as if he were making love to a woman, using gentle or forceful thrusts as required. As we near the pass, I start to feel nauseated. A yellow light bores into my eyes, replacing all other images, and the driver's voice sounds tinny and comes from a distance. I try to tell him I'm passing out, but I can't form the words.

Lucho stops the truck, comes around to my side, and helps me out, urging me to breathe deeply. We had climbed from a subtropical region to a subglacial

MI

altitude, and now we'll descend to Mancate, a smaller, more remote version of Miabamba. During Inca times, Mancate had been a resting place for Inca runners, and Lucho points out the ruins that had once given shelter to them.

We eat fish soup at a rickety table in the only restaurant in town. Lucho tells me he has agreed to transport more workers from Miabamba tomorrow morning. If he were to accompany me the rest of the way, he'd never make it back in time. He points out the road I must take and assures me it's not dangerous, adding that, if I start right away, I can get there by dark. What a revoltin' development this is.

The dirt road begins easily enough, and I start to feel more confident, thinking back to how I had handled the incident with the Guardia. What assholes! After I walk thirty minutes, the road ends at the foot of a mountain and gives way to a path. Rain falls as I climb through stands of coarse grasses that catch my clothes and whip my legs. I put on my wind breaker and forge ahead, ducking branches and climbing over rocks.

Lightning cracks nearby. Shivering, I take refuge under a rock outcropping. Rain mixes with my tears and snot. I might die right here, struck by lightning or bit by a fer-de-lance that can spring great lengths to strike its prey.

Father, forgive me for all the times I've hurt others, for all the times I've been ungrateful or selfish; I've been imperfect, but basically I'm a decent person. An old boyfriend, wanting to soften the blow of a break-up, once told me I was the most decent person he had ever met; I wonder if God thinks I'm a decent person.

*

When the rain and lightning stop, I climb steep stone stairs, afraid I might topple over backwards. The backs of my legs stretch like taunt rubber bands, and I must stop every few minutes to catch my breath. At the top is a structure, perhaps an Inca outpost. Someone has woven a roof to replace the one worn away hundreds of years ago. I change into dry clothes and decide to rest a few minutes before continuing.

*

The sun streams around the silhouette of a lean figure in the pyramidal door opening. I can't see his face, but I'm not afraid.

XXI

Vilcapampa

Here comes the dark night.
If I leave, I shall tumble.
Give me, give me a little shelter,
and at your side I shall slumber.

Ciro Alegría, from "Three Little Songs," *El mundo es ancho y ajeno*, 1941

"**I** have missed you so much," Rafael says, holding me. He kisses my face and hands. "I've been coming here every day for a week, hoping you would arrive, feeling guilty for making you risk the journey." He points to a piece of paper in the corner of the shelter, weighted down by a rock. "There is the note I left for you, but it must have been too dark for you to see it."

"Hold me a little longer, Rafael. There were times on the trail I didn't think I'd make it by myself."

"You came alone? Oh, Lydia, I'm sorry. I just assumed the person who brought you here had already returned to Mancate. I would have tried to meet you below had I known," he says, rocking me.

"I'm fine, Rafael, just tired and dirty. Most of all I'm relieved that we're together."

"Lydia, I need to hear everything—about my mother, Pachabuena, your parents, how it is with the Peace Corps—but now, it is enough that you are here."

"We will get to everything, sweetheart, I promise. As for your mother, she takes comfort in knowing you're safe, but she will never get over the loss of your father, or forget the way he died. Saturnina is still with her, and, when things calm down, we'll go to her.

"Lydia," Rafael says, getting to his feet, "for the first time in my life, I feel like a lost soul. My father is dead, my mother was attacked; I was not there to defend them, and now I am here, a safe coward."

"I understand how you feel, Rafael, but you had to leave. There was nothing else you could have done."

"Please, Lydia, I know you mean well, but you can say nothing that will take away my shame."

I extend my hand to him, and he pulls me to my feet. "Rafael, I did not marry a coward. If the villagers had not intervened, you would have been killed, too. Your mother would have lost you, and the people of Pachabuena would have lost their only physician. And maybe," I say, placing his hand on my belly, "I do have something that will ease your pain."

"You are with child?"

"Yes, Rafael. I wrote as soon as I found out, hoping you'd get word in Pachabuena."

He presses me to him again. "When will our baby be born?"

"I bet you can figure that out, *doctor Rafael*," I say, ruffling his hair, "but to spare you the calculations at this sweet moment, the baby will be born in July."

"I feel as if I am holding a flower in my arms—no two flowers."

"You are, my love, you are."

"Come, Lydia," he says, "I will take you to our new home."

After crossing a rope bridge over a deep, narrow gorge, we descend to the ruins of an Inca city that's so vast it spans two vegetative zones, spilling out into the jungle. A tall wall is partially visible through the lush vegetation. Knobby roots of towering tropical trees, like an old man's fingers, grasp mounds of rocks, as if at any moment they might be hoisted and flung at intruders. The farmers with whom Rafael lives think these ruins, not Machu Picchu, comprised Vilcapampa, the capital of the last Inca domain, and they have given their new community the same name.

The wall surrounds a quadrangle of houses. The first of the new settlers replaced the thatch roofs on the fieldstone houses and wove hammocks for sleeping. Our house is on the far end of the quadrangle, close to a large, communal garden. The mud Rafael used to fill the holes between the stones is still drying. There's a rustic table, two chairs, shelves for our personal things, and a few tin cups and dishes. Outside is a detached cooking area, also covered by a thatch roof, with a dome-shaped mud oven in the center.

The families who homestead here were eager to provide refuge to Rafael when they learned his family had helped Diego Torrente. They also valued the medical care he could provide. The dangers of life in Vilcapampa are many and include malaria and snakebite.

After a week of meeting the men and women of the compound, making small aesthetic adjustments in our house, and learning how to use the oven, I write home, trusting my letter to the man who makes the monthly trips to Mancate for supplies. I ask my parents to write using the Ahabi address in Miabamba and tell them it would be less confusing if they left my name off the envelope. The Ahabis will know the letter is for me when they see the return address.

*

Despite the nutritious meals I've tried to prepare, Rafael is losing weight and is spending every free minute experimenting with salts made from the bark of the *cinchona*, a tree native to Peru. The Indians call the salts *quina*. In addition to its usefulness in treating malaria, Rafael uses it to cool fevers, reduce pain, and induce uterine contractions during labor.

The people have little money, so instead of paying with *soles*, they trade medical treatment for prized vegetables or a freshly caught fish. Gradually, a natural system, known as *ayni*, emerges. People are mutually helpful and cooperative, but they can't ease my husband's grief.

I have tried to get him to talk about it, but he has shut me out from that part of his heart. "I'm losing you," I say to him after dinner one evening.

"Lydia, why do you say such a thing? That is crazy."

"Then talk to me, Rafael. Perhaps I'm selfish, feeling alone and uncertain of our future, when you're the one who has lost his father, the one whose mother has been beaten, the one forced from his home, but I feel like an unbaptized baby in limbo, or like I'm waiting to get out of purgatory, and I don't have my parents, either. How long must I live with only your shadow?"

"*Mi amor,*" he says, reaching across the table for my hands, "before you came, I cried myself to sleep every night, like an orphaned child. With your arrival, and the news of the baby, I hoped I would get stronger, but I am still tormented."

"Let me share your loss. Speak to me about it."

Rafael brings a candle to the table and lights it, illuminating the lines of sorrow on his beautiful face. "When I was younger and thought of the inevitability of my father's death, it was always in a detached way. When my father dies, I thought, I will carry on his legacy, not knowing God had another plan. God wanted me to know Him through the example of my earthly father.

"My father, my *taita*, as we Indians say, never preached. I did not have to read the Scriptures to know the person I should become, and, when I finally read them, I was amazed how closely my father lived the second most important commandment, to love your neighbor as yourself.

"In Peru it is common for boys to grow up fearing their fathers, but I never feared him because I knew he loved me, perfectly. I trusted his wisdom, knowing he would never betray my need for his approval by withholding it capriciously or by punishing me unfairly. Because of him, and the man he was with my mother, I grew up without any doubts about my identity.

"Now I feel stripped of all confidence. My earthly father is gone, and the God who gave him to me has disappeared. I've been pretending to be a man in this place, forgetting my weaknesses by caring for others who, in turn, treat me like a god. But at night, when you are asleep, Lydia, I cannot escape the hollow person I have become."

"Rafael, think of how much your father must have loved and respected you for you to speak of him this way."

"Yes, he told me before I went to the University that he considered himself the most fortunate of men to have a son on whom he could completely depend to bring love and honor back to him and my mother."

"And you have done that."

"Honor? What honor? My mother is injured and aging, and I should be with her. My father would be disappointed in my cowardice."

"No, he would be proud of the way you're taking care of your wife and future child, the way you're serving these people, and he would understand that you can't return to Pachabuena yet."

"He was always there, my closest friend."

"You want him to approve of what you're doing, but now you'll have to trust in the wisdom you learned from him."

"It's not just the loss of my father. I want to kill the men who murdered him, the men who beat my mother," Rafael says, pounding his right fist into his left hand, "but I am impotent. I was not afraid of losing my life if I had stayed in Pachabuena, but I thought of you and my mother, of the life we could still share, and I thought that my death would mean the end of my father's work, but now I am haunted by thoughts of revenge."

"I've never spent too much time on the Old Testament, but I do remember a line from Deuteronomy that may help us both: 'I have put life and death before you. Choose life.'"

Rafael stands behind my chair and puts his hands on my shoulders. "I had forgotten what a source of strength you are to me, Lydia. Let me draw strength from you. Let me lose myself in you. I have been in a desert."

                              *

On Christmas Eve, we gather with other families around a large bonfire. Some sing "Silent Night" in Spanish, others in Quechua. Rafael sings the English version with me. We share a common pot of *cuy*, sweet potatoes, and other tuberous plants and drink *chicha* made from casava.

Lying beside Rafael, under the black sky with a host of stars overhead, I dwell on images of childhood Christmases. On December 24, my father would leave work early and take my brother and me sledding at Washington Park. I remember, when we returned home, how the mittens would smell drying on the hissing radiator. We would sit down to steaming, homemade soup and heavy bread from grandpa's bakery downstairs, and for dessert there would be *stolen*, an oval-shaped, frosted, yeasty coffee cake with walnuts and candied emerald and ruby cherries.

On Christmas Eve, my mother always seemed to have a headache, and dad would suggest we take a drive to see the Christmas decorations, giving mom some time to rest. A light snow usually fell as we drove around, oohing and ahhing at the colored lights that followed the eaves of the elegant brick houses on Sherman Boulevard and outlined snow-laden fir trees in their front yards. We would end up in Wauwatosa, where my grandparents had moved when the bakery started to bring in a decent income. Grandpa used blue lights to outline their two-story stone house on Swan Boulevard. The lights made the razor-thin ice crust on the snow glow a celestial blue.

My brother and I visited the Bavarian crèche that my grandmother had arranged on top of her ebony baby grande piano. Looking up at it, we saw a miniature holy city, floating in angel hair on top of a black mountain. Caspar, Melchior, and Balthazar bore their gifts from the East, and shepherds and angels knelt at the crib. Alpine skaters glided on a small mirror, a respectful distance away.

By the end of our visit, Johnny and I hoped Santa would have reached our own neighborhood, although there was always some doubt as to whether or not he would stop at all. The longest flight of stairs in the world led to our apartment above the bakery. A passerby on this commercial street would never have guessed the warmth, excitement, and wonder within.

Given the weekly fights over unpaid bills that erupted on Tuesdays, when my dad got paid, I still don't know how my parents managed this ritual. But at Christmas, the bills were forgotten, and mother, having shopped for bargains all year long, and having hid them in in the backs of closets, placed gifts on one side of the tree for my brother and on the other side for me. They exceeded the tree's reach and spilled all over the living room.

As a boy, our father had told us he might only receive a single orange and a pair of gloves for Christmas. As I grew older, after Mass on Christmas morning, when my friends called to tell what they had received, I concealed my good fortune because they had received much less than I. Snuggling against Rafael, somewhere between the western highlands and the eastern jungle of Peru, I offer a prayer for my Milwaukee family.

*

The Vilcapampa farmers grow sugar cane, bananas, peanuts, casava, and coca. They also plant seed potatoes in clearings on nearby highlands, using the eye, or bud, of a wide variety of potatoes to ensure that all will not be wiped out in the event of blight.

Using the Doctrine of Signatures that attributes curative powers to plants based on their physical properties, the Spanish had referred to potatoes as "the testicles of the earth." Despite their reputed power to reinvigorate a tired man, the Spanish avoided potatoes because they believed they would become like Indians if they ate them, never guessing the humble Peruvian potato would one day become a staple for much of the western world.

*

Women do much of the agricultural work in Vilcapampa, hoeing every few days, giving careful attention to each plant. They don't approach farming as a large enterprise, weighing the probabilities of the yield of an entire field, but monitor each seedling, concerned also with the long-term productivity of the soil.

One afternoon, feeling tired, hot, thirsty, and very inadequate because of my awkwardness with the hoe, I sit down to rest. I don't want to complain about my back hurting because pregnant women here work without complaint till the moment they give birth.

Chakra Mama approaches, grinning, extending a baby finger to me. Does the Mother of the Field want to help me to my feet? If so, why just extend one finger? Magdalena explains that her grandmother is offering to transmit her agricultural wisdom to me. I reach up, and, as instructed, grasp each of her fingers with my whole hand, as though milking a cow. After thanking Chakra Mama, I return to my hoeing, prepared to tough it out, but the work is easier.

Vilcapampa women pride themselves on their strength and vigor. They clear the land with machetes before planting; sometimes they fish; occasionally they hunt. Frequently, after strenuous mornings in the field, and before returning to their homes to check on the food they have left simmering, they visit a secluded place in the river. I am honored when several women of different ages invite me to accompany them to the sanctuary where they bathe.

The air is heavy with the smell of dank soil, rotting foliage, and dripping ferns. Trees, weighted by thick vines that anchor bromeliads, dip their branches low over a mossy bank, shading the river. The women remove their simple tunics; I take off my cotton dress and superfluous underwear. The water relieves us of our hot weight and we are blessedly cool, like the small silver fish darting in the shallows among the large stones.

The women gravitate to the eddies between the
rocks. Some hug the rocks, dangling spread legs
behind them; others recline downstream, facing the
river's flow, bracing themselves with elbows dug into
the sand, their legs open before them in the shallow
water. Brown breasts and purple nipples float on the
river like tropical tuberous water plants. Oblivious to
their surroundings, the women close their eyes and
open wet lips, the spurting water quenching orchid
openings.

Magdalena invites me to join her near one of the
rocks. "Do you like?" she asks.

"I like," I say, thinking of what Father Burkholter
would say to me in the confessional at St. Anne's in
Milwaukee.

"The foam loosens women so they will be crazy to
have sex." She adds, "The *pusuqu* is very powerful."

"*Pu-su-qu*," I repeat. The name for foam sounds
like a lover's tantalizing invitation. He could simply
ask, "*pusuqu*?" Yes, oh, yes.

That evening I tell Rafael about my experience.
"Ah, so my Catholic school girl wife is losing her
inhibitions."

"Magdalena wasn't at all embarrassed about the
pleasure she got from the water. She wanted me to
have the same pleasure."

"Yes, because her understanding of good and bad
is different from the one you were raised with. My
father tried to raise me in much the same way, but
my mother teased him so much that he softened his
thinking."

"So you never counted impure thoughts and
touches before going to confession."

"*No, mi vida*. Here, people don't understand evil
to be the result of a corrupt human nature brought

on by original sin. Nature does have an opposing force, but even if it is destructive, it is not considered evil. There is reciprocity between these forces, just as there is reciprocity between men and women. It was the Spanish and the Church that first brought the Indians the ideas of demons and evil."

"I can imagine how the Spanish priests would have reacted to the river scene."

"They would have been excited but would have condemned all of you as witches. In fact, the sight of the women stimulating themselves would have confirmed their belief that witchcraft stemmed from lust, and, we all know, Lydia, that women have an unquenchable lust."

"You're absolutely right," I say, walking toward him. "*Pusuqu?*"

"*Brujita*, my little witch."

*

I begin holding Spanish literacy classes under the thatched roof of the communal hall. The Indian women have never been to school, and most of the mestizo women dropped out after third grade, so I pair women who know nothing of the alphabet with those who have a basic understanding. We meet after the noon meal, during the heat of the day, when the men take their siestas. To conserve my scant supply of paper, we use sticks to write in the dirt floor. As the women become more confident with sound-letter associations, I ask each one to dictate a story to me. They soon learn to read the stories I have transcribed—content that is meaningful to them. Sometimes we just have fun telling stories.

Magdalena tells of Asarpay, an Inca priestess who worshiped Apurima, the Oracle goddess for whom the Apurímac River is named. From the high temple, Asarpay leaped into the river so she would not be forced to view the profanation of Apurima's shrine by the Spanish army.

Epifanía, a plump, young mother with a baby at her breast, shares a story she had heard from her grandmother, about a woman who was turned into stone because she had committed adultery. The adulterous woman had been set upside down on the side of the road, with her skirts hanging down over her face, so everyone could see her shame.

Occasionally, Chakra Mama participates, keeping us spellbound with stories that hold moral dilemmas. She begins slowly, deliberately, telling us we must guard against becoming adulteresses, like a poor woman she has known. At this point, the students beg her to hurry up and finish the story.

Chakra Mama's friend had been toasting corn kernels, when, very unexpectedly, a kernel popped into her vagina. The woman removed it and fed it, along with the other corn, to a stranger. Was the woman an adulteress because the kernel had been in her private parts? Did she have to go to confession?

*

A farmer returns from Mancate with news that three hundred people have died in a Lima soccer stadium. The police were trying to put down a riot and used tear gas and dogs to control the throng, but they had kept the stadium doors closed, so fans who might have escaped were trampled at the door.

We also learn that Diego Torrente, instead of facing trial in a civil court, has been judged by a military tribunal. The tribunal called for the death sentence, and President Belaúnde would have had him executed were it not for an international uproar in support of Torrente. Instead, he will spend twenty-five years in a high security prison off the coast of Callao.

With Torrente in prison, the Guardia may have given up its search for Rafael. We talk about returning to Pachabuena after the baby is born.

The hand mirror I requested arrives with the news. Moving it about, at arm's length from my naked body, I try to imagine what I'd look like in a full-length mirror. I no longer have a waist, and my belly slopes out from under swelling breasts. Transparent skin, pulled tautly over the drum of my stomach and the knob of my belly button, reveals royal blue veins. I can't see my feet. Tucked away, hiding under my ostrich-egg stomach, is the anatomy that started it all. I wonder what my baby looks like.

When I was a child, my parents took my brother and me to the Field Museum of the Natural History Museum in Chicago. There was a display of miscarried babies with slanted eyes and tadpole heads. I studied them through porthole windows, like a voyeur in an aquarium, wondering if the babies had souls, and, if they did, were they floating in limbo because the babies had not been baptized.

*

As my time nears, I want to be alone. Feeling irregular cramping and dreadful back pain, I go to the river when no one else is there. Floating on my back, I feel a light pressure, as though fingers are kneading my belly. An urgent contraction follows, and I scream, scattering the macaws overhead. The tethered life within me slips out into the gentle current. Uterine fluid, river water, and colostrum make a liquid welcome for my screaming, amphibian child, whom I carry upon my buoyant breasts, while using gentle underwater strokes to get to the sloping bank. I rest against a tree trunk, surprised by how much it hurts when the baby's bud mouth takes my nipple for the first time.

XXII

The Mourning of Angels

There are such brutal blows in life, I just
don't understand.

César Vellejo, *Los heraldos negros*, 1918

GABRIEL is a happy, robust baby and has Rafael's
copper skin, black hair, and brown eyes tending
toward green. There is one odd thing about him,
however. The two toes closest to the big toe, on both
feet, are partially webbed, just like my father's. My
dad, always the joker, would demand that we pay
him a quarter to see his twin toes. Gabriel's feet
delight the village women. They want to play with
his toes, believing him to be part water baby, blessed
by the spirits of the stream in which he was born.

   During the mornings, I work in the fields, talking
or singing to Gabriel as he follows my movements

from the sling on my back. After the noon meal, I continue the literacy classes, nursing the baby when he's hungry.

Word about our community has spread, and new families are arriving. As they set up their households, the elders, those who have been here the longest, explain how land is parceled and how decisions affecting the people are reached. Ancient ways have re-emerged and have been adapted to suit the needs of the community. *Ayni,* for example, the system of mutual assistance, has proved to be a satisfactory way of ensuring that family requirements for food and shelter are met.

No special status is assigned to race or gender, contrary to practices in colonial times when the word of two Indian men or three Indian women had the weight of one Spaniard. In Vilcapampa, women and men have equal say in matters affecting the common good, and physical abuse of women is not tolerated.

There is much deliberation when controversies arise, and they are settled, although not always to everyone's satisfaction, through reference to the common good. And the common good will be enhanced—civil society will function more effectively—when all are literate, so the women I have already taught will, in turn, teach illiterate newcomers to read.

*

When Gabriel is two months old, we get word from Teresa that it is safe to return to Pachabuena. In preparation for our departure, Rafael has been training a husband and wife team to treat the basic ailments of the villagers, and he will leave the clinic with a supply of antibiotics, bandages, and pain killers. Saying goodbye is not easy because these generous people have become our family. There is a party in our honor the night before we leave, and our neighbors prepare *chupe*, a stew of potatoes, eggs, and chicken, a magnanimous gift given their economic circumstances and the scarcity of chickens. No matter how humble their financial or educational backgrounds, poor Peruvians are eloquent in their expressions of appreciation. Magdalena gives Gabriel a rattle she has made from a gourd, and Chakra Mama gives me a cloth pouch, holding corn and squash seeds; we will carry with us sustenance from the soil of Vilcapampa.

We leave our loving community, with Gabriel on my back, and Rafael carrying our necessities on his. In Mancate we negotiate a ride to Miabamba. Before climbing into the cab with Gabriel, I remind Rafael, who will travel in the bed of the truck with workers, about the roadblock I had encountered during my trip to Vilcapampa. The driver confirms it is still there.

A few miles outside of Miabamba, Rafael signals to the driver to let us out. The workers have told him about an old rope bridge that may still be functioning. We thank the men and quickly leave the road, following a path to the bridge that hangs low and shredded over the Urubamba. If we reach the other side, we can take a narrow trail along the cliffs until we reach a new bridge leading to the center of Miabamba.

Seeing the dilapidated bridge, Rafael first suggests I walk to Mancate with the baby, risking the roadblock. He will meet us at the train station after crossing the bridge. But I have no papers identifying

Gabriel, and the Guardia will be suspicious about the baby's father. Am I stealing this baby who looks more Indian than gringo? I also fear running into the same guards who had threatened me when I first traveled to Mancate.

Rafael steps out first, his feet on the two main ropes that stretch between the boulders on both banks. The river is narrow here, but its flow, strictly channeled by the boulders, increases in force and depth. If he falls, he won't survive the rocks and whirlpools. Rafael grips the hand ropes. If the bottom of the bridge gives way, he can hold on to them. I want to close my eyes. Dear God, protect him; protect us.

Minutes later, the longest minutes in my life, Rafael reaches the other side and calls for me to cross. I take a few tentative steps, but my balance is thrown off by Gabriel's weight, and one foot and leg slip through the woven floor of the bridge. We fall to the tattered bridge floor, and now both of my legs dangle beneath it, above the convulsing water. Gabriel screams from the jolt. Somehow I must pull my legs out through the twigs and ropes. I reach out to the foot cables in front of me, pulling with all my might, until, inch by inch, I extract my legs from their torturous web.

Trusting that Gabriel is secure on my back, I'll try to cross the rest of the bridge on bleeding knees. Now I can't avoid looking at the hungry river that sends tongues of spray to weaken my grasp, to lap in the sacrifice of an innocent infant.

Over the thunderous din, I hear Rafael shout, "Lydia, look at me! Don't look down! *Sí, mi amor,* you can do it!" The woven twigs and rough ropes further cut my hands and knees, until finally, Rafael grips my arms and pulls us to safety. "Don't ask me to do that again," I say.

*

Weary and hungry, we reach Pachabuena on the evening of the third day of our journey. My mother-in-law has aged. Her lustrous black hair, graced by a few silver strands when I last saw her, is white. She is thin and has lost her proud bearing. Despite her initial display of happiness upon seeing us, and at meeting her grandson for the first time, she is a woman weakened by sorrow. We respect her grief and give her the privacy it demands.

*

As we settle into family life, Teresa holds Gabriel more often, responding to his laughter and babbling, singing to him, taking some joy in his responsive, plump baby body, feeding him the tasty, mashed fruits and vegetables she has prepared. Color returns to her cheeks, and she gains weight.

With part of her family restored to her, Teresa reclaims the stature she had earlier enjoyed in Pachabuena. It was not the people who denied her the role of wise woman and teacher, the role of *amauta*; she had relinquished it. Now Teresa sits in a rocking chair, holding Gabriel, patiently listening to her neighbors' problems, occasionally asking questions to clarify an issue. Wives and husbands leave smiling, or single men and women return to their homes with straight shoulders and a sense of purpose. Teresa demonstrates "spiritual strength," the meaning of "Supay," her father's surname.

More aware than ever of the potentially powerful roles women fill in their families, I begin literacy classes for the women of Pachabuena, who, in turn, teach the alphabet and a basic vocabulary to their children. Rafael takes over his father's work, exhausted each night, but content to be home with his family.

Although I am fulfilled as wife, mother, and teacher, I have an unyielding desire to see my family. My parents should know their son-in-law and grandson, but there are many complications, among them Teresa's safety and well-being, and the risk Rafael would run by trying to secure the necessary travel documents. Now I understand why Peruvians trust only their families and not the politicians and elected officials who get carried away by power, authority, and greed. Without a reliable and trusted government to solve social problems, you solve your own, within the municipality of your own extended family.

*

Over a year ago, I entered Pachabuena and saw the men breaking the soil with their foot plows, and the women, bent over from the waist, placing the sacred kernels in each hole. Before the planting, the women had prayed to Saramama, the goddess of corn, daughter of Pachamama, and the men had prayed to Illapa, the god of thunder. The blessings of both male and female gods are needed for a bountiful harvest, and, according to the same beliefs, the division of agricultural labor by gender is essential as well. Women are not to touch the plows, or they might break them in a stony field, but they can irrigate the fields, their agricultural lives metaphors for their family roles; they incubate the seedlings, keep them from harm, and water them when dry.

The evening before this year's planting, the men gather at the *bodega* and get drunk, later stumbling home to their wives and beds. Horacio Lodo, the guard who worried me last year because of his spying on Rafael's family, returns to his wife, too.

In the morning, on my way to buy eggs, I hear a woman sobbing behind a reed fence. "*Buenos días*," I say, getting close to the fence. "Can I help?"

"*Buenos días*," she says, stifling a sob, peeking around the gate. "*No, señora Lydia, gracias.*" Her face is pulpy, cut in several places, and discolored, and she is holding her arm.

"You need help. Please come with me to the clinic."

"I can't, Señora. Everyone will see me."

"Well, then, let me bring some bandages here."

"*Gracias, señora.* You are very kind."

I hurry to the clinic and bring back an antibiotic and some bandages. "You need stitches on this cut," I tell her.

"Please come into the house, Señora," the injured woman says. "—Just a bandage, please—I am afraid my husband will be home soon."

"Did he do this to you?"

"He meant nothing. He was drinking."

"Does this happen often?"

"Not so often."

"You knew my name. I'm sorry, I don't know yours."

"I am Perpetua Mejía de Lodo."

"You are married to Horacio, the guard?"

"*Sí, señora.*"

"But this can't continue, Perpetua."

"What business is this of yours?" Horacio Lodo says, storming into the house. "What are you doing here? I don't remember inviting you," he hisses.

"Your wife needed help," I say.

"I can take care of my woman."

"Yes, I see how well you take care of her," I say, gathering my things.

"You think you are so good, think you have the right to come into someone's home and meddle in their business," he says, gesturing wildly, unsure of his footing. "You rich people are all alike."

"And what about you? Do you think you are better than your wife because you are a man and wear that uniform? You have no right to hit her."

"Listen, woman. I don't care if you are married to that Communist traitor. Stay out of our business."

"And you stop beating your wife! I promise I will report you the next time you do it. Do you understand?"

A sickening laugh leaves his throat. "And what do you think they will do, gringa? She is my woman. And maybe the 'higher authorities' will want to question your stinking husband. Now get out of here!"

"I feel sorry for you, Horacio," I say, leaving.

I buy the eggs and return home. Teresa is cleaning vegetables for dinner. "Daughter, what is it?"

"Horacio Lodo beat his wife last night, and I'm sure he'll do it again."

"*Hombre sin vergüenza.*"

"He injured her badly, mother. He is shameless!"

"Lydia, he is a little man, kicked around all of his life. He thinks the uniform bestows authority on him, but everyone knows he is pitiful. The only authority he has is over his wife, but he does have power to cause trouble. Please be careful."

"I could have killed him, mother. I could kill him now."

"Shhh, Lydia. I understand your anger, but there is nothing you can do. I would talk to him, but he would not pay attention to me."

"Maybe Rafael should speak to him," I say.

"If you tell Rafael, he would challenge Horacio, but you must realize, Lydia, that it could go badly for Rafael."

"Then there is nothing we can do?"

"Maybe you have already caused Horacio to think about his behavior, and you know, Lydia, life always has a way of punishing the wicked."

"And punishing the good, like Horacio's wife and Dr. Miguel."

"But good will come of that, too. I did not think it would, but now Rafael is here, and I have a daughter and a grandchild. Come, let us take flowers to Miguel's grave."

＊

Two days later I am sterilizing equipment when Perpetua drags herself into the clinic. A stream of dark red blood that she has tried to staunch with rags pours down her legs. Rafael gets her to a cot and examines her, deciding she has had a miscarriage. He uses sterile gauze to control the bleeding. Later he will do a dilation and curettage.

I take soup to Perpetua after she has rested. Rafael has been watching her closely and asks if anything has happened that might have caused her to lose the baby. With tears in her eyes, she looks up at him, then at me, before turning away, saying she can think of nothing. I don't want to betray her, but under these circumstances I can't keep her secret from Rafael and ask him to come to our room, where I tell him about the incident with Horacio.

"You think the miscarriage is due to the beating?" he asks.

"I think so, yes. I'm not sure he punched her in the stomach, but you can see what he did to the rest of her."

"Why did you not tell me about this, Lydia?"

"I spoke with your mother, Rafael. She thought, and I agreed with her at the time, that we would be endangering you by getting you involved."

"But this guard not only beat his wife, he threatened you."

"Rafael, listen. As a North American, I didn't think he would bother me, but he could hurt you. Now I wish I had listened to your mother and not told you."

"I will speak to him today," he says, returning to Perpetua. But Horacio is at her side, trying to pull her out of the bed.

"Horacio," Rafael says, calmly. "Perpetua needs her rest. She has lost much blood. Let her alone."

"She is my woman, and I will tell her what to do. It is no business of yours. By the way, where have you been touching her? You keep your hands off of her."

"Do you want her to die?" Rafael asks.

"From what? From a little blood? Women are supposed to bleed."

"Horacio," Rafael says, still calm, "I'll ask you one more time. Leave your wife alone. She can go home in a few days."

"And who is going to cook for me? Tell me that you *maricón*," he says, calling Rafael a queer.

Turning to his cowering wife, Horacio yells, "Woman get out of that bed and go home now!"

Rafael opens a drawer and pulls out a small gun. "You will leave the clinic now, Horacio. Perpetua will stay here until she is strong enough to come home. I mean you no harm, but I cannot allow you to interfere with my work."

Horacio goes, saying, "You'll be sorry, just like your father."

*

A week later, in the middle of the night, there are loud thuds at the door. Teresa runs to our room. Rafael tells us to lock ourselves in the bedroom with Gabriel while he investigates.

"Please, Rafael, be careful," I plead.

"*Qué Dios te guarde*," Teresa says, quickly making the Sign of the Cross over him.

We hear an angry exchange of men's voices. "Mother, stay with Gabriel, I must go to Rafael," I say.

"They are dangerous, Lydia, be careful."

One of the men is pointing a rifle at Rafael; the other circles about him, taunting him, calling him a Communist queer, asking him where his gringa bitch is.

"Here I am, Horacio. You are really macho when you have a gun," I say, slowly walking toward him.

"Ah, perfect, you are in your nightgown. I know your problem; you've been wanting a real man," he says, grabbing my breast. In an instant Rafael is at his throat, but the second man cracks Rafael's head with the butt of his gun, and he slumps to the floor.

MII

Horacio is about to finish Rafael, but I reach behind me, grab the fire poker, and bring it down on Horacio's arm. I hear him scream before feeling the explosion of pain in my head.

*

Upon arriving at the house early the next morning, Saturnina, who had spent the night with her boyfriend, knows something is wrong when she hears Gabriel's mournful cries. She enters through the back door and rushes to the bedroom, finding the baby. Teresa is bound and gagged. They find me on the floor of the living room. My eyes are swollen, my nightgown is above my waist, and dried semen stains my legs. Blood darkens the floor where Rafael had fallen.

It takes me a while to understand my circumstances, and when I do, I gather the strength to ignore the crushing pain in my head. We try to open the front door, but there's a heavy weight against it. Saturnina and I push until we see that Rafael is heaped against it. I squeeze through the opening.

His body is cold. I lie beside him, cradling him, as we had done with each other on cold nights. Turning his body toward me, I see the dried blood that cakes his nose and mouth and the torn and swollen flesh above his eyes. His golden skin has been torn, pummeled, and kicked. I trace the raw circles of cigarette burns on the face that had radiated so much love and take into mine the burned and torn hands that had tenderly healed others, the hands that had sweetly caressed me, the hands I now kiss for the last time. Rafael's shirt is still damp with thickened blood.

I open it and see the gaping wound in his chest, like
the opened side of Christ. "Today thou shalt be with
Me in Paradise," I think. A note has been pinned to
his bloody shirt: "Communist dog." I moan in despair,
understanding Christ's last words, "My God, my God,
why hast Thou forsaken me?"

*

We bathe the body of this precious man and reverently dress him before placing his body in the open
wooden casket, set upon the same table where we
had all happily dined when our men were alive.
Teresa and I want everyone to see what has been
done to Rafael.

At the vigil, we pray for his soul and for those
who have taken his life. The weeping villagers place
roses and lilies beside his body.

After the funeral Mass, as his body is lowered into
the earth beside Dr. Miguel, Father Martín prays for
Rafael's soul.

May the Angels take you into paradise;
may the Martyrs come to welcome you on your way,
and lead you into the holy city, Jerusalem.
May the choir of Angels welcome you,
and with Lazarus who once was poor may you
have everlasting rest.

*

After a long night of drinking, Horacio began to beat
Perpetua. Hearing her screams, and this time, armed
with sticks and hoes, neighbor women shouted for
him to stop. He confronted them, yelling obsceni-

ties, but there were too many women; they beat him to death. Animals and birds of prey feasted upon his remains, the most ignominious of deaths in the Andes.

*

Each day is a burden to overcome. Getting out of bed is the biggest step I take all day. What is next? A bath? Yes, I can do that. Then feed and dress Gabriel. Talk to him. Hold him. Yes, I can do that. Cook, clean. Keep busy. Yes, I can do that. At night, waiting for sleep, I recall the circumstances surrounding Rafael's death. My intervention in Perpetua's situation had resulted in his torture and murder. There is no solace. Evil has won out over the sublime goodness of my husband. The Jesuits taught me that the word "God" derives from the word "good." All people seek the good, even though some mistake evil for their good. Those of us who choose rightly find God. Raphael was my good. Now my good is gone. In my dreams I see grotesque beasts from the bowels of Satan, trammeling the Archangel.

The beasts have vanquished me, too. Not with beatings, burns, and unspeakable assaults on my body, but with the torture of Rafael's absence, the vivid memory of how he died, and the knowledge that my son has lost his father.

I dress in black as the practice of *luto* requires. Saturnina helps me with Gabriel. I force myself to play peek-a-boo with him, to laugh with him, and I think of taking him home to Wisconsin by Christmas, but I can't leave Teresa.

Teresa no longer holds or feeds the baby. She has lost her husband and son. To love and lose

Gabriel, her third archangel, would be too much. An inconsolable sorrow consumes her, and I'm not fit to help. She eats little and remains in her bedroom.

On a sleepless night, I leave Gabriel in my bed, go to the kitchen to prepare some tea, and notice the light burning in Teresa's room. "Mother, may I come in? I've brought you some tea."

"Yes, of course, Lydia, thank you."

She wears a plain white gown, and a thick white braid falls over her left shoulder. On her dressing table is a photograph of herself as a young mother, standing proudly between her husband and son. She is barefoot, and her sleek raven hair touches her elbows.

"May I talk with you a while? Gabriel is asleep and I feel so alone."

"Come sit beside me, daughter. Forgive this old woman for forgetting that you have lost your husband, and that Gabriel has lost his father."

"But you have lost your husband and your son."

"We must not compare sorrow, Lydia. No heart can really know another's suffering. I know how much you loved my son, and I know, even more, how much he loved you and Gabriel."

"You're reading the Bible."

"Yes, I am trying to understand why men seek power."

"Power, why?"

"If I can understand the need some men have for power, perhaps I will be able to better understand our loss."

"The men who killed Miguel and Rafael?"

"Yes, those who left us widows, and Gabriel, fatherless; the men who torture; the men who beat their wives; the men who think they have a right to a woman's body; the men who exploit the poor. From where does this evil come?"

"And you'll find your answer in Scripture?"

"The God of the Old Testament is authoritarian, a God in whom men may find justification for the subordination of others. But Christ offers a different image of God in the New Testament. He possesses the traits that are most beautiful in men and women. Jesus is strong, yet he weeps; He is just, yet compassionate; He is demanding, yet merciful."

"But if God is merciful, why does He allow us to suffer so much?"

"It is easy to think that our suffering is unique; that what we suffer is more sharp, more profound than the suffering of others. Before our losses, we had no trouble believing in God, in asking others to bear their burdens, but you and I, newly bereaved, search for answers to quell our doubts."

"Is that what you're doing, too?"

"Of course. If I ask God why He allowed such a horrible thing to happen to us, I must also ask why He permits the daily indignities inflicted on the poor and weak. But they do not suffer because it is God's will, but rather because of the will of those who seek power and abuse it."

"But what's to become of us, mother? What about this sadness that clenches my heart?"

"Did you know, Lydia, that the Indian women in Peru believe that only very valiant women give birth by themselves? That is how you gave birth to Gabriel. You are a courageous woman, and you and Gabriel will be happy again. I am sure of it."

"In school I read about the kind of love that embraces the world—rich and poor, men and women of different races."

"Yes, Lydia. Its Greek name is agape. That is the love that will cure this world."

"I love you very much," I say, kissing her cheek, smoothing her hair.

"I love you, too, daughter, but I think it is time for you to return to your family with Gabriel. I know I am keeping you here, but Saturnina will take good care of me."

"You are my family, too."

"I am an old woman who may soon die, but I have loved you as my daughter. You must return to your country and make a new life for yourself. You will teach Gabriel about his father and grandfather, and you will tell him, too, how much his grandmother loves him. Now get into bed with me. We will warm each other."

I rest my head on my mother's breast.

*

Gabriel is Peruvian, an Andean, the grandchild of a noble pair whose love transcended race, culture, and language. He is the son of a man whose courage, integrity, and kindness I will forever honor. God willing, we will return to Pachabuena in time to live and work with Teresa, so that Gabriel may know her wisdom and grace. In the meantime, I'll need the support of my northern family—my parents, brother, Susan, Joey, and Claire.

Before I close my eyes on the flight from Lima to Miami, I study the fertility charm I had bought in Puno, and I re-read the letter Rafael wrote to us from his cell before his death, the letter Perpetua recovered and gave to me before we left Pachabuena, the letter which began this story. ". . . but our spirits must not be vanquished by their ignorance or by the evil they do."

Acknowledgments

FOR their love, guidance, and emotional sustenance, I am indebted to my parents, Dorothy Seitz Silke and John Eugene Silke. Among the living, and in the order I received their help, I thank my husband Joe for his unflagging support. Thanks to Sandra Bly, to whom I entrusted the earliest paragraphs, and to Johnny Delgado, who told me many years ago, "Patty, girl, don't let anyone take your day." Thank you Lynn Miley, for being an early reader and for telling me, "It's a go." Heartfelt appreciation to my good friends Mary Lowe-Evans and Ron Evans for their professional insights and validation. Loving thanks to Nancy Gilliam whose sensitive ear and gentle advice smoothed many rough edges. Thank you, Jack Brooking, for moving me forward. *Mil gracias* to Julia Almendárez Johnson for patiently answering my calls regarding Spanish language usage. Thank you, Katrina King, for your personal assistance in the Special Collections Department of the University of West Florida library.

And, how fortunate I was to have Bonnye Stuart as
my copy editor.
Pensacola, April, 2001

Selected Bibliography

Adorno, R., T. Cummins, T. Gisbert, M. van de Guchte, M. López Baralt, and J. Murra. *Guamán Poma de Ayala The Colonial Art of an Andean Author*. New York: Americas Society, 1992.

Alegría, Ciro. *El mundo es ancho y ajeno*. Buenos Aires: Editorial Losada, S.A., 1961 (first published in 1941).

_____. *Novelas Completas*, segunda edición. Madrid: Aguilar, 1963 (La serpiente de oro first published in 1935).

American Women's Literary Club. *Cook Book, Libro de Cocina*. Lima: 1959.

Aquino, María Pilar. *Our Cry for Life, Feminist Theology from Latin America*. Translated by Dinah Livingstone. Maryknoll, New York: Orbis, 1993.

Arguedas, José María. *Los ríos profundos.* Buenos Aires: Editorial Losada, S.A., 1958.

Bingham, Hiram. *Lost City of the Incas.* New York: Atheneum, 1965 (first published in 1948).

Blanco, Hugo. *Land or Death the Peasant Struggle in Peru.* Translated by Naomi Allen. New York: Pathfinder Press, 1972.

Bourque, S.C. and K. B. Warren. *Women of the Andes Patriarchy and Social Change in Two Peruvian Towns.* Ann Arbor: The University of Michigan Press, 1981.

Centro de la mujer Peruana, Flora Tristán. *Para que ese dolor te calme.* Lima: 1993.

Cieza de Leon, Pedro de. *The Second Part of the Chronicle of Peru* (1554). Edited and translated by Clements R. Markham. New York: Burt Franklin, 1964 (first published in 1873).

Cisneros, Jaime Luis. *Biblioteca hombres del Perú Mariano Melgar and José Galvez B.* Lima: Hernán Alva Orlandini, 1964.

Cobo, Bernabé. *History of the Inca Empire.* Translated and edited by Roland Hamilton, Foreword by John Howland Rowe. Austin: University of Texas Press, 1988 (original finished in 1657).

_____. *Inca Religion and Customs.* Translated and edited by Roland Hamilton, Foreword by John Howland Rowe. Austin: University of Texas Press, 1990 (original finished in 1657).

Day, Dorothy. *By Little and By Little the Selected Writings of Dorothy Day*, Robert Ellsberg, Ed. New York: Alfred A. Knopf, 1983.

Garcilaso de la Vega, "El Inca." *Comentarios reales de los Incas.* Lima: Librería Internacional del Perú, S.A., 1959 (first published in 1609).

_____. *The Royal Commentaries of the Inca.* Alain Cheerbrant, Ed., translated from the French by María Jolas. New York: Avon, 1961 (first published in 1609).

Guillén, Alberto. *Deucalión.* Lima: Librería Francesa E. Rosay, 1920.

Harrison, Regina. *Signs, Songs and Memory in the Andes Translating Quechua Language and Culture.* Austin: University of Texas Press, 1989.

The Huarochirí Manuscript a Testament of Ancient and Colonial Andean Religion. Annotations and Introductory Essay by Frank Salomon, transcription by George L. Urioste. Austin: University of Texas Press, 1991.

Hemming, John. *The Conquest of the Incas.* London: Macmillan, 1970.

Lara, Jesús. *La poesía quechua.* Mexico City: Fondo de Cultura Ecónomico, 1947.

Lara, Jesús. *Poesía popular quechua.* La Paz: Editorial Canata, La Paz, 1956.

MI

Las Casas, Bartolomé de. *Brevísima relación de la destrucción de las Indias*. Seville: 1552. Translated by John Phillips in *The Tears of the Indians*. New York: Oriole Editions, 1972 (first published in 1656).

Mariátegui, José Carlos. *Siete ensayos de interpretación de la realidad Peruana*. Miraflores, Peru: Librería Editorial Minerva, 1972 (first published in 1928).

Markham, Clements. *The Incas of Peru*. New York: AMS Press, 1969 (reprinted from 1910 London edition).

McIntyre, Loren. *The Incredible Incas and their Timeless Land*. Washington, D.C.: National Geographic Society, 1975.

Neruda, Pablo. *20 Poemas de amor y una cancion desesperada*. Mexico City: Progreso, 1955.

Palma, Ricardo. *Tradiciones Peruanas completas*. Edited by Edith Palma. Madrid: Aguilar, 1961 (first published in 1875).

Poma de Ayala, Felipe Guamán. *Nueva crónica y buen gobierno*. Prologue by Franklin Pease. Lima: Casa de la Cultura del Perú, 1969 (first published as "Nueva corónica y buen gobierno" in 1615).

_____. *Letter to a King a Peruvian Chief's Account of Life under the Incas and under Spanish Rule*. Translated and edited by Christopher

Dilke. New York: E.P. Dutton, 1978 (first published in 1615).

Portal, Magda. "Mi descubrimiento de Flora Tristán," in *Flora Tristán una reserva de utopia.*" Lima: Centro de la Mujer Peruana, Flora Tristán, 1985.

Prescott, William H. *History of the Conquest of Peru.* Philadelphia: J.B. Lippincott Co., 1874 (first published in 1843).

Rachowiecki, Rob. *Peru a Travel Survival Kit.* Hawthorn, Australia: Lonely Planet Publications, 1991.

Saint Joseph Daily Missal. New York: Catholic Book Publishing Co., 1966.

Silverblatt, Irene. *Moon, Sun, and Witches, Gender Idologies and Class in Inca and Colonial Peru.* Princeton: Princeton University Press, 1987.

Turner, Clorinda Matto de. *Aves sin nido.* New York: Las Americas Publishing Co., 1968 (first published in 1889).

Valderrama Fernández, Ricardo and Carmen Escalante Gutiérrez, eds., *Andean Lives, Gregorio Condori Mamani and Asunta Quispe Huamán.* Translated from the Quechua by Paul H. Gelles and Gabriela Martínez Escobar, Introduction by Paul Gelles. Austin: University of Texas Press, 1996.

Vallejo, César. *Obra poética.* Américo Ferrari, Coordinator, Collección Archivos, UNESCO, 1988. ("Black Heralds" first published in 1918.)